tommy's tale

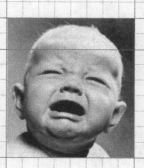

A Novel of Sex,
Confusion, and
Happy Endings

tommy's
tale

ALAN CUMMING

books

AN IMPRINT OF HARPERCOLLINS PUBLISHERS

*it***books**

HarperCollins books may be purchased for educational, business,
or sales promotional use. For information please e-mail the Special
Markets Department at SPsales@harpercollins.com.

A hardcover edition of this book was published in 2002 by
ReganBooks, an imprint of HarperCollins Publishers.

FIRST IT BOOKS PAPERBACK PUBLISHED 2014.

Designed by Cassandra J. Pappas

The Library of Congress has cataloged the hardcover edition as
follows:

Cumming, Alan, 1965–
    Tommy's tale : a novel / by Alan Cumming.
        p. cm.
    ISBN 978-0-06-039444-8
        1. Young men—Fiction. 2. Fatherhood—Fiction. 3. New York
(N.Y.)—Fiction. 4. London (England)—Fiction. I. Title.

PR6103.U48.T66 2002
823'.92—dc21

2002017890

ISBN 978-0-06-232161-9

14 15 16 17 18 WBC/RRD 10 9 8 7 6 5 4 3 2 1

For Susie and Andrew

a glossary of tommy terms

B&Q	a chain of home improvement superstores, much like Home Depot.
Beadales	a liberal, arty school in England, full of rock-star offspring.
Bender	a homosexual, or an extended period of debauchery.
Blue Peter	a legendary BBC children's program.
Brass monkeys	very cold.
Caning it	prolific use of drugs or alcohol.
Champneys	a health spa for the affluent and media conscious.
Charlie	cocaine.

Conkers	horse chestnuts, dried, then attached to a string for battle.
Disabled loo	washroom for the handicapped.
Dries	theatrical jargon for forgetting lines onstage.
Garage	gas station.
Islington	a borough of North London, where Tommy lives.
Mimsy	nothing much of anything.
Muscle Mary	a man who spends an inordinate amount of time in the gym.
Off book	theatrical jargon for word-perfect.
Rimming	oral pleasure given to the anus.
Snog	suck face, smooch.
Stonker	a wide-ranging noun to express size and/or excess, as in "a stonker of a night."
Space hopper	hoppity hop.
Spots	zits.
Vest	T-shirt.

Introduction to the New Paperback Edition

*T*ommy's Tale was first published in 2002, and I spent a lot of that year and some of the next explaining that no, actually it was *not* a thinly veiled memoir but was indeed—as we'd rather defensively stated on the cover—a novel.

In hindsight, I realize that I had been girding my loins even earlier than the book's publication for the endless quizzing about which parts of Tommy's story were mine, which themes were hewn from my virile experience and which merely plucked from my equally fecund imagination. In the film I wrote and directed with Jennifer Jason Leigh, *The Anniversary Party,* I cast myself as a novelist with a book (unseen by the camera but actually sitting on a shelf in the house in which the film took place as part of the set dressing, which we'd personalized to add authenticity) entitled *Tommy's Tale.* And during a particularly nasty row our two characters had at the top of a canyon, I screamed at Jennifer the very line I would gently but firmly repeat to reporters across the globe for a very long time to come: "IT'S A NOVEL!!!!!!!!!"

And it was.

But obviously you must have realized I like to play with what's real and what's imagined. I am an actor, after all! It's what we do! Doesn't a story resonate more strongly with an audience if they are led to believe it's true? Aren't we intrigued, or titillated even, when a well-known person writes a fiction about a world we can easily imagine them inhabiting? The answer to both questions is, of course, yes.

I think one of the most striking things about becoming famous was the realization that people went from being interested in my work to being as interested, if not more, in me. You become a "personality" and not just an actor. An audience no longer looks at you innocently or objectively once you become famous. Instead you are imbued in their minds with previous roles, things you've said in interviews or on talk shows, and gossip about your laughingly named "private" life.

I went into writing the film and *Tommy's Tale* thinking it might be interesting to play with all that. What if I merged what the audience knows or thinks it knows about me with a character who appears in many ways similar to me?

At one point in *The Anniversary Party*, my character is described as "a sexually ambivalent man-child." It was, and arguably still is, an accurate assessment of me. It was also a direct quote by someone describing me in real life.

In *Tommy's Tale*, the eponymous hero is a bisexual party boy, a phrase that could still describe me to this day. Well, the boy part is stretching it a bit, I suppose.

What I'm getting at is that just as I feel an actor is more effective when he allows the audience to see him, the person, as well as the character he is playing, so then a writer, and especially a writer whose personal life his readers know something of, can more effectively and authentically create a world because we are all predisposed to think he is writing his own truth.

But here's the rub. In *Tommy's Tale*, I did more than that. Not only did I make Tommy someone whose aura and behavior could logically be aligned to the reader's presumptions of my own, I also used people and themes from my real life to inhabit his narrative. Of course, there were also many parts of that novel that were completely fictionalized, as were certain characters. I was having my cake and eating myself too, as it were.

So although I was right all those years ago to scoff at the doubters who assumed I had just regurgitated onto paper a few tawdry months of my life, I am now able to share with you (perhaps in the light of the chapter from my new book you will find at the end of this story—an actual, for real, totally no-fiction-anywhere offering) that *Tommy's Tale is* a thinly veiled memoir.

There is nothing Tommy does that I have not done, aside from the job he holds and the way the story concludes. All those years ago I purposely averted attention away from this because I didn't want the book to be viewed merely as a journal of snorting and shagging and thereby overshadow the real theme of the story, and the reason I wanted to write the novel in the first place: fatherhood.

My twenties and thirties were spent in various stages of obsession about becoming a father. Sometimes it was actively physically trying to make it happen, other times it was investigating adoption. But it was something that was a constant in my being for a very long time, and that is what I wanted to write about. How do you deal with those feelings, especially as a single bisexual party boy-man?

Which of course poses the question: How did I, Alan, deal with those feelings? Well, I suppose two things happened. I got older and I got content. Rereading this book reminded me of the utter yearning I had to be a dad, but honestly it is no longer a part of me. I now have no desire to have children, and I feel very relieved that none of my attempts in the past bore fruit, for all the relationships I was in while trying ended pretty badly, and any child involved would have suffered as a result. The fact that now I am in the most successful relationship of my life and have lost the desire to be a father does not go unnoticed by me—or my therapist!

All of the main characters in the book were based on people I knew and loved very much. Only one of them is no longer in my life, and he is, ironically, the person I wrote myself a happy ending with in these pages. I realize now that his character was the most fictional thing I wrote in the whole book, and sadly my least successful piece of creative visualization. I even dedicated the original edition to him. Still, as Tommy finds out, we all make mistakes.

So here I am now, in 2014, finding myself putting the finishing touches on an actual memoir. It is a very personal book centered around the summer of 2010, when my life was turned upside down by revelations my father made, as well as by my finding out, via the BBC-TV show *Who Do You Think You Are,* that my maternal grandfather died in Malaysia playing Russian roulette. Yes, you read that right.

Both books, my memoir and *Tommy's Tale,* are essentially written from my perspective but at very different times in my life, and with very different intentions. Now, in 2014, Alan is stepping out from behind that thin veil, in no uncertain terms. Of course, partly it's crucial for me to do so, as the story involves not just very intimate and graphic details of my childhood but also how my fame has been the cause of the biggest and most upsetting schisms in my and my family's lives. Just as I needed the alter ego of Tommy to be the buffer that would ensure what I really wanted to say was heard, so now I must be more revealing, more transparent, more vulnerable in order to tell my real story.

Writing *Tommy's Tale* was revelatory to me in that I was able not only to discuss an issue that I felt very strongly about, but was able to present the world I'd lived in in all its dirty, honest detail. *Not My Father's Son* would not have been possible without Tommy giving me a helping push off the self-revelation cliff.

Both books are based on the events of several months of my life that I will never forget and would not have missed for the world. I hope you enjoy me thinly veiled *and* totally nude.

a fairy-tale prologue

Once upon a time there lived a little boy who couldn't wait to grow up and have fun. He wished and he wished for the day when he would be able to leave his childhood behind, and eventually, a bit later rather than sooner, his wish came true.

The little boy became an adult—at least in the eyes of the world. He was old enough to have left his parents' home, he had a job, he paid taxes and he had sex—all the typical things grown-ups do—but the difference with him was that he felt like he was pretending to be a grown-up. On the outside he could feign it, but on the inside he knew he was still a little boy.

Years passed, and he managed to hide his secret from most people except those who grew very close to him, and they didn't seem to mind too much. But he did. He fought his little-boyness. He tried to think like other grown-ups and to like the things they liked and to laugh at grown-up things. He let other people dress him in grown-up clothes and furnish his home in a grown-up way, but it was no use.

Finally, one wintry day, he snapped.

He woke up and looked at his life and he realized it was a sham.

"I am a little boy!" he cried. "I am a little boy! What's wrong with that?"

He went to a cupboard and opened the box in which he had locked up all his special little-boy things. There were some toys and a book of fairy tales, a tin with conkers and shells and a game called Kerplunk (which he'd been dying to play with for years but was afraid his friends would think him stupid, as on the box the game came in it said "Ages 5 and Up"). He took the little-boy things out of the box, placed them on his shelves and every time he looked at them they made him smile.

And after a little while, when he had stopped panicking about the possible consequences of his actions and had begun to feel comfortable with his new little-boyness, he had what can only be described as an epiphany.

"You know what?" he said to himself in the bathroom mir-ror, "I've never been a little boy. That's just it! All these years I've been ashamed and the fact is I never was a little boy in the first place. I had to be a grown-up when I should have been a little boy, and now that I'm a grown-up my little-boyness has exploded out of me. I've lived my life backwards."

And indeed he had. The little boy had never known his fa-ther. In some ways this was lucky, for he was not a good man. But the responsibility he felt because of his father's absence and its ensuing difficulties for himself and his mother fell heavily on his narrow, boyish shoulders too early. At the end of each day he would climb to his room in the attic of their house and take out his box of special things from beneath his bed, play with the few toys and leaf through the compendium of fairy tales. To soothe himself he would think of his own situation and problems as a fairy tale, and soon he would be transported to a sleep far, far away from the sad and scary grown-up world this little boy inhabited.

Why had he stopped doing that? the grown-up little boy now wondered.

He lay in the bathtub for a while, staring at the ceiling, and soon tears started to slide down his cheeks into the water. But it was a good kind of crying, for although he was crying in sadness for having been forced to assume grown-upness, he was also crying with joy that he could now embrace being a little boy.

"There's nothing wrong with being a little boy," he sobbed happily. "It's fine. I'm fine. From now on I want always to be a little boy and have fun."

And he did. This little boy had lots of fun. But if ever something bothered him or interrupted his fun, he would soothe himself as he had done in that attic room all those years ago, by turning whatever it was into a fairy tale of his own, a modern fairy tale. And then things didn't seem so bad.

That little boy's name was Tommy, and this is his tale.

1
h.e.i.

You know what I really hate most of all in the whole wide world? More than people who don't bother to vote and then carp on about taxes and how all politicians are the same? More than people who think that if you're bisexual it means you'll fuck absolutely anyone (especially them)? Much more than the concept of circumcision (female or male)? What I hate most of all in the whole wide world is that *feeling*. The feeling you get when you wake up one afternoon and the first thing you think of is some hideously embarrassing incident from the night before. (Let's just call them H.E.I.'s from now on, shall we? It sounds more chic and is easier and less painful to repeat.) It's the absolute pits. And it's always happening to me. This one, though, is a stonker. Last night had started so well too.

What happened the night before . . .

There was a massive queue for the club. It was a Friday, I suppose, and we should've known better, but still. I used to enjoy
a queue too, but ever since Charlie told me his club-queuing
theory, all the joy of the anticipation and the camaraderie had
gone out of it. Now I feel like a helpless and abused pawn in
the cynical game of nightlife commerce. Here's why: Charlie
says that queues outside clubs are only PR devices. It's not that
they're absolutely jammed to the rafters inside or anything, it's
all about making the people who are driving past in their cars
think they're missing out on something really exciting 'cos hey,
look, all those people standing around in the cold wouldn't be
doing it for nothing, would they? He's right, you know. In all the
thousands of times I've waited in long, nonmoving lines in the
freezing cold, there has never been a single time I've got in and
the club has been full enough to merit making me wait for that
length of time.

Bastards.

And last night was a case in point. It was absolutely brass
monkeys. That's the thing about clubbing in London—the
bloody weather. And tonight I'd miscalculated yet again and
was wearing just a skimpy little vest. I persuaded Charlie that
we should take our e's while we were waiting, and miraculously
he agreed. He was normally more into wandering round a club,
getting his bearings and feeling settled before imbibing anything stronger than a Corona, but I reasoned that with a queue
of this length we were wasting a lot of potential off-our-faces
time inside, and if we dropped them now we'd be coming up
and starting to fly just as we paid the hugely inflated entrance

fee and ran to the bar for bottles of overpriced water to quench the dehydration. Also it would take our minds off the cold. So we did.

You just never know with an e what level of experience you're going to have. It can be anything from an "Oh, that was nice" to a "Jesus, what happened?" This one was pretty intense. As I'd hoped, it started outside, a sort of tingling and an overwhelming need to stretch and yawn. Then everything started to get a bit blurry, but I do remember the glowy feeling, that sensation of warmth and the imminent and unstoppable euphoria. Oh yes, it was a particularly vintage glowy feeling actually. And by the time we made it to the dance floor, wave after wave of chemical benevolence was seeping outward from my tummy and washing over my entire being. I was up, I was off, I was high, call it what you will, but I was still me. I was just a more vivacious, smilier and happier me than I had been an hour or so previously. I felt at my best like this. Content, carefree and yeah—hackneyed though it may be—full of love.

You know, people who don't do drugs like this think they're really scary and violent experiences, but they're so not. They're what the word *sensual* was invented for. And last night, Dame Sensuality came down from the clouds and sat on my face and I drank hungrily of her.

It got a little too intense at one point and we needed to have a little sit-down, so we went off the dance floor and through to the chill-out lounge with its less fit-inducing lighting and more trancey vibe. We fell into a sofa and watched people. The e was playing tricks with my eyes, and I was enjoying the strobing effect. A girl was swaying to the music near me but leaving a little trail of herself behind her with every turn. It was like one of those effects they used in pop videos from the early eighties, and I liked it. Then suddenly I seemed to be in the middle of a conversation with Charlie that I didn't remember starting:

"I couldn't believe it," he shrieked.

He was shouting in my right ear hole, spitting tiny gobs of beery sputum against the side of my face. (Actually, it felt *amazing*.) I turned my head to face him and the music suddenly seemed twenty decibels louder. Wow! That was weird. I turned back and . . . yes, much quieter. I turned to him again . . . boom! Wow. It probably had something to do with where I was sitting in relation to the speakers, and the changing position of my head meant that either one ear or two was in direct fire of them, so therefore, depending on a very delicate movement of my head I was going in and out of a sort of weird speaker sound-cusp thing! Or maybe it was just the drugs? Whatever, my aural pre-occupation prompted Charlie to bawl even louder. I was having major rushes, and I knew that my F.B.M. wouldn't be far off. That's nearly the best thing about ecstasy for me, the F.B.M. It stands for Fabulous Bowel Movement, and if the e is good I have one about forty minutes or so after I've taken it (depending on when and if I've eaten, obviously). But I digress. Back to Charlie . . .

"I couldn't fucking believe it! She took me into a dark corner, stuck her tongue down my throat and then she said it."

"What?" I shouted too loudly. I didn't really care what she had said, whoever she was. But I was quite enjoying the feeling of Charlie's breath up close, his smell and his bristles.

"She said," and here Charlie paused for maximum effect, "and wait for this, she said she wanted to make love to me!!"

Eeeyyooaach! The two of us rolled around on the arm of the clapped-out sofa we had plonked on to wait for the e to kick in. We hate that phrase. *Making love.* It disgusts us. It appalls us. We knew we would never make love to anyone. And if we ever said we had or were going to, we each had carte blanche to execute the other on the spot. Our lives would be over if we made love. We would never make love. Sure we would love, and we did, often. Especially on nights like this. And we would easily have sex, or fuck, or screw, or shaft or whatever other verb I'm not going to grapple for. Oh yes, we'd do all that and then some more. We were party boys. We had fun. But never, ever ever ever did we *make love*! Not with each other or anyone else. No sirree Bob.

Making love sounds like a hobby, don't you think? Like a kit you'd buy from B&Q. It sounds like a Marks and Spencer frozen meal. It sounds like death, and if you didn't get it you were out of the picture. Anyone mentioning that dread phrase was instantly non grata, relegated to the bottom of the pile of weekend-cardigan-wearing, barbecuing, trying-for-a-family young couples that we so despised because we were scared we'd turn into them. (But the way we were going, fat chance when you think about it.)

Nobody *makes* love. Love either happens or it doesn't. And if it's just a euphemism for fucking the arse off someone, then what's that all about? Why can't we be more honest, more graphic about our animal urges? Let's drop all the crap, we thought. We all fuck, we all like it, so why wrap it up in tissue paper and call it making love?

And finally (I know I've banged on about this one—pardon the pun—a bit much so early on, but it *is* important) what, if anything, do we actually *make* when we are engaged in this activity? I'll tell you . . . moany noises, messes on the sheets, stains on our pants. That's what. So fuck off, you love makers. May your genital organs turn to sugar icing, and your visages to those of John Boy Walton and Jane Seymour.

You see, Charlie and I are a sort of self-appointed sexual truth police. Any whiff of dishonesty or pretense is outed and pilloried immediately. As is, equally, any attempt to suppress openness.

But now, reliving last night's H.E.I. and realizing why the light of day is cold, I wish I had broken my much-vaunted rules, suppressed some openness and shut the fuck up.

Actually, I lied . . .

Even worse than the *feeling* of an H.E.I. is the *seeing*. The seeing of the person you had the H.E.I. with the previous night lying next to you in your bed, snoring. And even worse than that, Charlie was not just with me for the H.E.I., he was the *object* of it.

(Incidentally, I know I'm prevaricating about telling you what this H.E.I. actually is, but be patient, please. When you find out you'll more than understand my reticence.)

Isn't it funny how you can hate someone in a second? Just like that, they're dead meat. You despise them. You want them as far away from you as they can go, never to return, when the night before, hours ago only, it was love! Big love! The love that oozes from your pores and every bit of your body shudders with it.

That's what I felt that day about Charlie.

It was a rainy London Saturday. There was a little girl murdering some old Spice Girls hit in the playground at the end of our street, so I knew it couldn't be a school day.

As soon as my eyes were open my ears were ringing with the things I'd said to him. God, what happened to me? My toes were literally curling with the embarrassment. But, you know what? I pretty much still meant what I'd said. Yeah, that was just it.

With all my heart. All my body. All my *cock*.

And there, I'm afraid, we get to the most worrying aspect of the matter. Because here is just a little selection of some of the things said by me, Tommy, to Charlie, last night, in the Heat of the Moment:

"I love you, Charlie. I want it to be like this always"—not too bad, I suppose, though a little daytime soapy.

"You're the best thing that's ever happened to me"—starting to get scary 'cos first of all it's not true, I don't think, and secondly it's the title of a song by Gladys Knight and the Pips.

"I can't remember ever feeling like this"—technically true, yes, I'll give you that, but surely one of those phrases that should be banned when you're on drugs. But all this was nothing whatsoever compared to . . .

"I'm yours, you know that, don't you?" and finally . . . oh Jesus Christ . . .

"My cock is yours."

God, I can't believe I said my cock was his. What was I thinking? Did someone hypnotize me and ingest my thoughts with soft-porn vocabulary?

I mulled it over for a moment more, and then realized that it was also in the light of last night's conversation about lurvemaking that the above proclamations left me feeling so shameful, and weirdy, and like the wrong music was playing to the video of my life.

So let's get it all straight (as it were)

Here's what happened: Whilst coming up on a class A drug I laugh with my friend about a girl who was trying to shag him using the phrase "making love." I come home with the same friend and in the course of having sex with him, spout phrases equally as naff as the ones we had earlier scoffed at, culminating in me telling him that my primary sexual organ now belonged to him. He doesn't seem to notice anything wrong with this and maybe even quite likes it. This morning I hate Charlie and want him to go away.

But not just go away, I practically want him to die. Now my stomach turns at the very thought of even touching him. He looks like shit, he's breathing fumes that could wither a hardy annual right in my face, and I wonder if I pretend to be asleep for long enough he'll just get up and go, and only bother me with a sloppy kiss on the forehead and a few mumbled endearments about how I was right about the water thing. (More about the water thing later.)

How can this have happened? What's wrong with me? Why did I need to say those things? I'm not that kind of person. It's not that I'm afraid of intimacy, I don't think—although I suppose it depends on how you define intimacy. Me, I'm a rimming-on-the-first-date sort of boy, and that's pretty intimate, but I suppose it's been a while since I've needed to do the other kind of intimate, the harder kind, the kind where you *say* things. So I may be a little out of practice, but even so. Normally, rather than word it in a porny version of a Hallmark card, I'm usually pretty frank and honest with people when I have to tell them how I feel about them. And in this case I didn't have to, it was all voluntary! Charlie hadn't said a word! I just spewed out all this stuff about how I was his, and so was my you-know-what. And what makes it even more disturbing, if that's at all conceivable, is that I will *never* be his. Not Charlie's, not anyone's. No part of me. Uh-uh. 'Cos even if I felt it and really believed that I wanted it, my experience has taught me that *nothing* is forever.

And I am a man and therefore a bit of a dog.

And why commit myself to something that I know I'll never be able to keep to because of biological accident (being a man) or just plain old can't-get-away-from-it desire (being a dog)?

Besides, I like being on my own. I like not having to tell someone where I'm going and what I'm doing. I like not having to remember to call if my plans change. I like being able to shag who I like, boy or girl. I like being able to hide if I want to. I like not being owned. Don't I?

Millions of little thoughts were whizzing around my mental periphery. Some of them quite scary.

Scary thoughts

1. I am in love with Charlie, as in properly, as in not just like I love him like I know I do, but *in* love. With Charlie! (This is the most scary.)

2. I have lost all the senses of humor, irony and wit that I
   ever possessed in some bizarre drug-related incident.
   (Not beyond the bounds of possibility.)
3. I am imagining it all. (Please, God.)

And less scary . . .

1. I have done too many drugs this week and I was a
   bit more out of it last night than usual, and anyway
   everyone says stuff like that on e and especially when
   they've been caning it a bit all week (though not
   the cock-possession bit), and this morning I'm a bit
   grumpy 'cos of all of the above and so I'm crashing
   and I just need to clear my head and have a little bit
   of time for myself and so Charlie has taken the brunt
   of it all. Yeah. Must be.

I turned over and had another good look at him. He was stirring
toward wakefulness. I watched his eyes twitching beneath their
lids, his lips slowly parting and closing, his tongue scraping the
roof of his mouth in a desperate attempt to encourage some saliva into that dry place.

Poor bastard. He's really dehydrated. How many times have
I told him? I can't understand how people let themselves get
into such a state. Mornings like this could so easily be avoided
by the adherence to a few simple rules. Let me rephrase that.
Charlie's dry mouth, dehydration and potential headache could
so easily be avoided by the adherence to a few simple rules, on a
morning like this. Spot the difference?

Tommy's water rules

1. Drink water all the time.
2. Carry a liter bottle around with you all the time to encourage the above.
3. Especially drink water when you're drinking booze.
4. And even more especially when you're doing drugs.
5. Drink loads before you go to bed.
6. Have bottles by your bed so you can sip in your sleep.

Everybody should do it. Princess Diana swore by it. It's good for your skin, it stops you getting headaches, it's brilliant. I think of a bottle of water the way I think of my backpack or my fags—it's one of the essentials I can never leave the house without.

But Charlie? Oh no, not even at 4 A.M. last night when we'd finally collapsed onto the bed—sweating and spinning and shouting (God, I must apologize to Sadie)—even then he'd refused the offer of a slug of my Volvic.

"You know I never touch the stuff," he'd said, his eyes straining to focus on the bottle I was waving in front of his face.

Then there was one of those time-lapse things where you are actually carrying on the conversation, but you've left so long a pause the other person thinks you're onto something new, and so completely misinterprets your next statement.

"You'll regret it in the morning," said I.

"What?"

Charlie seemed immediately sober for a second or two, and then his eyes opened a bit wider and really pierced into me. (It's at moments like these that I think Charlie wants a bit more from me than I want from him.)

There was another pause. Slightly awkward this time. I filled it with:

"Not drinking water, you stupid fuck," and we laughed a sort of slurred laugh and started to take each other's clothes off.

We always did it a certain way: sitting up, kneeling, on the bed, foreheads together, arms round the bottom of the other's back. Then one of us said "Go," and we grabbed the bottom of the other's shirt and pulled it off as quickly as possible, whilst continuing to keep our heads pressed together as hard as we could—thereby making the bit when the neck of the T-shirt flew up past your nose and over the top of your head really, really sore.

But sort of amazing if you were off your face.

And we always were, 'cos who'd go out of their way to experience that sort of sensation when they were sober?

Oh God, Charlie was totally waking up now. He started to rub his eyes maniacally. It was a habit he had that I was sure he was going to regret in later life. He rubbed so vigorously he was bound to be damaging something—his retina or his iris or something. And sometimes he did it when his lenses were in. Anyway, this morning his eye-rubbing ritual was a sign for me to close mine. I'd decided the best way to deal with all this was to pretend none of it had happened, and sleep it off. Well come on, wouldn't you? I said my *cock* was *his,* for fuck's sake!! I'd snooze through till about five, then get up and have something to eat with Sadie before she went to work. Then a nice bath, a spot of telly and Bobby would be home from his studio and we might have a joint, then go and join Sadie for a couple after her show comes down. And then decide what to do for the evening. But today, with the way I was feeling right now, a quiet night in and a complete avoidance of chemicals was starting to look like the best plan.

Okay, sorry. If you're going to stick with this, I've realized I'll have to clear up a couple of things . . .

Things you need to know so far

Hello. My name's Tommy. I'm twenty-nine. I've got green eyes and brown hair, but you'd hardly know 'cos I keep it really cropped. Just had it done on Friday actually, so it feels like a baby hedgehog right now. I'm skinny. Everything else about me is sort of normal, but then of course I suppose that greatly depends on your idea of normal. To me, I'm pretty normal. I live in a flat in Islington, London, with . . .

SADIE

Sadie is thirty-three and mad. I've known her since art college, where we literally bumped into each other in a corridor on our first day, both lost, both late for our first ever art history class. I've loved her ever since. She's little and has dark hair and when she smiles her little pixie face looks like it's doing what it was meant to do. Sadie did textiles at college, and since then she's had loads of different jobs but she's never been totally fulfilled in any of them and it's really starting to bother her. I told her I'm not fulfilled either but then I don't look to my job to provide fulfillment, but she doesn't listen. She's on a sort of quest. She's been an assistant designer at a carpet company (as our hall and stairway can testify), a stylist for various photographers, an arts and crafts counselor at a drug-rehabilitation day center and a personal assistant for a TV newsreader, amongst many other jobs. The latter was a little detour from her previous career trajectory, but really juicy on the gossip front because it turns out Mr. Serious Foreign Affairs Correspondent keeping us all abreast of the horrors in Bosnia and the like spent most of his free time exhorting strangers to perform horrors on himself in a sex dungeon in Vauxhall! Sadie had to have him paged there once when his boss from the TV station called her in a panic because they needed him to comment on a big earthquake in Guatemala. She works in the wardrobe department of the Almeida Theater just down the road at the moment, and has done so for a while. Dead handy, but she wants to get out of the world of wardrobe and do something she really wants to do, except the thing is, of course, she doesn't really know what that is. But she'll sort it out, Sadie. She's the best. Every good laugh I've had for as long as I can remember has involved Sadie. People thought for ages we were a couple, and we could have been I suppose, but we loved each other too soon and there was never any time for sex to get in the way. We're inseparable like a couple, and Sadie swears the reason she hasn't got a boyfriend is because everyone thinks she's spoken for by me. I tell her the reason she hasn't got a boyfriend is because she's in her early thirties and doesn't hang around enough straight men. She's even the reason I'm lying in my bed having a stupid panic attack about telling Charlie my cock is his (wait till I tell her, she'll die). 'Cos it was through her I met him, at some showbiz party she'd been invited to at Planet Hollywood. Anyway, I also live with . . .

BOBBY

Bobby, I think, is thirty-five. (He's a wee bit cagey about the specifics.) He has shortish blond hair and goes to the gym a lot.

He's ostensibly the most normal of the three of us because his job is making lamp shades, but the interior design thing is just a ruse because he's really mental. Sadie and I saw him in a club one night and because he was dancing so madly and making us laugh so much we went over to him and told him we thought he was great and he had to be our friend. It was as simple as that. Sometimes you just *know* with people, don't you? You just know when someone's going to be really sexy, or you just know if someone's really clever, but most of all you just know when someone is really kind. Bobby, it turns out, is the kindest person we've ever known. He is one of those people who genuinely gets more pleasure giving than receiving (but enough of his sex life, ha-ha) and ever since he has been in our lives Sadie and I have sort of relaxed somehow. It's as though with him around we're complete, we're safe. If anything goes wrong, Bobby will be there and his very presence makes things better. It's a special gift he has.

Anyway, soon after we met him it turned out he was being turned out of his flat and we just happened to have a room free in ours due to Stinky Eva Braun having moved out (an anally retentive former flatmate named Heidi who we found via an ad in *Time Out,* and who turned out to not only have a cleaning fetish that she expected us to share, but also b.o.—a terribly un-fortunate combination because the benefits of the first affliction were cancelled out by the second one, BIG time. We eventually forced her out by being so untidy that she practically hyperven-tilated every time she came home. And so sweated more too. Yuck).

But Bobby fits in fine, and has done for about two years now. He's really self-sufficient too, you can take him anywhere and not worry that he won't find anyone or anything to talk about.

I love that about him. It's such a relief to have best friends who are low maintenance, don't you think? He was an army brat, you see, and quite used to being the new boy in the playground having to make friends or sometimes even learn a new language, so chitchat at parties is a piece of cake for our Bobser. His peripatetic childhood also means he has an amazingly unsentimental attitude toward possessions. He told me once that because his family would always be moving to some other army base in some other country, the things he held precious kept disappearing. It upset him so much until he realized they couldn't have been that precious in the first place, and then he felt much better. His room, apart from the furniture, contains only clothes and books. Not a knickknack, not a Mermaid Barbie, certainly not the tons of junk I have strewn around mine. Sadie once made him a sash that said "Perfect Flatmate" on it, and he is. We just love him. Except we've made a new rule that if he's going to bring back men and do weird sex stuff with them, he can't leave them tied up in the bathroom anymore. Sadie nearly shat herself once when she got up for a pee in the middle of the night. Bobby had gone downstairs to get a drink and left some poor bloke on his own! He says that's part of the whole thing—tying them up and then leaving them there for a while so they don't know what's going to happen next. Apparently he's really good at it. I must say being tied to the radiator in a stranger's flat and then said stranger pissing off for a fruit juice isn't causing stirring in my loins. I want them *there*.

What else can I tell you about him? He's a great kisser—yes, he and I have been known to have a snog on the odd inebriated occasion, just for the sensation, mind; nothing happening in the underwear department. And to give you a better picture of the wonder that is Bobby, his lamps sometimes don't have real shades—instead he goes round phone boxes in Soho pinching those cards with prostitutes' telephone numbers, then clips them onto a metal frame and the bulb goes inside. They're my favorite sort of lamp so far, actually. I think it would be great to have one by your bed, and wake up each morning and see "On Your Knees 5 Minutes from Here" or "Have You Been Naughty? Matron Is Waiting to Spank You" staring out at you.

What else?

Oh yes, I work as a photographer's assistant. To earn money.

Okay, got the picture? Now, back to bed . . .

I felt Charlie stretching next to me. Through the one eye I had open ever so slightly I saw his feet poking out the bottom of the duvet and heard his arms bashing against the headboard. And then he turned in to me, and I felt his bristles against my earlobe. (He was practically Neanderthal considering the number of times a day he had to shave.)

There was a pause and then he whispered, "Have you got a match?"

I tried to pretend I hadn't heard him, but I laughed and spoiled it. I opened my eyes and turned round to look at him. "Yeah," I said. "Your face, my bum."

We both cracked up. We say that all the time. It was the first verbal interaction we ever had, you see, at that party at Planet Hollywood. I had come back from the loo and Sadie was talking to him. I was desperate for a fag and was rifling madly through my pockets for my lighter but to no avail and so I said to him, "Have you got a match?" And he looked at me, all serious and really good-looking in a kind of North London–immigrant–attitudey kind of way and said, "Yeah, your face, my bum."

That was when I knew I liked him.

And now I knew I still liked him. He was smiling at me and trying to get his hands down the bed to tickle me without me seeing, and I thought: What the fuck am I playing at? He's great, Charlie.

And I realized that of all the scary thoughts I mentioned before, it was the less scary one, the one where I've been overdoing things a bit and need to have a few nights in, that was the right answer. So I should just chill out about all the other stupid scary stuff and enjoy my day off.

Yeah.

Cool.

Everything is as it should be.

But there was still the matter of the cock thing. His hand brushed against it as he drew his arm up to rub his eye again. But before he started the rub, he looked at me all sheepish and said, "What planet were you on last night? Jackie Collins?"

We both roared, and I gave my blushes full rein. I love Charlie. He leaned over and kissed me on the head. I closed my eyes for a second and when I opened them he was looking at me, his eyes all doleful and his lips pursed like he was going to say something important.

"I wish it *was* mine, Tommy."

Charlie had a habit of doing this—saying things, knowing full well that the only response I could give was going to be hurtful to him. But maybe he didn't know. Maybe that's why he kept on saying them. I swallowed hard, not knowing how I was going to put this.

"But I know it isn't, don't worry," he said, saving me.

"A bit of it is, Charlie. Quite a big bit," I whispered.

Then I sat up and kicked the covers off. I reached down and put my cock in the palm of my hand.

"This is your bit here," I said, measuring with my thumb and index finger. Charlie smiled.

"That *is* quite a big bit," he said, and leaned his head on my belly.

"Would you like to inspect it further, sir?" I pushed his head down before he had time to say anything more.

Yeah, Charlie's all right.

2

finn

Finn was carefully cutting out pictures from *Hello!* magazine and sticking them onto a big sheet of yellow paper. So far, he had most of the Norwegian royal family as well as various B-list TV presenters who had gathered at a "top London nite-spot" (sic) to celebrate the launch of one of their brethren's first foray into fiction (a sex thriller set, would you believe it, amidst a TV station's echoey corridors and back passages—though, sadly, never in the anatomical sense). It was a bizarre concoction of faces—the pale Scandinavians, smileless and formal, next to the sweating, orange-skinned, grinning-for-England media types. Finn though, was being his usual philosophical self about it all.

"I'm putting one smiley person next to one not-smiley person to show that life is sometimes happy and sometimes sad.

And when you're in a sad bit, you shouldn't worry 'cos you'll be smiling and having a drink and hugging your friends again quite soon," he said, without looking up.

"Morning, Finn. How was your week?" I asked, picking up a glass off the draining board and heading for the fridge. God, I needed orange juice bad.

"Fine, thank you, Tommy." He glanced up at me and smiled. "You look like you had a big night." Then he inhaled sharply, as if about to speak again, but changed his mind because his attention had now been taken up by the picture of a pretty boy-band singer who had been about to be outed by a tabloid newspaper so then came out "voluntarily." Finn sighed out his breath and was still for a minute.

"Do you see this boy? He used to do it with girls and now he does it with boys."

"I know," I said, opening the fridge and surveying the culinary car wreck inside. "That's nice for him, isn't it?"

Finn looked up at me, his dark eyes unblinking, a few bits of toast debris on the edge of his lip. "Do you ever do it with girls, Tommy?"

Here we go, I thought. Stony ground. "Yes, I do, Finn, sometimes. Do you?"

He snorted and rubbed his eye—a family trait. "Don't be dippy." There was a little gurgle of suppressed laughter and then a pause. "Does my dad know you do it with girls?"

I was busying myself, sniffing old cartons of milk and orange juice and moving Chinese take-away boxes to one side. For an eight-year-old he was really good at confrontation. "Yes, Finn, he knows."

"Doesn't he mind?"

"Why would he mind?" I asked, feeling at once more curious and less safe at this turn of the conversation.

"Because you're my dad's boyfriend, and I don't think you should be doing it with girls when you're supposed to be doing it with him."

I froze for a moment—easy when you're half in the fridge, of course—and took stock of the situation. Okay. Finn is sitting at *my* kitchen table, chopping up *my* friend's *Hello!* (unread, I might add) and, frankly, my idea of a fun Saturday morning does not include getting a lecture on fidelity from a minor.

I went over to the table and sat across from him, pushing the cuttings and scissors to one side. We looked at each other for a moment, then I cleared my throat and began.

First of all, I was going to put him right about the B word (*boyfriend*—okay, yes, I do have some semantic issues). I never actually *felt* like a boyfriend, you see, and certainly never referred to myself as one. I think it's the word itself as much as the actual thing. It's so *mimsy*. Two of the most insipid words combined into one—"boy" and "friend." And that's not what Charlie was to me—he was a friend, but it wasn't like we were ever going to go to Ikea to buy candles together or anything. And he was thirty-nine, so you could hardly refer to him as a boy—even though he did his best to act like one sometimes. It wasn't like we didn't shag other people or even have sort of minirelationships with other people. What we had was sort of a friendship involving sex. We were each other's shags.

Oh fuck, all right. We were boyfriends. So instead, I said:

"Finn, I am your dad's boyfriend, that's true."

"I know that," he interjected snappily. "I mean . . . duh!" He stuck out his tongue and looked down at the grinning celebs. Oh fuck, I thought, where are we going with this one?

"I just don't think you should be doing it with girls. It's not fair on my dad." His voice squeaked upward as he said "my dad," and I thought he was going to cry. Although his head was down I could see the chin wobbling, but he recovered quickly and looked up, challenging me to mention the tear half in, half out of his left eye which sat there quivering.

"Finn, please, I . . . I . . ."

I couldn't fucking believe this. I had been awake for all of ten minutes, during five of which I had been racked with anxiety about my drug-induced B-movie dialogue and during the other five—okay, so the other five were quite relaxing, but nonetheless *draining*—and now someone in short trousers is probing me about my sexual habits as an alternative to collage making. I tried again:

"Finn, your dad and me are special friends and, well . . . we understand how important it is not to be tied down to each other too much,'cos that makes people unhappy . . . and, so, sometimes we see other people and that means that when we see each other again we, eh, are all the happier that we are with each other and we get on better. You see?"

Not bad, I thought. Not bad at all, considering (a) the time of day, (b) last night, (c) the postorgasmic energy low and (d) that I had never really thought about this subject before.

Finn considered all this for a minute, then picked up the scissors and flicked a page over to a grinning former Olympic gymnast who was opening her home and heart for the first time after her recent divorce. "I just want you to be my second dad, Tommy. And I think my dad does too," he said softly. The tear finally gave up and plopped onto the gymnast's sofa.

Jesus Christ, I thought. Jesus fucking Christ.

What could I do? Finn looked so forlorn sitting there pre-tending to be interested in the mag and swallowing really hard so he wouldn't blub. I wanted to pick him up and hold him and tell him it was going to be all right, that I'd love to be his second dad, that I almost was already, wasn't I?

But I didn't. I couldn't. I was frozen by it all, it was too much, it was too *early*. And also the thing that was at the back of my mind but I could never have said is that maybe, and more likely probably, it wasn't going to be all right. I wasn't going to be his second dad. I didn't know how long I'd be in his dad's life, at least in the way I was at present.

And yet in admitting that to myself, I also had to look at the possibility of Finn disappearing from *my* life, and that was the scariest thing out of all the myriad of new and confusing concepts that my short chat with Finn had thrown up. And for fuck's sake, I had only come down for a glass of juice! I didn't even know he was here. Sadie usually took him down Upper Street to let me and Charlie have a lie-in on Saturdays, but then I remembered she had a fitting or something (or wardrobe drama as we'd call it later), and she had to go in early.

So how long had he been sitting there on his own then, the wee soul? His dad and I upstairs sleeping off our e's and him down here chopping up *Hello!* That's not right.

This morning was really doing my head in.

"Hey," I said, trying to sound chirpy. "Howzabout trying out Bobby's new Nintendo Game Cube? He left it out for you."

"I know. I've played it already and got to level six."

Whoops. Subject closed.

Aw, come on, Finn. What do you want me to say? That I'll marry your dad and we'll all live happily ever after in a cottage with roses round the door? (Hey, I didn't say this, I just thought it, so chill out.)

"Well, how about a game of Kerplunk?"

His eyes lit up and he was out of his chair like a shot. "It's on the shelves," I said to his back as he sped into the living room.

3

wet thoughts

I had a lovely bath. It was great, our bathroom. Really stuffed with things, so that when you were lying back in the tub all woozy and calm with the heat, there were loads of things to look at. Mostly products. Between them Bobby and Sadie consumed enough skin- and body-care products for a small third-world country. And because they bought so many, the shopgirls kept giving them little sample jars of new ones, and that made our shelves bulge even more, so that sometimes the bathroom looked like a small Clarins or Clinique outlet. Occasionally I'd have a rifle through and smear on some eye benefits or I'd do a bit of toning. Especially after a hard night. My favorite was a face cream, or serum to be precise, of Bobby's which you put on and a couple of seconds later you felt your skin tightening and you began to realize what it must feel like to be Zsa

Zsa Gabor or Kirk Douglas. Bobby said it felt like he was ten years younger. I said it felt like someone had come on my face.

There were loads of bits of junk we'd picked up on our travels strewn around too. Bits of funny-shaped wood we'd lugged back from day trips to Brighton or somewhere beachy, and flashing police lanterns that had long ago stopped flashing which we'd pinched from roadworks on drunken walks home.

And postcards. Millions of them. Stuffed into the frames of pictures and poking out from behind the mirror. The best was a 3D Pope John Paul that Bobby had sent us from a weekend away in Italy once. If you closed one eye and moved your head back and forth the pope blessed you.

We didn't have a towel rail per se. We had a naked male mannequin in the corner onto which we threw a garish collection of towels. It appeared very haphazard, but there was a system: Bobby's was over the head (because he gave the most, geddit?), and Sadie and I had an arm each—hers was right (because she always was) and mine was left (to match my leanings). The whole ensemble looked like a Muslim lady who'd dropped a few tabs of acid. It was very us.

I think it is the bathroom that most accurately reflects the personality of a house's occupants. And, bizarrely, society seems to have dictated we make the decor as impersonal as possible in the room that is the most personal. I hate that. A bathroom with too many white tiles and not enough things in it can seriously weird me out. I like clutter. I like to see where people have been and how they live when I visit their toilet. I find myself losing interest in them very quickly if it's all spotless and guest soaps and so neat you're scared to dry your hands, as it will muck up the towel arrangements. I want to pull open the cabinets and throw things around. I want to see old magazines and coffee cups and pictures and *life*. It can still be neat, I just don't want it to feel like a morgue. In my dream home, I'd have a bath in the middle of the lounge, and I'd lie in it and watch TV and chat to Bobby and Sadie and drink nice white wine.

I loved having a bath at the end of a bender. It felt very cathartic, washing away the sins I'd committed, the laws I'd broken. Sponging away the coating of booze and fags and chemicals I'd sealed myself up in for the last few days, letting fresh air back into my insides and energy rush out through my pores.

I loved to think back and tell myself the story of all that had happened—the conversations I'd had with strangers, the things that made me laugh, the cab rides, the music. There would always be loads of things I'd forgotten, so it was good to recap. We all live life so fast these days that we don't even process what we're doing a lot of the time. And we hardly write things down anymore—I stopped keeping a diary years ago after an old girlfriend found it and read that I'd kissed her big brother at their mum and dad's silver wedding anniversary party—so I try and do mental recaps of my life as often as possible so that maybe in the future I'll have a little file directory in my head that I can access and remember my glory days.

The bath is the only place I can shave without hating being a man. It's such a stupid thing, the daily scraping of little bits of harmless hair off one part of your body just because someone (Who? Society? "Them"? Fashion editors? The *Daily Mail*?) has decreed that it's unsightly and downright scruffy to walk about in the world with a bit of stubble. (Unless you're George Michael, of course. He gets away with everything. But then he's of Greek origin and therefore has big hirsute issues to deal with, so that's okay then.) But me, I only need to shave every couple of days, but blow me if the day I don't do it turns out to be the day I'm on a job with Julian—my boss, the photographer, but more of him later—and we're photographing some poncey old nob in a stately home and Julian will be tutting at me all bloody day and telling me my appearance is inappropriate. It's sore to shave. You do it when you wake up, and that has never been a good time for me to concentrate on anything so potentially dangerous. I just hate being a man when I'm shaving. And hey, okay, I know compared to period pains, childbirth and bikini-line waxing it's nothing, but all the same it really pisses me off. But at leisure in the bath, I almost like it. Here I can relax, the steam softens the bristles and makes them easier to get off, and the hot water soothes any potential rash which normally runs rife. And you can loll around and do it slowly and keep doing it till you're really smooth.

Smooth is the new thing now. A lot of men I know shave their chests or get them waxed. Or their backs, if they're cursed with a hairy one. Yuck. I knew a bloke at art college who was so hairy that when you gave him a cuddle and rubbed your hand across his back it sounded like a Brillo pad being rubbed against a blackboard. Nowadays, at the very suggestion of back hair, men go racing to the nearest electrolysis outlet and have it eradicated. What's that about? What is this obsession with looking hairless, and therefore more childlike? Don't you find it worrying? I know it's been something women have put up with for generations—you should see how much consternation a hairy armpit causes on a fashion shoot—but now it's men's turn to feel weird about natural things that happen to their bodies. I'm never going to shave my chest. Well, to be honest, I only have one little tuft between my nipples and a few strays above there, but one day soon I know they'll all join up, and then I definitely won't shave them. And anyway, there is no bigger turnoff than rubbing your face along someone's body and coming away with a stubble rash. Man or woman.

Shaving and stubble brought my thoughts back round to Charlie and Finn. As they were leaving after many games of Kerplunk (we have a Saturday league, you see), Finn had hung back at the door, and as he was pulling away from kissing me good-bye he looked deep into my eyes and said, "Think about what I've said, Tommy. Please."

Fuck. Talk about guilt trips, eh?

It was kind of hard, lying in the bath and mulling over emotional threats I had just had from someone who was born when I was twenty-one. Fuck. And then I thought of Charlie, and what he might feel about all this. He didn't start relationships with people seeing them as a prospective "second daddy," did he? I didn't think so, but actually, we'd never really talked about it. I just thought he was even cooler and sexier than I had already when he told me he had a son. And when I saw them together for the first time I thought him cooler and sexier still. Finn is such a great child because Charlie treats him like an equal. If there's something Finn doesn't understand, Charlie explains it to him, and maybe because he is so frank with matters of the heart and his own sexuality, Finn is the most unprejudiced child—no, person—I have ever met. I know it's really annoying, but isn't it also fantastic that at eight he can chide me for sleeping with girls when I should be sleeping with his dad? And Charlie did that, Charlie made Finn the way he is, a beautiful, honest boy, just like himself. And also Charlie's a gardener! I have always had a thing about gardeners. It's just their whole silent, ulling-things-over-for-hours-upon-end-with-their-hands-immersed-in-the-soil thing. They seem so together because they've had all that quiet time to sort themselves out. I find together a very sexy attribute. Maybe because I am so un-together myself, I hear you ask? I certainly didn't feel very together right then. I felt wet and cold.

I turned on the hot tap, and all seemed well again. Until yesterday I'd had a carefree existence. It was great. I had a laugh with Charlie, we went out, did drugs, had great sex, had a laugh, I saw Finn, I had a laugh. And now today, today, since the second I opened my eyes, the pair of them had turned into ogres of potential angst, pain and—oh no, the worst of all—responsibility.

I decided to think happy thoughts, and leave all the heavy ones till another time. A time when I wasn't so tired, and hungover, and a time that wasn't a Saturday. Sundays are the days for heavy thoughts. All rain and nothing good on the telly and everyone depressed 'cos they've got to go back to work the next day and so if they let themselves go down far enough they'll break into their demons box and DEAL WITH THINGS. That's what Sundays are for.

So instead, I kept within the same vein, but thought back to happier times:

The night I met Charlie

Sadie took me along as her date to a party at Planet Hollywood thrown by some posh actor who'd been working at the Almeida and who was going back to America. They always had posh American actors at the Almeida. Posh English ones too. But by posh American actors I mean rich and famous movie stars, and by posh English ones I mean people I'd seen on the telly a lot and then read interviews by them saying how they only get paid three hundred pounds a week to work at the Almeida but they don't care because they get to take such great artistic risks.

Yeah, risking sounding like a wanker.

Anyway, at the party we ran into this girl called Pauline, who I'd met before through Sadie. She was a sign-language interpreter and always worked the performances for deaf people at the theater. We'd chatted in the bar a few times and one night we came back here and had a few drinks. Before I met Pauline and had only heard about her from Sadie, I had this picture in my head of a sort of a skinny middle-aged lady with a silk scarf and a cameo brooch and rosy cheeks and really really keen. Well, wrong. Apart from the keen bit. Pauline was keen all right. But there was no cameo brooch or silk scarf, and instead she was in her late twenties with short dark hair and a great, womanly body. You know the kind of body women used to have in the fifties? And the kind women would have nowadays if they left themselves alone and didn't go on diets all the time and practically live on a step machine? Well, that's the kind of beautiful body Pauline had. A curvy, fulsome, womanly body. Something to hang on to.

I remember she had a gold chain with a crucifix hanging from it, and when I suckled on her nipple it slid across her breast and into my mouth. I let it stay there, chewing on it and chewing on her at the same time. It felt really dirty somehow, the heat and the swollenness of her and the coldness and the crunch of it. And her moaning, and me chewing on Jesus and that rising feeling in my stomach that I always get when I know that I'm going to fuck someone. (Doesn't happen in your stomach when you know you're going to *get* fucked, incidentally. It starts more in your head then, and works down. It's like a decision you've made rather than an inevitability. I must ask some girls if it feels the same for them.)

Anyway, we were at it like rabbits, me and Pauline. All night. Really all night. I know that when people use that phrase they're usually exaggerating. Here's what I think they really do:

"At it all night" (but not really)

They go to bed and fuck. Start to doze off and maybe have a bit of light frottage (but almost certainly no coming) before . . . big-time sleeping. Then they wake up, feeling horny, and fuck again before coffee.

At it all night with Pauline

Go to bed and fuck. Talk and fondle for a while, gradually starting to talk and fondle dirty, leading to . . . fuck again. Bit of a loo break, followed by major oral scene, leading to . . . fuck again. Then some chatting seguing into oral and digital stimulation by me of her, which would've led to . . . fuck again. Probably. But I only had a three-pack of condoms.

Then she pisses off, leaving me completely (and literally) shagged out and with only five minutes to get on my bike and down to Julian's studio in Old Street to set up for a shoot with some TV weather girl who has a makeover book out. I didn't even have time to shower, and at one point I had to hold up a reflector really high whilst standing right next to said weather girl, thereby exposing her to the full waft of my unwashed and sex-sated armpits. Even I thought I smelled foul, and I'm me. Poor girl kept smiling though.

So the Planet Hollywood gig is the next time I see her. (Pauline, not the weather girl. Although I haven't seen the weather girl either. I think she graduated to her own chat show on cable, bless her, and we don't have cable. Bobby won't allow it on moral grounds.)

She bounds out of a crowd up to Sadie and me just as we're laughing about the way people leave straws in their drinks glasses and don't use them, then constantly get poked in the nose or the eye (spectacle wearers are particularly funny) by said straw, but feel they can't just throw it in the ashtray as if it's somehow part of the whole experience, like the ice cubes and the lemon.

Okay, I know it doesn't sound funny now, but me and Sadie can find everyday, absurd stuff like that hilarious for hours. If you know where to look there is weirdness all around you. Sometimes even if we're not hungry we go into restaurants and just hoot at the menu descriptions. You know you're in for a good time if old stalwarts like "crunchy salad" and "a mélange of vegetables" appear. Our favorite of all time was when a car we had hired broke down and we had an unexpected night away at a little hotel in Great Marlborough. On the menu that evening was the supreme "pasta served on a bed of rice." Talk about carbo overkill.

Pauline didn't get the joke either when we tried to describe it to her, but we chatted for a while, sort of awkwardly in that way when you've shagged and one of you (in this case me) hasn't returned the call. After a couple of more drinks it was fine though, and her hand rested more and more often on my thigh, and when she said she was going to the loo, I said I was too, and this is where it gets a bit seedy.

A seedy bit

Okay, remember I was drunk, as was Pauline, and the last time I'd seen her we had been totally uninhibited with, and obviously very into, each other. So I noticed that the disabled loo was free and so we popped in there together and had a bit of a snog and a feel, and we sort of stumbled across to the toilet, and she sat down on the lid and I stayed standing in front of her, so her face was at my waist level. Right, I'm going to tell you faster now:

She opened my fly and starts to, you know . . . whilst I took out some charlie I had in my pocket and proceeded to cut up a line on the top of the cistern. Yes, I know, I'm getting a blow job whilst doing coke in a disabled toilet. (But at least she was a signer for the deaf. Okay, not funny.)

Now I have to be honest, I was really getting off on the sleaziness of it all. Sex in toilets has always excited me, especially disabled ones because you're being even more bad. And coke, partly because I do it so rarely, has something of a seventies, Studio 54, up-against-a-wall-shagfest sort of vibe to it. So I was really surprised when Pauline, on hearing my snorting, and no doubt feeling my body arch to get my head down to the top of the porcelain (God, thinking about it now, I could have choked her), suddenly spat me out, pushed me out of the way and rasped, "Are you doing drugs, Tommy?" Picture the scene. I have coke spilling out of my left nostril, a ten-pound note jammed up my right, her saliva dripping on to my (unfortunately very light gray) trousers from my fast-shrinking penis, and on top of it all I am being given a lecture on the evils of drug taking by a furious woman wearing a crucifix, in the disabled toilet of Planet Hollywood.

And there is someone knocking at the door.

I laughed.

I never saw Pauline again.

She said she never did drugs and would never even talk to anyone who did, so I said she'd better go home then, as most of the people there were off their faces so she was going to be pretty hard up for conversation partners and, anyway, wasn't alcohol a drug? She seemed to have no problem shoving that down her throat. But she was off, leaving me to pick up the contents of my pockets that had scattered across the floor (Oh! That must be how I lost my lighter!), hoover up the last few grains still left on the cistern and dry the wet patch from my trousers under the hand dryer. After a few minutes I made my way back to the party, wired as much by the intensity of Pauline's anger as by the coke. (It was pretty crap stuff.)

And there, talking to Sadie, was a beautiful man: tall, slim but tough looking. At first I thought he was Indian but it turned out he was Greek. His hair was black, short and shiny, and he had the most amazing arms I'd ever seen—they were muscular, but long and elegant at the same time. Charlie caught me staring at his arms and wouldn't look away. That was what did it, really, that refusal to look away. I thought he looked a bit scary, a bit of a lad, but then he said the match thing and I knew it was all a sham. The three of us started mucking about straight away, and he thought his favorite thing on a menu was "a medley of fruits."

He came home with us and all three of us clambered onto Sadie's bed and snorted the rest of my coke off a copy of *Nicholas Nickleby* that Sadie was plowing through. I remember Sadie sliding her finger across the cover of the book, rubbing the residue on her gums and saying Dickens had never tasted so good. We stayed up for ages chatting and grinding our teeth. At about five in the morning, Charlie and I made an emergency run to the service station on Upper Street for chewing gum, but before we'd even got to the front door we did major snogging. It wasn't just coke-crazed snogging though. It was something special, gentle almost, a promise of more. I looked up from the snog and he was staring again, unblinking and sure. When we got back, laden with gum and juice and sweets we knew we'd never eat but the packaging had looked so appealing under the neon of the Shell shop, we didn't go back in with Sadie. He came into my room. We chewed gum and passed it back and forth, and rammed our tongues far, far down each other's throats. So far I thought my jaw would never close. The next day I had major stubble burns, but I didn't care.

The next morning he left early to get Finn ready for school. I went next door and crept in beside Sadie.

"How are you, precious?" she'd murmured.

"I'm high on charlie," I said. "Both of them." I cuddled up close to her, happy and sleepy and sure that Charlie would be a new member of our family.

Because that's what we were, me and Sadie and Bobby. A family. We loved each other and looked out for each other and knew we'd all be in each other's lives forever. Our love was unconditional, like a family's, and we could infuriate each other in a split second like families, but we never ever took each other for granted. And that's the difference.

I remember family Christmases at my grandparents' when I was a little boy, ugly affairs, brimful of underlying sibling violence in the living room—where the men drank and slumped into sofas passing the time till the first argument, like dogs waiting for a fight—and gastronomic power games between my gran and the younger women in the kitchen. When my cousins and I were being put to bed, my mum and my aunts would whisper bitchy comments to each other that would always culminate with this old mantra: you can choose your friends, but you're given your family.

This way Bobby and Sadie and I had the best of both worlds—friends we chose that became our family.

I can't even remember what my real family actually feels like anymore. All I have are just some vague memories like the Christmas bitching or the silent meals or the seemingly never-ending nights in front of the telly, hoping to avoid a slap before bedtime and wondering why God had chosen to punish me with being an only child to an angry father. My old family sucked. I was so happy to get away, so happy to find like minds and so wary to let anyone else in who might spoil our little secret world with their ordinariness and lack of understanding, just like my biological, ordinary, nonunderstanding family had.

But Charlie made it. Not totally, of course, 'cos he doesn't live with us, and as there's no way I'm going to live with anyone I'm shagging again—I tried that once before and let's just say it's not my thing—we'll never be able to fully test him out. But he gets top marks in all areas thus far. He is helped of course by having Finn. Finn has boosted his ratings a great deal. He's only eight but really sussed. He loved our flat because of all the colors and toys and junk lying about. On the nights that he stayed over we'd have a chat while he had his bath and count the postcards and chat about this and that.

After his bath, Finn stood naked in the corner beside the mannequin with towels draped over him, and his dad would come in and wash his hands, then pretend to be terrified when this new tiny mannequin suddenly came to life and grabbed him, laughing and yelling.

Finn was an example of how the new family works. (Which basically means that the old ways *don't* work.) He's got a gay dad (not a bisexual anymore, Charlie says, he feels he's swung over completely to the land of Dorothy) and he only sees his mum twice a year at most. (She's a cook at a hunting lodge in Chile. She went on a find-yourself type of holiday just after she and Charlie split up, duly found herself and now only comes back sporadically. Usually for family weddings, rather ironically. She's really nice, actually.) But Finn has a large extended family in us. We see him a lot and he stays over most weekends. Which is great. Mostly. I mean, it's hard when you realize how attached he is and everything. And if—no, when—Charlie and I stop seeing each other, I think I'll have to ask him for visiting rights. No, I'm serious almost. And if I didn't, Bobby and Sadie would! Last week, at one of our boozy, flatmates-only dinners, Sadie and Bobby and I got all teary and said how much we loved him, and they said that every time they knew Charlie was coming round to see me, they hoped Finn was too.

I loved the way Finn thought. No topic was too obscure or taboo. We'd sit down to watch telly and suddenly we'd be talking about death, or who had invented trousers. He came into my bed one morning and said to his dad, "Did you have sex with Tommy last night?"

I was mortified, but Charlie took it all in his stride: "Yes, I did, Finn. Why?"

"Because the pair of you smell of midnight sweat," he'd said, and snuggled in between us. Midnight sweat. I loved that phrase. It was just perfect.

Finn loved rubbing my head when my hair was short because

he said it felt like Velcro. He was such a sensual child, always stroking his fingers along things and describing experiences by how they felt, not by what had happened. And maybe why Finn and I get on so well is because I've always thought of things in that way too. I've never been able to be rational. I can only say how I feel: Once I went on holiday to Yugoslavia, when it still was Yugoslavia. It was beautiful. Beautiful and scenic and hot and the people were nice. But it just *felt* wrong. And what happened? A few months later it was war-torn and the hotel was blown up and the locals were being raped and killed by their former neighbors. I always trust my instincts. Even if they're wrong, because wrong things happen for a reason too.

Like once I was so in love within about three days of meeting someone, BIG love, like forever love and no one else. Sadie and Bobby, I could tell, were a little alarmed and worried for me, but they didn't say—what could they say? I was happy and it *felt* right and I wouldn't have heard them anyway even if they had plucked up the courage to burst my bubble. I was following my heart.

But then of course it all went horribly wrong and I woke up one day and looked across the pillow at a woman (for she was) I didn't know. Her breasts—onto which I'd cried tears of happiness when she'd whispered that she would always look after me—seemed the breasts of a stranger, of a girl in a magazine. And that was when I realized the moral of the story of that person: we have to look after ourselves. We can be supported and helped and cherished and all those other self-help-book words, but really we have to look after ourselves. God, sounds a bit jaded, doesn't it? But that's what life has taught me. And I like it.

Someone sent me an e-mail about what the Dalai Lama said at the new millennium, and my favorite bit was "remember the three R's—respect for yourself, respect for others and responsibility for your actions." He's got it pretty sussed, old Lammy.

But Finn was a different matter. He couldn't look after himself. He had to rely on others, adults, those who knew better. And suddenly I was one of those who knew better, or who should know better. And that was a first for me.

The water had turned really, really cold, and the streetlights now sent eerie shadows across the walls.

Fuck me, what was happening to me today?

The Finn panic

Was it possible that I was only seeing Charlie so I could keep on seeing Finn? Was I only carrying on seeing Charlie so that Bobby and Sadie could keep on seeing Finn? Could I bear the thought of not seeing him? Could Bobby and Sadie bear it? Was I being emotionally blackmailed to carry on a sexual relationship against my will by my two best friends?

And that was only for starters. After this morning and last night I was on a bit of a paranoid roll. How about: Would I ever be able to downgrade my relationship with Charlie to a platonic level? (That way I'd still be able to see Finn. Charlie too, of course.) Should I ask Charlie to live in the flat so that we all get to see more of Finn?

God, I am really weird.

But worse: Maybe I want to stop seeing Charlie?

And then, oh my God, I can't believe I'm saying this:

Maybe I want to have kids of my own?

But with whom?

And when?

And also, fuck me, this is bonkers:

Would Finn mind?

I was shaking. Really shaking. What the fuck was happening to me? I'd gone from all the cock-belonging-to-Charlie stuff, to the your-dad-and-I-are-just-shags, to the how-could-I-live-without-them, to I-want-a-child-of-my-own. All in about fourteen hours! That's not right. I turned the hot taps on for a very long time.

Maybe I need to relax more.

Maybe I'm not sleeping enough.

Maybe I'm overanxious.

The cavalry arrives . . .

Just then I heard the front door slam shut and Bobby's cry of "Daddy's home. Anybody in?"

"In the bath, Bobser," I yelled.

I listened to him leaping up the stairs and bounding across the landing. He pushed open the door and stood silhouetted like a contestant on *Stars in Their Eyes* as the steam swirled around him. He lit up a joint and inhaled deeply.

"Oh, Bobby, you are a lifesaver. You have no idea how much my mind needs to be altered right now," I said, sitting up, so glad to have him near. "D'you want to come in with me for a bit?"

"Yeah, okay, love, don't mind if I do."

I turned the hot water on yet again as Bobby threw off his clothes and climbed in the bath with me. He had a great body, sort of borderline Muscle Mary but not into Stretch Armstrong territory. His head was still on the same scale as the rest of him.

That's what I find scary about muscle queens—the way their heads look like they've shrunk.

I moved down to the taps end of the tub to make room for him. That was a rule in our house—second in the bath got the no-taps end. (In my dream home the bath in the living room would have taps on the side, thereby eradicating for both bathers any possible tap/cranium chafing.)

Bobby let out a huge sigh as he eased into the water. He passed me the joint and I took a massive hit. I closed my eyes and lolled in the dual high of the hash and the nicotine. When I opened my eyes I looked down at Bobby's crotch and said, "Has your cock got bigger?"

"I wish," he replied. "I've just trimmed my pubes at the base of it to give an illusion of greater length."

I made a mental note to do the same to mine, and then remembered my no-shaving-of-body-parts rule. Cocks are different though, aren't they? God, I can't stop talking about my cock today.

I loved the way Bobby said words like *illusion,* or *suitable,* or even *Sue.* He put a "y" before the *oo* sound so it came out like *illyusion* or *syuitable* or *Syue.*

"Good idea," I said.

"You okay, Tom?" asked Bobby. When he asked me how I was, I always felt he meant it. I'd never had an older brother, but Bobby felt like one. Not just his age but his size made me feel safe and protected when I was with him.

"Yeah, cool," I said. I wanted to tell him about the panics, but now wasn't the right time. I'd tell him and Sadie the "my cock is yours" bit later, but I'd make it funny and self-deprecating and a sort of "this is how much I was out of it" story. And it didn't seem right to be discussing fatherhood with a naked gay man in a bath.

"Cool," I lied again, and handed Bobby back the spliff.

We chatted for a while about the wonderful world of lamp shades, and I began to feel a little more normal, weirdly enough. He'd sold nearly all of his last collection of shades at his last show. (Yes, there are lamp-shade *collections*.) He had it in one of the bars at a members' club in Soho, so it was quite chichi. I had helped, chatting and charming the customers, a little dish-cloth stuck provocatively down my jeans to use when handling the bulbs I'd screw in and out of various shades so customers could see "the two-tone effect that light gave the fabric." It was a laugh. Bobby was now starting a new collection of lamps made of religious scenes, so he had been scouring churches all day looking for naff postcards to give him inspiration. He had a great job because he could do that if he liked—just walk about looking at stuff. But you have to be really disciplined as well, and Bobby was. He went to his studio every day by ten, and if you met him for lunch he'd be the one who'd be looking at his watch after an hour, even though you were the one who had a boss. His motto was "Everything in moderation, including moderation." I thought that was great. Pity I didn't use it more often. Bobby and I sat in silence for a while, enjoying the wet and the warmth and the easiness of doing nothing with each other. Occasionally Bobby ran his hand along my leg, stroking the hairs as they wafted back and forth, and it felt comforting, like I was his cat, and he was so comfortable with touching me that he even forgot he was doing it. Like a cat, I fell into a sort of woozy trance (yeah, and the pot may have helped that state too!) so that when Bobby stood up to get out of the bath the whoosh of the water and the sudden apparition of this manliness in front of me made me gasp and sit up, as though I had been asleep all along and none of this had really happened.

(But don't worry, it had—we aren't going to go into some weird *Matrix*-like territory here.)

My gasp must have been a little more audible than I had thought, or would have wished, for Bobby said, "Are you okay, Tom? You seem a bit jumpy."

"No, really, I'm fine," I lied again. Why did I lie? Why not tell Bobby? Why not say I was confused and scared and worried that I was being emotionally blackmailed by an eight-year-old whilst at the same time teetering on the brink of some sort of existential crisis about my sexuality and the beliefs therein that I had previously thought were at the very core of my being?

Actually, nah, best not bother.

"I'm fine, really. Just had a bit of a weekend. Is there any more left of that joint?"

"That's the way." Bobby chuckled. "Hair of the dog, my darling."

He stepped out of the bath and passed me over the ashtray with the remainder of the joint in it. I lit up, exhaled and felt immediately better. I watched Bobby drying himself and checking himself out in the mirror. It was just impossible for him to look in a mirror or a window or even the kettle without pouting. Sometimes we played games and the forfeit if he lost was to look in a mirror and not pout, but he just couldn't. I said it was a biological thing that some homos are born with. Like getting a hard-on when they see a cute boy or taking their tops off when they congregate in clubs, pouting in any reflective surface was an instinctive, natural urge passed down in their gay genes, and it ought to be embraced rather than mocked. But it was still really funny.

Bobby caught me looking and pouted all the more. I laughed, he did too. First just a wee giggle, then before we knew it, full-blown guffaws and snorting. We were off. Soon we had no idea why we were laughing. What was funny was that we *were* laughing. And it felt so good. All the tension just drained out of me. I felt elated. The funk I had been slipping into was disappearing down the drain with the bathwater, and I was ready to face another day. Even my body felt better for the laugh. My face had stretched and felt alive again and my stomach muscles ached, but in a good way.

The world just looked better all of a sudden. You know how that can be.

Phew!

4

a fairy tale about fear of the unknown and drug use

Long ago, in a land far away, there was a dark forest. And in that forest there lived a really cool little elf. This elf had things sussed. He lived alone in a tree above a lake, and every morning he woke with the lark (who had a nest in a neighboring tree) and he set off into the forest to find food, friends and, most of all, adventure.

Adventure was not hard to come by in the forest, certainly not for this particular elf.

First of all he would take a shower under the waterfall that spilled into the lake from the mountains to the north. It was always icy cold, even on the deepest summer day, but the elf didn't mind—in fact, the colder it was the more he loved it. Standing under the gush of icy wetness each morning made him feel alive. If for some reason he had to miss out on that daily ritual there would be something off-kilter about his day, and no matter what time it was when he got home he would run down the hill, rush round the lake's edge to the waterfall and plunge into the vertical stream. Then, and only then, his day would be complete, or so he felt.

You see, this elf knew how to live. He had learned a long time ago the importance of allowing joy into his life. For it is something you allow, you know. There is so much joy out there to be had, and most people are bereft of it because they are simply scared of letting it in. And of course the longer they are without it the more scary it becomes, and so the harder they try to keep it away and before you know it they have lived a life empty of joy. Imagine that! Actually, you don't have to. Just look around you or think of some of your friends.

Most days the elf would meet up with the other elves and they would run up and down the hillsides, bouncing and wrestling on the soft carpet of pine needles that lay everywhere in their land. Sometimes they would go to the part of the forest where the magical berries grew, and there they would spend the entire day gorging on them, then gaze into the air, seeing the most beautiful sights and thinking the most illuminating thoughts.

Best of all, the little elf liked to spy on pixies who lived on the other side of the dark forest. A lot of people think elves and pixies are the same thing, but they're not. The differences are small but crucial. An elf, for instance, would never be seen dead dancing round a toadstool.

On his pixie-spying days he would hide in a tree or a bush near the places he knew they congregated and listen to them talking in their funny accents and watch them as they ran and dived and wrestled—just like he and his elf friends did.

One day it occurred to him that if he enjoyed spying on them, they, equally, might enjoy spying on him. And sure enough, a few days later, just as the elf was entering the grove in the forest where the magic berries grew, he spotted a pixie darting behind a tree.

"Hey!" he cried, for unlike his friends who were afraid of the pixies, this elf knew that there was nothing to fear but fear itself.

After a few false starts due to a mixture of fear and shyness, the pixie emerged from behind the tree and the two started to chat very amicably. They got on so well that the elf asked the pixie to join him in the grove and to partake of some magic berries.

"Oh, never!" whispered the pixie, stopping in his tracks.

"Why ever not?" said the elf.

"I have heard about those magic berries," explained the pixie. "You elves eat them and then you sit around laughing or thinking you see things that aren't really there."

"How do you know the things aren't there?" said the elf, confused. "You've never eaten them."

"But I've seen you. The berries do strange things to you."

"Exactly," said our elf, getting more and more exasperated. "That's the point, surely?"

"But aren't you ever afraid?" asked the pixie, looking deep into the elf's sparkling eyes.

The elf thought for a moment. "At first, a long, long time ago, I think I may have experienced a little trepidation. Fear of the unknown, I suppose. But now? Oh no. I'm not scared because it isn't a scary thing. It's nice. I see things and I think things and I feel things and everything I see and think and feel helps me to live more contentedly the rest of the time."

"Oh, I see," said the pixie.

There was a pause. The elf picked a handful of berries from the tree under which they had been having their confab.

"So, are you going to try some?" he asked the pixie, a knowing smile creeping across his elf face.

5

Sadie

"Oh, how gorgeous! My two favorite boys!"

Sadie was sitting on a bar stool, her arms outstretched to welcome us. The Almeida Theater bar was nearly empty, as the play hadn't finished yet, but Sadie seemed to be done for the night, for there was a fat glass of white wine in one of her still-outstretched hands. She kept them outstretched until Bobby and I reached her and she pulled us both to her (incidentally ample) bosoms.

"Come and suckle, you naughty things," she said. Her little pixie face was beaming with delight.

"Don't you have any socks to wash?" I asked.

"Oh, a multitude, my darling, and some particularly stinky dance belts too, but not for another fifteen minutes till the show comes down. I'm just having this small libation to gird my loins for the rigors to come. As you can see, I'm still in uniform."

She held up the piece of cord she was wearing around her neck which had an assortment of safety pins, scissors and other director of wardrobes' paraphernalia attached to it.

"How was the show, Sade?" Bobby inquired, egging her on to one of her impromptu monologues.

"Well, they're a lovely house, apparently, and standing room only, this being a Saturday. A lot of laughs, thank God, as our leading lady can get very grumpy if the masses aren't appreciative of her comic excesses."

"Any dries, love?" I inquired. "No, at last it seems as if we're all off book. It's been a bloody struggle, as this play's an Everest to climb, but I think I can say that we're all finally at the summit."

We all loved this silly, theatery talk. Our favorite game was to abbreviate a play's title the way some of the more poncey actors did when talking to each other about their glittering careers. So, *A Midsummer Night's Dream* became simply *Dream*, *All's Well That Ends Well* became *All's Well,* and *Hamlet* and *Macbeth* became *The Gloomy Dane* and *The Gloomy Thane*. We, of course, being us, liked to go one step further. *As You Like It* became *As, The Glass Menagerie* became *Menage,* and so on. It was on a par with finding "on a crisp bed of lettuce" on a menu funny, and we could do it for hours. The last play that had been on at the Almeida was *'Tis Pity She's a Whore,* which of course we called simply *Whore*.

Sadie sipped her wine, swilled it around her mouth before swallowing, then said, "Lovely finish." We giggled. "Any wardrobe dramas?" I said.

"Only a minor incident involving the Dame," Sadie replied, grinning. "The Dame" was Sadie's name for the leading actress. She wasn't actually a dame, though she acted as if she were, and the mention of any of her thespian peers who actually had the title was met with a face so black you'd think all the lights had been switched off, and a tirade of four-letter words about the unfortunate, yet titled, actresses that would make a sailor blush. It had even made me blush when, at the first-night party last week, I had foolishly brought up a film I had seen with one of the dames in it.

"The Dame asked me to wash her dressing gown, which, you know, is not exactly my job, as dressing gowns are not strictly speaking articles of wardrobe, are they, boys?" Sadie smiled.

"This sounds like an excuse, Sades," said Bobby.

"Oh, believe me, my Bobby dazzler, it is! You see, I forgot to read the washing-instruction label, and it turns out that the gown, like its owner, is of a very delicate nature. By the time it came out of the tumble dryer it looked like something from Baby Gap. The Dame was furious."

"What did she say?"

Sadie was trying hard not to laugh. "It was a classic. She said, 'To err is human, but to err with a silk this expensive is not. Young lady, you had better shape up or ship out!'"

We all fell about at this. "Shape up or ship out! That should be your new name for her, Sadie," I said. "Dame Shape Up or Ship Out."

Just then the bar doors opened up and members of the audience started to come in, sated with drama and gagging for a pinot or a cabernet. (It was Islington after all, no Lambrusco was imbibed here.) Sadie rushed off to sort out the actors' laundry.

"Be careful not to err," I giggled.

"Wear rubber gloves, darling, I heard a story about someone getting crabs from having a jock strap land on their nose during a Chippendales concert" was Bobby's parting shot as she left.

We ordered drinks and sat at the bar, eavesdropping and

laughing, still feeling the aftereffects of the joints we had smoked earlier. Bobby had a vodka and cranberry—the alcoholic beverage most homosexuals prefer. I was won over by the special wine of the day which I saw chalked up on a blackboard behind the bar: "Sémillon Chardonnay—smooth, fruity, with a buttery aftertaste."

"That sounds right up my street," I said to the girl who was serving, and a small area of her upper lip uncurled itself briefly to reveal a canine—I think on her planet that was a smile. "Make mine a large glass of your special, a vodka and cranberry for my father here . . ."

"And fuck you too, boy wonder," Bobby said under his breath.

". . . and a glass of water with no ice to ensure my boyish good looks remain untarnished for another few years."

The girl showed all her teeth finally, but grudgingly. I loved a challenge.

"You know, if you insist on this infantile practice of still fucking girls, you really shouldn't hang around with rabid queens like myself, Tommy boy," said Bobby, after the girl went off to get our order.

"Stop being self-persecuting," I replied. "And anyway, hanging out with you is much more fun than fucking someone like her. Mostly."

"You are too kind," Bobby snorted.

"I can always fuck her later when you've gone home."

"That's my boy."

The bar was really full now and after we'd got our drinks and I flirted a little more with the girl (whose name, I prised out of her, was Sasha), we swung our legs round on the stools and faced the crowd so we could do a bit of people watching.

· If you were going to make a film and set it in the bar of a theater in Islington, North London, and the people in front of me were extras, you'd think it was too hackneyed and unbelievable that one group of people could so fulfill all the clichés about themselves . . .

The Islington types in the bar

Type Number 1: The tatty old bohemians. They were here long before Tony Blair moved in and the area became synonymous with the ideals of his New Labour, New Britain; long before it became a gentrified melting pot of poverty and power, artists and artisans and focaccia and fried eggs. They were the neighborhood stalwarts—teachers or social worker types who lived in the less swanky bits of the borough and had kids with names like Saffron and Jake and who longed for the old days when *socialist* wasn't a dirty word but whose staple diet, at the same time, included couscous and ciabatta. If I ever sat next to them in a café or passed them in the street, I suddenly was wafted back to the seventies and wanted to grab a placard and shout "Maggie Thatcher, Milk Snatcher." They were all right, but you didn't want to get stuck talking to them for too long.

Type Number 2: The old poshies. At the opposite end of the spectrum from the tatty old bohemians in outlook and financial circumstance but similar in that they were here before it was groovy too, the old poshies are a breed unto themselves. And indeed this may account for some of the physical peculiarities that some of the group possesses—the chin that is a vertical line from the mouth to the upper chest, for example (mostly, thankfully, displayed in the male of the species), or the mouth in a perpetual state of semi-grin (or semi-sneer, depending on the general countenance of the wearer), and this accompanied by a lavish use of the word "splendid." (This is available in both sexes.) These are old-money types, whose homes, if you ever get past the shiny front door (and I've seen a few for, believe me, they all enjoy a bit of rough with a bit of rough), will remind you of those pictures of Edward and Mrs. Simpson once he had abdicated—a sort of suburban opulence that takes you back to an era of mews houses and servants' quarters, except that now the mews is rented out to someone who makes lovely pots that they sell in Harvey Nicks and the servants' flat is kept for the children when they pop home from uni for the odd weekend.

Type Number 3: The new money. They would have been called yuppies in times gone by, but thinking of them as young, urban professionals now is wrong because, despite the weekends at Champneys and the vitamins and the slimming, black Paul Smith and Prada wardrobe, they are no longer young. They work in the media—and if you are thinking what the fuck does that mean exactly, then join the club. It's another of those nebulous things I've always tried in vain to get my head around, like the stock exchange or why someone has never told the queen how weird her hair looks. There are a few photographers, and people from ad agencies or PR companies that I sometimes see at shoots, who hang around and whisper things into stylists' ears which are then ignored. You know the sort. They used to be funky and radical but then they got rich and a little chubby and now they drive cars that are really more suited to the outback of Australia, and they breed designer kids with names like Saffron and Jake and live in . . . Islington.

Type Number 4: The scraggy types. I'm afraid to say that Sadie and Bobby and I would definitely be included in this section. (Like you hadn't sussed that earlier—who else but scraggy types would hang their towels on mannequins and have a very slim grasp of the contents of their fridge?) Vaguely arty types— actors, artists, or wanna-bes—that sort of thing, our common bond being that we don't earn very much money, certainly not enough to live here. So we scraggy types live in the scraggier parts of the area unless we have sugar daddies or mummies, or are only pretending to be scraggy and really belong to Type Number 3. We are the dispossessed of Islington, and we are proud. We can enjoy being near good restaurants and shops that stock Alessi corkscrews and Tintin watches—they are nicer to browse round than chippies and pawnshops, frankly, and they all have cute staff—and at the same time we have the satisfaction of bitching about how fucking expensive everything is and how even if we did muster the cash for a lunch in Granita, we'd never get a table anyway 'cos it's always full of the inhabitants of types 2, 3, and, on special, celebratory, push-the-boat-out occasions, 1.

So we had the best of both worlds, and I liked it. Even walking tonight to the bar, Bobby and I had come out of our flat that looks onto a council estate, then walked along Liverpool Road with its Georgian terraced homes, some newly painted and reroofed with little cypress trees in pots lining the steps to the front door, and right next door to them all but derelict versions of the same house with the windows broken or boarded up, the perfect location if you ever wanted to make a film set in a crack den.

Rounding the corner we have on one side a down-at-heel shop run by a Chatty Kathy Pakistani family, where we would buy the newspapers and bacon and juice for our brunch on the way home from clubs early in the mornings (maybe they weren't that Chatty Kathy, maybe we were just incapable of communicating at those stages of the night), and across the street a twee little interior design shop which had in the window one of those armchairs you see in TV commercials for boiled sweets where some pervy old duffer gets out a bag and proffers them to his grandson and then the next thing you know the little boy is sitting on the pervy duffer's knee. Well dodgy if you ask me, but there you are. This shop also seems to specialize in those little fringey bits that you can dangle round the bottom of said armchair or hang from your pelmet. (Isn't that just a great word? I must mention it to Sadie the next time we have one of our "bed of lettuce"–type conversations.)

Then we walk through another, older council block, a less 1970s-ugly one this time, with a big communal garden in the middle of the square, teeming with scruffy kids with broken toys, pop through a little archway into a kind of scary thin alley, and lo, behold, we are in Almeida Street, another world. The cars are newer and shinier, there are no kids on the street like in the council bit we just passed through (Saffron and Jake are probably at interpretative dance class) and down the end, nearly on the corner of the main drag of Upper Street, we have that den of bohemian iniquity that is the Almeida Theater. What a journey through the highs and lows of British society we have had.

But enough of demographics, it's time for another drink

Whilst I had been lost in my reverie of cultural anthropology, Bobby had started chatting to someone, one of those men who, before his hair had started to thin too visibly, had made a preemptive strike and shaved the whole lot off. A few years ago that look would have definitely had him down for a friend of Dorothy's, but nowadays, with gay culture infiltrating the mainstream, and straight men getting in a tizz about nose hair and sporting tattooed Chinese symbols on their (usually bared) shoulders, it was getting a bit hard to say for sure. When I tuned in to their conversation a little closer and heard the words "lamp shade" being used very liberally, I got the picture. Straight men don't talk about lamp shades in bars. Unless maybe they are in the lamp-shade business and at a lamp-shade convention. But come on, how many straight men are in the lamp-shade business?

It turns out this guy's name is Mike and he had bought several shades from Bobby's last collection.

I could see that Bobby had designs for Mike that were not merely on paper, and so I left them alone for a minute to go back to the bar, both for a refill and another stab at melting the iceberg that was Sasha.

She was stretching up to get a glass and her T-shirt slid up over her belly a little. She had a very sexy belly. I love bellies on women. I'm not a big fan of them on men, however, unless they're really big, and I'm in a pin-me-down-'cos-I'm-Daddy's-bad-little-baby kind of vibe. Anyway, Sasha caught me looking and smiled, with all her teeth.

I smiled back, but with no teeth, a sort of "yeah, I was looking at your belly and I'd like to fuck you" smile, you know the kind. She held my gaze, then reached up and got another glass. This time I saw the white mark from where her g-string had been when she'd been lying in the sun. She was a lovely olive color, but the tan-line thing made me really horny.

"What would you like?" she asked, showing no teeth, doing for all the world the same "yeah, I know you saw my tan line and I'd like to fuck you too" look that I'd done to her. I was in. Just then Sadie bounded up to me.

"Tommy, quick, you have to come downstairs. You'll never believe it!"

"I was just getting a drink from Sasha, Sade," I said, giving her a hard stare, hoping she'd get the picture.

"Why are you looking at me like that?" she responded, a blank look on her face. "The most amazing thing has happened! Quick!"

"Another white wine?" asked Sasha, trying to save me, I think.

"He'll get a white wine in a minute, Sasha, this is an emergency," Sadie said over her shoulder as she grabbed my hand and tugged me toward the exit sign. She could be very determined when she wanted to be.

Downstairs in the wardrobe room, Sadie locked the door and turned to me. "You'll never guess what?"

"Yes I will," I said, pissed off. "I'll guess you've ruined my chances with that barmaid upstairs."

"Were you giving her the look of love, little Tommy?"

"Big time, until you barged in like a manic gym mistress. Didn't you get my signals?"

"You know you are a constant mystery to me, my darling," said Sadie, ruffling my hair.

"Jesus, Sades, I couldn't have been less subtle," I snapped at her from nowhere. Sadie stopped in her tracks and blinked a few times, then said:

"She'll still be there when we get upstairs again. Are you okay, Tom? You seem a little bit tense."

God, I'd forgotten about all the tension stuff. The whole Finn thing and the what-was-I-doing-with-my-life and all that. Now that I come to think of it, I *was* overreacting a bit about the flirtus interruptus. Sadie was obviously desperate to tell me something juicy and I was raining on her parade. If I was going to give myself an on-the-spot, amateur psychological assessment (and I didn't want to, believe me), I'd say my desire to ensure I got laid tonight in a meaningless, dirty and semi-anonymous manner was due to the fact that I was more eager to have Sasha's pussy in my face than I was to mull over the feelings that had been shooting round my psyche all afternoon (and had been temporarily erased by a cocktail of pot, laughter and a Sémillon chardonnay with a buttery aftertaste). Oh dear.

"No, I'm fine, Sade, really. Just a bit tired. Had a bit of a latey last night with Charlie."

"Yes, I know. I wish you liked being gagged when you have sex, Tommy, you really are a noisy little fucker."

"Sorry, Sadie," I said, and we both giggled. "What's the big scandal then?"

"Well," she said, pausing for effect. "I was doing my wardrobe duties in the Dame's room after the show as usual."

"Shape up or ship out?"

"Yes, shut up, this is fabulous. She left straight after the show came down tonight, as she was meeting her agent in the Ivy for a light supper."

Isn't it funny how posh people say "supper"? It really gets my goat. It makes me think of boarding schools and matrons wandering up and down rows of ancient oak trestle tables admonishing little boys in boaters who are trying to keep down some hideous stew. Supper. Vaguely biblical too. Again a long wooden trestle table, but this time bread being broken off in big chunks and passed from one hessian-wearing bearded man to another. It does *not* conjure up sole meunière and a bottle of Chablis in the Ivy with Joan Collins at the next table. Anyway, I digress. Sadie was getting to the good bit.

"She'd brought in a lovely ensemble to wear for the

occasion—sort of an oatmeal two-piece, long frock coat to cover up the bulges . . ."

"Yuck, enough of the wardrobe eye, get on with it."

"So." Sadie's eyes sparkled and she had to fight back the grin that was bursting to spread across her little face. "She'd left the clothes she came to work in all across the floor of the dressing room—she really is an old slut, you know, Tom—and I was dutifully picking them up, a look of resigned servitude crossing my countenance . . ."

"Natch," I said. "Get on with it."

"When this fell out of her pocket and landed on the floor!" She held up a little plastic bag with a small amount of white powder inside it.

I leaped up and examined it closer. "Fuck me!" I cried. "The Dame's a coke head!"

Ten minutes later

The bar was still really busy. As we pushed open the swinging doors (with our crotches—the weirdest things seem funny on drugs), the melee of sounds from the postplay drinkers washed around my head, and I had a flashback to swimming galas when I was a Boy Scout and everybody screaming and the screams echoing back and forward against the tiled walls of the municipal pool.

Fuck! The Dame gets good stuff!

The decision to steal it had been instant and irrevocable because (a) everyone knows it's finders keepers when it comes to drugs, and (b) it wasn't as though the Dame was ever going to come into work and accuse anyone of stealing her cocaine, was it?

We stopped in the middle of the bar and immediately felt that everyone else was staring at us, which was, of course, true—we had just burst through the swinging doors (crotches first, let's not forget), shouting and laughing, stopped just as immediately, turned in to one another in a remarkably obvious "we're paranoid" manner, then fallen silent apart from an unusually large amount of sniffing, accompanied by the nervous flickings of our fingers rubbing our nostrils and surrounding facial areas. So of course they were looking. We might as well have had a billboard attached to our heads saying "We just snorted coke in the loo!"

Bobby was still deep in conversation with the lamp-shade aficionado, and anyway, when he had turned round with everyone else in the bar at our entrance, he had raised an eyebrow and turned away a tad too quickly for me to think—even in the middle of this major and instant high I was on—that he would welcome me and Sadie if we had gone over and joined him right that very minute. My legs were tingling. I could feel the coke starting to slip down the back of my throat, and it felt fabulous.

"Quick, let's go and sit at the bar and chat to that girl you want to fuck," said Sadie, rather too loudly, I thought, but it was nice for her to take control of the situation, and for us to have something to do. It felt like we'd been standing there for ages. Bobby said later we hadn't, and that he only heard a snatch of Sadie's sentence, but I think he was too intent on getting inside Mike the bald man's boxers to be an accurate witness.

Anyway, luckily there were two free chairs at the bar and we climbed on them and started to just *jabber*. That is the only verb I can think of to use to describe it: Jabber. I started.

Tommy's jabber

"Jesus Christ, Sadie, this stuff's strong, isn't it? Mine's started to run down the back of my throat, has yours? I love that feeling, don't you? It's like you think it's going to be really horrible and you worry a bit but then when it happens, when you sort of give in to it, it isn't too bad at all, it's actually a REALLY GREAT SENSATION! But I wonder if it's great more because you think it's going to be weird instead of just being great anyway, like before, like always. D'you see what I mean? Like, I wonder if it's actually just *all right*? Just okay, nothing to write home about? But because you worry that it's going to taste funny and maybe make you gag a bit, you actually are more predisposed to thinking its fabulous when it turns out to be not nearly as bad as you thought it was going to be in the first place? Do you ever think stuff like that, Sadie? Ha, ha, I've just remembered something funny that Charlie said. He said: 'When you suck someone's cock for the first time do you ever gag just to be polite?'

"I had such a good time with Charlie last night, but you know what, Sadie? I got really fucked up and I said, oh God, you'll never guess what I said. It's a bit dirty, do you think I should say it here? Am I talking too loud, do you think? Fuck! I feel amazing, don't you? That girl's tummy is really turning me on. You know, earlier, when you came in here to tell me about the coke—I still can't believe we are snorting really great coke that was in the pocket of the Dame's trousers—oh yeah, sshh, yeah, sorry, I *am* talking too loud, amn't I? Anyway, remember when you came in and Sasha was giving me the look of love, well it was really amazing, you know? It was one of those moments where you really feel alive, and sort of all buzzing happens in your head and you feel all primal. We really sort of connected in some way and even if we never say anything else to each other again in our entire lives—Hi, Sasha, can I have a glass of water, and can Sadie have a . . . a glass of water too—well, even if we never talk to each other again after she brings the waters, we will still have connected in some really basic, human way and in years' time we will be walking along the street and our eyes will meet and something will stir deep, deep within us, and we'll just *know.* We'll remember tonight and we'll get wet. Yeah, we'll get moist downstairs, Sadie! God, have you noticed how I have started to sound like a Jackie Collins novel recently? No, really I have. It started last night with Charlie. Thanks, Sasha. Did you see that, did you see that? She so wants to fuck me. Sadie, I want to ask you something. It's about Finn. I love Finn. You know, I really do, like more than just aw, he's a cute kid and stuff, but we have such great chats and actually today, Sadie, he said stuff to me that made me feel really weird, it really sort of . . . well, it really made me think, you know? Think about how I feel about Charlie and what I'm going to do in my life and sort of if I want to . . . you know, because I'm nearly thirty, and I know it's not the same as for women and stuff, but I've got to think about my situation, if, you know, I ever wanted to have a kid of my own. And I'd want to have a stable relationship to bring a child into . . . did you see that? She looked at me just as she went through the door. Where has she gone? Do you think I should follow her? I'm going to. I'll be back. Will you be okay? Great, right, wow, I am off my fucking face."

Sadie's jabber

"I'm really stoned. Are you really stoned? It's great, isn't it? I'm feeling really bonkers, Tom, really bonkers, are you? Yeah, it's running down the back of my throat too, I wonder if that means it loses its potency, or does it still get into your system when it's in your stomach? One of the stage managers swears by snorting it up his bum, well not actually snorting it of course! That would be the domain of people in brothels in Bangkok or in John Waters films. Did you ever see that one when the man makes his bum hole go into all these weird shapes? It was really weird. And I think he could actually make it do *noises* too. Anyway, Ivan the stage manager puts coke up his bum instead of his nose because he says it gets into your system quicker because there are tons of membranes or something up there and also you have the benefit of not sniffing all the time after you've snorted. Thank God! Imagine if you sniffed out of your bum hole! Eeeyyuuch! Are you as stoned as me? It's great, isn't it? God, that girl really is staring at you, isn't she? She's new, you know, we're not sure about her yet. The jury is still out. Isn't it funny how we all test people? You know what I mean? Like in America, they are so much more open to new people, at least they give the illusion of being. Here we really take our time to warm up to people. I don't think that's a very nice trait that I share with my countrymen. I am going to make a concentrated effort from now on to be nicer and not to wait until I've made up my mind about people before I give them the benefit of niceness. And I'm going to start with the Dame! I'm going to walk into her dressing room on Monday night and say 'Your Majesty, I thank you for my sore nose of the other evening, you are a true asset to this theater!' She's not so bad really, just a bit frustrated. Like a lot of actresses her age. Well, you know, she hasn't quite got the career she would like—don't we all know it—and she doesn't have kids or anyone special in her life and I think she worries about getting older and being lonely. Fuck, yes, this is really good coke. All hail the Dame. Ssshh!

"But you know, it must be awful. I think a lot of women do that. When they're young they are so busy trying to make their way and have a career and all that and they never think of children and then when they're older they realize they have missed out on something but it's too late to do anything about it. It's really tragic, Tommy, really tragic. I mean, I feel a bit like that too. Yes I do. I just don't want to turn into one of those women who are great fun and wear funny clothes and bring bowls of homemade hummus to dinner parties and everyone loves them because they're like the mother they wished they'd had. Oh God, what am I talking about? I *am* that woman already. Oh fuck me, Tommy, I really want a baby! I just do. I really want one. Gosh, you too? And I'm fed up waiting for Mr. Right to come along and impregnate me. Mr. Right has left the building. Mr. Right only exists in Hugo Boss adverts. Mr. Right is certainly not going to get off the tube at the Angel and trot up our street and fuck me. God, you've got more of a chance with Mr. Right than I have. Maybe we could have a time-share scheme? I think that girl wants your pants and wants them bad, okay, see you later."

A moment of reflection

Okay, yes, obviously, now, from the aerie of the future, with the benefit of hindsight, I do notice a striking similarity in some of the key issues that Sadie's and my jabbers threw up that night. And of course, I can see now that a more sensible man—a ruthless one too, mind—but a sensible man could have taken action right there and then and asked Sadie to consider maybe having his baby, and all would be well, we'd have stopped a lot of unnecessary angst and wrapped this whole thing up and been on to the denouement by page 100.

But come on! I was off my fucking tits! Do you think Sadie would have taken me remotely seriously in the state that I was in? And what sort of legacy would that be for a child? Oh, your parents thought of having you after stealing drugs, then getting really high and self-pitying whilst propping up a bar. I don't think so.

Anyway, it wasn't like that. You don't think that way on coke. It isn't a linear experience. It's all instant, you don't have time to be introspective. It feels like you talk constantly. I mean, you sort of *do,* but the other person (if they are in jabber mode too) talks back, and you sort of have a conversation but not really, and so the feeling of isolation and *jabberiness* is even more intense. And then there's the laugh thing. If you become aware something is funny, your body takes over and you hear a kind of hysterical, shrieky laugh emitting from somewhere and then you realize it's from inside you. It feels like you are impersonating someone laughing. Don't ask me why. It's weird.

So all in all, I wasn't the man to discuss with any seriousness a practical way to realize a half-baked desire that may have been borne of previous overuse of drugs. And Sadie, her pupils huge and her smile glued to her face like a rag doll, was in no state to reciprocate.

Maybe it was the biggest mistake of both our lives. Maybe it was a blessing. Whatever—as I said earlier, even bad things happen for a reason.

And I was horny, and let's face it, if I had been trying all day to avoid thinking of the aforementioned stuff I was hardly about to delve deep into it now, was I? Especially when the gorgeous Sasha is giving me her come-to-the-toilet eyes and I have a little bit of coke left and all I can think of is how nice it will be to feel her pussy juice on my face. Maybe I could even experiment with that bum thing Sadie was talking about?

6

the disabled loo

The biggest difference between a disabled loo and a—no, I will not say normal—a nondisabled loo is that the former is just so *spacious*. Of course there are all those handrails, but the most startling thing is there are just *acres* of room. I am writing this as though you have never been in a disabled loo. I hope this is not the case—they are a wicked luxury that everyone should know of. But even if you haven't, I hope you can understand that the assignation that Sasha and I were about to have, whilst losing some of its cramped, bang-your-head, sweaty, oops-excuse-me, no-you-go-first quality, was going to be an altogether much more languorous, better lit, sumptuous and, yes, *spacious* experience because of the type of toilet facility mentioned above.

I actually had to guide Sasha to it. She was all for just popping into the ladies and taking our chances, so I could tell that

73

I was the veteran from the word go and therefore immediately took control. I locked the door and turned to look at her. For a moment there was silence. I loved this time. The lull before the storm. Just those few seconds when you could look way, way down inside someone and know you were going to have them.

"You are a dirty bitch," I said, without moving.

She smiled, not quite sure what to do. I smiled back and walked over to her, pushed her against the wall and kissed her. She had beautiful lips and her mouth tasted fresh and dewy. Our tongues explored each other's mouths and my hand went down to her crotch, feeling her heat.

"Do you want some coke?" I asked. Her eyes lit up. I knew the answer. "Do you want to take it a different way from usual?"

Sasha, it turns out, is another in that long line of girls who, contrary to popular opinion, love a bit of bum action. The coke was administered with my finger and then to make sure it had got where it was going I gave her an oral check. She was leaning face-front against the wall, her arse stuck out like a pervy Betty Boop, her little suede skirt flung to a far corner of the loo. I was on my knees behind her, one hand clasped around the ankle of her little black boot, the other round my cock. Then we tried some coke on her pussy, and that was a great success too. If you've ever partaken of the same, you'll know the wondrous qualities that cocaine has on the mucous membranes of the vagina. My wishes came true and then some. When I came up to kiss her mouth my face was *dripping*. I was having such a good time.

There was only a little bit of coke left, so we put it on my cock so that Sasha could get some. Now I had tingling everywhere. We were both sweating and various body parts were fairly numb so that meant we were a little more vociferous than we might have been. At one point she was on the floor, her head was against the door and I was kneeling astride her, my hands grabbing on to the door handle for support while I fucked her face.

Good clean fun.

Really.

And then we were cleaning up afterwards. Have you heard of a pearl necklace? Well, this was more a pearl veil. After I came she spread it all over her face with her fingers. I had her juice all over my face and down my chest and on the crotch of my black jeans—it was drying now into one big, nice milky-white stain. Fabulous.

"Let's just stay here and chat for a while," I said. My teeth were grinding and I could feel the red splotches exploding across my face. I looked in the mirror—another nice disabled-loo touch, your own hand basin en suite—and I looked like an advertisement for not taking drugs. My eyes were saucers, I was pale, with only the aforementioned blotches breaking my otherwise alabaster complexion. My mouth was a constant whirr of grinding, and I was covered in a mixture of sweat, cum and vaginal juice. I felt great.

"I think you are fucking sexy," I said to Sasha.

"Well, you know, Tommy, the feeling is really mutual," she replied kindly, a damp paper towel at her temple. "You look like you're all cookies and cream but you are a very dirty little boy, I'm glad to say." She laughed and pulled another towel from the dispenser. "Do you have a girlfriend?"

"No," I snorted. "No, not for a while." I immediately thought back to India. You remember page 44 where I said I'd fallen BIG for a woman after three days and then she turned out to be not the person she told me she was, and I was left disillusioned, hurt and broke? That was India. I could feel a black mood coming on. Coke could do that if I let it. India could too.

"Actually, at the moment the nearest I have is a boyfriend," I said.

"Oh really?" She was unfazed. "Is he that big guy you came in with who's now chatting up that bald bloke?"

"What, Bobby? Don't be daft. No, he's my flatmate, my best friend, well, my equal best friend. No, my sort-of boyfriend's called Charlie, and he has a little boy called Finn."

"Ooh, sounds complicated." She had finished washing up now and turned toward me curiously, her little cheeks still red from our sex. She sat on the edge of the sink and looked at me. There was silence for a moment. One of *those* silences. "It sounds like you're a little confused, Tommy."

I laughed. One of those laughs I mentioned earlier where you're in the middle of laughing and you hear yourself and you think, Who is that desperate person?

"Well, yes, I am confused, but not in the way you think," I said, knowing that being obtuse was a stupid idea because she was only going to ask me to explain and if I really did I would . . . what, what would I do? . . . I would, you know, I might . . . cry.

Yes, get this. In the disabled loo of the Almeida Theater, Islington, London, England, U.K., our little Tommy might burst into tears in front of a girl who he has only clapped eyes on less than an hour ago, a girl whose every orifice he has had his tongue down, a girl whose pussy juice is still wet on the neck of his T-shirt, whose sweet-smelling bum hole he can still conjure in a nanosecond; our Tommy could cry in front of this stranger, isn't that weird? And for why? Because she had said he sounded confused and she, this stranger who had just gagged on his penis (and it wasn't the Charlie type of polite gag), she was the first person who had said that to Tommy in many years, and even though he knew the kind of confusion she thought he was suffering from was far different from what was really going on—these tears would not be about whether he preferred boys to girls—the fact that she had cared enough to listen this far and mention the word *confusion,* and the look of genuine care and concern on her little moist face, and the fact that he had just gone to a place with her that made them so close at this moment, all this made Tommy start to cry. Yes, no, he really did. Big, blubby tears and heaving sobs formed years ago way, way down in the very pit of his stomach. Tommy lost it. Tommy lost it so bad he can't even bear to talk of himself in the first person right now. The girl tried to help him, she cuddled him and kissed his forehead, but Tommy was inconsolable. He was shuddering. He was emitting noises that shocked even him, so it was no surprise, but no less depressing, when the girl made her excuses about having to get back to work and started to leave.

But before she had gone, when she had managed to lever his eyes toward hers by lifting hard on his chin, she had said, "What is it? Can you tell me what it is?"

"I want to have a baby," whispered Tommy, and started to wail again, because he felt ridiculous. He felt like the girl who after one bout of sex starts talking about marriage and children and then of course the boy thinks, Fuck me, panics and leaves, just as Sasha (the boy in this instance) was now leaving and I was left alone looking in the mirror (a bad idea if you want to stop crying, believe me) and wondering what the fuck I was going to do.

———

What.
The fuck.
Was I going.
To do.

battling on

A long time ago, when I was a little boy, the father of one of my friends at school died very suddenly. My mum told me that the Angel of Death had come and taken the man away, and whilst I understand that she thought that was the best way to explain away the massive coronary he had suffered, my boyish imagination led to visions of this Angel of Death hovering outside my bedroom window every night just as I was dropping off to sleep.

The wife of the man (and the mum of my friend) would appear at the school gates to collect her fatherless brood and a respectful silence would descend over the other mothers. Even as their children spilled noisily from the schoolroom nothing was said, I think because grown-ups are under the misapprehension that children will not be affected by silence but will be by hearing the truth. Of course quite the opposite is true—it's only as we approach our parents' age that the truth gets harder to deal with and we yearn for the unspoken and the silent.

I remember the day, a couple of weeks after the incident, when the silence began to be replaced by a mild murmur. This signified, I think, that the normal rambunctious postschool interaction would soon be back in force, and served as a kind of warning to the bereaved mother that she had better buck up and gird her loins, because her allotted time for mourning would soon be over.

Anyway, on that day, one of the other mums laid a hand on the widow's black-cardiganed arm, just as me and her son were hopping into the backseat of the car. "How are you doing?" the well-wisher mouthed, almost inaudibly, her eyebrows knitted into an "I'm concerned" pattern.

"Oh, you know," the widow replied, stoically. "Battling on."

I never forgot her choice of words. Battling on. It had the ring of watching an old black-and-white film starring John Mills on a rainy Sunday afternoon, one with images of war-torn London, with everyone sleeping inside tube stations because of air raids, and desperately fucking each other in the dark.

That was exactly what I was doing those next few days after the disabled-loo incident: battling on.

Obviously the coke hangover made it a little harder to get out of bed the very next morning, but even the day after that and the day after that it was a real struggle to get up at all.

When Sadie had asked me if I was coming downstairs for our flatmates-only dinner on Sunday night, I'd mumbled an excuse about having a sore tummy through the bathroom door to her.

"Have you been vomming, my angel?" she asked.

"Yeah," I lied back, in that tone that I hoped also communicated "and vomming is such a humiliating thing to happen to anyone, so you'll understand and forgive me if I need to regain my dignity, alone, in my room, for the rest of the day."

On Monday I waited until I knew Bobby would have gone to work, then crept round the flat as quietly as I could so as not to wake Sadie. I just couldn't handle talking to anyone. And it wasn't just the embarrassment factor, 'cos I didn't think Sasha would tell anyone. But even if she did, so fucking what? At least I had been honest, at least I had *connected* with her, at least I was alive! It's not every day you have a stranger finger you anally with a class A drug, come on your face, then burst into tears about his desire to be a father, all within the first hour of meeting you, is it? No, it wasn't the worry of anything to do with all that that had me scuttling around in my undies trying to avoid my best friends—it was that I was *depressed.*

I'd been depressed before, of course. But I'm talking about really depressed. Not just feeling a bit down or sad, a depression that has something to do with biorhythms. I'm talking about the kind of depressed that floats in upon you like a fog. You can feel it coming and you can see where it is going to take you but you are powerless, utterly powerless to stop it. I know now. I used to think that people who had it should just go to the gym, or read one of those books with titles like *Feel Really, Really Scared, but Make It Work for You* or *I May Be Fucked Up Because of My Childhood and Things That Happened That I Have Suppressed, but Hell, I Can Talk About Them and They Will Cease to Be My Problems.* But now that I am older and, in at least this case, wiser, I know that the best thing to do is just ride it out. I know it will pass. I hope it will pass and I pray it will pass. No, I know it will pass. And I think I know by now how to handle it.

Tommy's depression rules

1. Masturbation: The moment you wake up, masturbate. Whenever you find yourself in the same chair looking at the same piece of the wallpaper for more than five minutes, unzip your flies. Masturbate, masturbate, masturbate. It's God's antidepressant. But anyway, Jesus Christ, who *doesn't* want to wank as much as possible, whatever mental state you're in?

2. Seclusion: Don't see anyone, they'll only ask you how you're feeling and you will either (a) lie, and say you're fine or (b) tell the truth but talk nonstop for hours about all the fucked-up things that have been swirling around your head for days, making the poor listener completely punch-drunk, confused and, no matter how sympathetic they may be to your plight, utterly bored and looking for the first opportunity to run from the room screaming, and in your delicate state it is hard to put even the most minor of rejections into perspective.

3. Writing things down: That is the best way to let it all out. The pen and the paper will not judge, will not yawn; you will not worry that they have missed the last tube home and you should offer them the taxi fare to Enfield. You can scream, you can jabber, you can talk and talk and talk until you eventually find out WHAT IT REALLY IS, and you will disturb no one else because you are screaming and jabbering and talking on paper.

4. More masturbation: Watch porn, fuck yourself with carrots, in fact take the entire contents of your fridge and either smear it over yourself, fellate it or dare yourself to sit on it. Really. Go mad. Think of all the photos you have seen on the Internet and reenact them. This will help you in various ways:

(a) Sex, even with yourself, is just great. Sometimes especially with yourself. (b) Everything looks rosier when you are out of breath and covered in your own semen. (c) All those food products will be fabulous for your skin, and (d) clean fridge, clean mind. Or something like that.

5. **Writing more things down.**
6. **Even more masturbation.**

They've always worked before. In the past—when I had been in the fog and had followed my normal rules, and my hands were tired from both task 3 and tasks 1, 4 and 6—I would always have some epiphany, some door in a dim and dark wing of the house of my mind would be opened, and I would go back to the real world different, clearer—not totally un-fucked up or completely sorted or anything like that, but just a bit more knowing of myself, a little bit cleaner, a few knots in the wood having been sanded out, a little clearer, a little calmer, a little less scared. That was how it used to be.

This time, though, was different. This time Tommy's depression rules didn't wash, I discovered, because I *knew* why I was depressed, and there can be no epiphany when you already have the answer. I knew why I was depressed, and that was the depressing thing.

Why Tommy is depressed

Okay, here goes: I'm depressed because I have realized that I really, really want something, I want it in an ancient way, a primal way. I can't fucking help myself, and believe me I have tried. I want a child.

Now that, under normal circumstances, would not be a reason to reach for the sleeping pills. But here's the rub: I don't want—and I don't believe I can sustain—the type of relationship necessary to have a child.

I don't want to be tied down. I couldn't live with one person forever. I couldn't say I would only have sex with just one person forever. I couldn't say I would stay. I just couldn't and I know. Because I have felt it and said it before, and have then run out the door as fast as my legs would take me. And as I ran, I didn't feel remorse and guilt. Those come much, much later. No, I felt joy, I felt glee, I felt the wind in my hair, and I laughed, for I had escaped the big bad dragon who was going to pin me down and enslave me for the rest of my life.

So I don't want to pretend to be capable of something that I know I am not, and that is depressing? So I am honest with myself and that is depressing? That's depressing!

So let's recap: I want a child, but I don't want to be in a relationship and I *really* don't want to live with anyone. I can't have a child unless I have a relationship, but I don't want a relationship.

Okay, so what are my options here? How about I have a child with someone, anyone, and as soon as we have the baby I can end the relationship and go off with it? Yeah right, how many times have you heard of the man getting to keep the child? The woman always gets the kids, even if she's a descendant of Lucretia Borgia and has the nurturing instincts of Medea. No, sadly, getting pregnant behind your partner's back is a pleasure only girls get to experience. Which brings me to another point—is being a man and wanting a child on my own wrong? Is it against nature? Fuck it, no, it's not. And even if it is perceived as weird, well, fuck you, it's time for a change, and watch how good a father I'm going to be.

But why don't I want a relationship?

Ooh, hard one . . .

I know, I know! I don't necessarily *not* want one, I just don't want one as a means to an end of getting a child. Yes, that's it! Maybe I might have one, but I want the child thing to be a separate issue. God, when you come to think about it, Charlie has got it sussed, hasn't he?

So I just don't want to be forced into having a relationship that might—well, let's say undoubtedly will—go wrong just to enable me to fulfill my primal male instincts. Unless of course it's a relationship with someone really—and I mean *really*—understanding. And in order to be *that* understanding they would have to be someone who is so desperate that no one would want to touch them with a barge pole. I know I'm being harsh here, but let's face facts: no one actively thinks it's okay that their partner doesn't believe in commitment, fucks around with anything that moves and only wants you in their life so your child feels like less of a freak in the playground. And here we come to another point. It *is* male, it *is* primal. God, it's one of the most masculine feelings I've ever had, this. This wanting, no, needing to look after and care for and just give loads of fucking love to a little, helpless baby. It's like a duty, not a desire.

So why does it feel so weird? Why do I feel like a freak when I talk about it? Why do I need to be coked off my tits and with my trousers round my ankles to even begin to talk about it?

Well, maybe because the public's perception of someone like me is not someone who should be entertaining such thoughts. I am from the "outskirts of society" (a phrase I have always enjoyed, invoking as it does an image of lots of pierced, tattooed people crawling through the undergrowth about to enter the city and do depraved things to innocent readers of *OK* magazine as they slow down in their cars at crossings to give old people the right of way). I am a sexual deviant. I am a drug user. I am irresponsible and untrustworthy and I should never, never be left unsupervised with a child, let alone allowed to take one home to society's fringes to do God only knows what to it.

Yeah, and look how good a job all you straight, clean, together people are doing of it.

Of course we could always go the route of adopting. Hello? And the number of single sodomites you know who have passed the adoption agencies' criteria is?

And then there's also the thought to contend with that I might be absolutely terrible at bringing up a child. I could be the worst fucking father ever. My selfishness in wanting to have a child in my present circumstances does not augur well for a lifetime of the selflessness and slavish devotion to someone other than myself that parenthood requires. I am fucked. I am fucked because I am listening way, way deep into myself and hearing what my mind and my body wants, and my ancestors have wanted for generations. But because I am me, Mr. Modern Man, Mr. I Cannot Tell a Lie, I am stuck here on the number 19 bus, several stops past the one I should've got off at, sitting immobile, wishing I was dead, longing to get my cock out and just jack off there and then. I wish I'd stayed in bed. I wish I'd called in sick again. I wish I'd called in and said I was never coming back to work. I wish I could stay in bed forever and just wank until I die. Suddenly I noticed there was no one else on the top deck. It was midmorning, we were stuck in a jam because of an accident at the top of High Holborn. Of course I got the hugest hard-on ever known to man. I know, I know, I'm in the midst of this crisis and all I can do is think with my dick, but you know what? That's what this is all about in the first place. If I was pretending *not* to think with my dick, I could be part of a nice little couple right now, straight or gay—the straight one fucking away condomless and the girl lying with her legs up against the wall afterward, the gay one holding hands and writing a check to an adoption or a surrogate agency, then fucking condomless when they got home—and all this would just be the imaginary riff of some pop novelist. But I have and this isn't and so I pull my cock out and I'm so shaking and horny and animal and vibrant and messed up that a couple of seconds after I have it in my hand I've shot all over the back of the seat in front of me and it's dripping onto an empty packet of Cheesy Wotsits lying on the deck.

I lick my hand. This is who I am, and there is fuck-all wrong with it. I get off the bus and walk back to work. The coming elation lasts for a little while as I set up the lights in the studio and put on the coffee machine in the greenroom and take the croissants that are delivered every day out of their boxes and put them onto a big plate. Yeah, I am okay, and I can see the light at the end of the tunnel.

But as I am taking the croissants and coffee into the studio and setting them on the low table where the models or celebrities chat with Julian before they go into makeup, I begin to realize that this end of depression is different from the others. There is no epiphany, no little box in the corner of my mind-attic that has been cleaned out. Oh no. This time, the only calm comes in the sureness that the reason for my depression will never go away. It will always be there, a huge black cloud that I will run from and dodge but never escape its rain.

I was realizing all this as Julian came into the studio and started to talk to me. Even though he was standing right next to me, I was seeing him from far, far away, from the other side of the room in fact. I could sense that his eyes were sparkling and his lips were moving, but nothing was registering.

The thought of the rest of my life in the thrall of this cloud was making my legs weak and Julian became like the last frame of a silent movie when the image gradually decreases into a little circle surrounded by black, until finally there is a pinprick of the image and then, as the orchestra plays its last note, the screen goes to black, and I was on the floor at Julian's feet and the croissants were thudding down all around me like Daliesque French resistance parcels being parachuted into wartime France. . . .

8

the good news

The good news is that I am not dead. I am not writing this from beyond the grave à la one of those annoying novels or films where in a sneaky sting in the tale the main character, who you have been rooting for, suddenly pops his or her clogs and you are left with a really wishy-washy, half-baked narrative device that encourages you to believe that people who have hitherto been recounting their experiences as live, flesh-and-blood human beings have suddenly died very conveniently, and just as conveniently have access to a laptop computer from their afterlife resting place. I hate that.

Please let me assure you, dear reader, that I stay alive until the end of this book. There is no death here. At least not in the conventional sense. There is perhaps the death of love in a future chapter, there could, I suppose, be the death of Tommy's innocence in a few chapters but that will be accompanied by the birth of a slightly different and therefore newer Tommy. But anyway, the matter in hand is this:

Why Tommy fainted

1. I have not had a proper meal since Friday night. It is now Wednesday.

2. Copious amounts of coffee, American Spirit Yellow cigarettes, chewing gum and a cup of miso soup every day or so maketh not a healthy diet.

3. Cocaine makes you not want to eat. Anything. Apart from chewing gum.

4. I have not been sleeping well. (See above.)

5. Massive amounts of masturbation and the spilling of seed therein can seriously weaken a boy who is already experiencing the effects of 1, 2, 3 and 4 above.

Since the H.E.I. with Sasha in the disabled loo, I have been avoiding (a) people and (b) food. The good thing about this evasion combo is that the (a) part means no one tells you how shit you are looking and the (b) part facilitates going to the loo less and thereby lessens the chances of engaging with those in (a) who would have told you you look like shit.

Of course there is also the matter of the other drugs I've been imbibing—after the Dame's stash had been decimated I made a phone call and had a delivery of a slightly less pure form of cocaine that some people might call *speed* but which I—delusionally—think of as *cocaine manqué*. Like sort of when there is a power cut and you have to use candles. That sort of thing. Yes. Scuzzy, old candles that burn very quickly and fill your room with toxic, noxious fumes that you will spend years coughing up or working on the Stairmaster at the gym to rid your lungs of. I say you, because fuck it, there is no way I will ever go near a gym.

Basically, the amount of stuff I was putting up my nose was capable of keeping a normal person awake for weeks, and to diminish the appetite of a scavenging dog to that of an anorexic model on the days prior to fashion week. I probably ate more food by *breathing* than by actual mastication.

So, all this combined with my recent light-headedness on the top deck of the number 19 and the slowly forming feelings of nausea brought on by the wafting smells of the coffee and the croissants makes it a wonder I stayed vertical at work this long.

What happened next

The first thing I saw when I came to was Julian's arse, and believe me, it's not the sort of visual you want to have as you reenter consciousness. That sort of saggy, public-schoolboy-gone-to-seed derriere has never been attractive to me, especially when combined with the too-tight slacks Julian persisted in wearing, even when his belly had given up the fight and thrust itself over the waistband, like a volcano that had started to erupt but then thought better of it.

He had been kneeling over me, concerned, bless him, then turned away to reach for his mobile phone which was on the coffee table next to the sofa now covered in mashed-up croissants. He was presumably going to call for an ambulance. I was out for about a minute, which is a long time when you are a posh and privileged photographer unused to making your own tea or reserving your own dinner table and suddenly faced with the potential death of the very person who normally does all those tasks for you. He was well freaked out. However, my stirring and confused scream at the sight of all that corduroy-slack-clad loose flesh wobbling toward me caused him to leap backward, terrified, falling on the table, further decimating the croissants and staining said slacks with several mugs of piping hot coffee.

"Oh, Tommy, thank God you're alive," he gasped.

Julian wasn't normally prone to such disaster-movie-style dialogue. He was much more a pupil of the English school of not being able to express his feelings (especially to other men) aside from a gruff slap on the back (well done/good to see you/ good catch, etc.) or a firm handshake (with, occasionally, the other hand grasping your forearm to express extraspecial gravity or force of feeling, thereafter never discussed again). Basically, Julian was a repressed toff who, because of a childhood allergy to horses, had taken up photography as a hobby, retreating to a specially converted darkroom in one of his parents' estate's outhouses whilst his siblings, their pasty thighs astride their mounts, giggled at him and waved as they set off across the dewy pastures.

And that, I think, is half of his problem, or half its solution. Perhaps because of that early bout of puffy eyes and runny nose, but more likely because of a pathological fear of opening his legs that wide, Julian missed out on the thrill of the ride.

I know it's trite, and I always hate mincy old queens who go on about how straight men would all fall to the pleasures of gay-dom if only they knew what was good for them, but, in this case, they have a point—Julian just needs to get fucked up the arse.

Hard. Many times. Then I truly think he'd be so much happier. His curiosity would certainly be satisfied, and that could only be a boon for me of a Monday morning (see below).

However, I digress. He's not the sort of chap to say, on seeing an employee recover from a minor faint, that he was so happy that said employee had not shuffled off his mortal coil. But, as I have said, he thought there was something really wrong, and I'm going to think that it was my friendship, happy-go-lucky attitude and smiling face he would have missed and not the fact that I controlled everything about his working life and without me he wouldn't be able to function. It's true. Don't let the job description "photographer's assistant" fool you. My assisting went so much further than handing him rolls of film, pressing light meters and telling him what the stop was. In addition to being a stupid clod with figures, and thereby relying on me for practically every piece of arithmetic connected with taking a picture (and there can be a great deal), Julian had also somehow passed on all responsibilities of adulthood to yours truly. Therefore, I paid his bills (by phone, it wasn't brain surgery, but *still* . . .), I told him when his friends' birthdays were coming up, I called the florist on Mother's Day, I basically reminded Julian every day of how to be Julian. On Fridays I had to print out a list of numbers and instructions for him to follow until we met again on Monday. I had banned him from calling me on weekends after one too many nights of me having my mobile rammed against my ear in the chill-out room of some club talking Julian through the process of how to get his car back after it had been towed or explaining how his burglar alarm worked, or even (and he must have been really drunk this time) directing him to the club where I was because he wanted to buy some coke, as the girl he was with—a wafer-thin catwalk mannequin with bad skin—

wanted to "get absolutely bloody wasted and fuck like a bunny."
(His words, not mine.) As it transpired, the evening did not turn
out as planned. I did deliver the goods into Julian's sweaty palm
on the club's pavement, he doing a hackneyed performance of
someone obviously being passed drugs but acting nonchalant,
but after he got the girl home and they got naked and he'd cut
up the lines with his American Express platinum card (a nice
touch, I thought), the girl hoovered up her share and before
Julian got to first base she had run to the toilet and barfed up
the entire Caprice dinner and stayed there, head down the pan,
for the next three hours, weeping and vomiting, whilst Julian
ground his teeth and tried to resist the urge to fuck her from
behind. "It was a bloody nightmare, Tom," he'd told me. "I was
high as a kite, and I had a bloody great stiffy, and there's this
filly" (yes, he actually calls girls fillies) "arse up in the air in front
of me and I can't do a bloody thing with her."

Julian got a great vicarious thrill from quizzing me about my
exploits, and was given to girlish squealing at the really seedy
ones. Especially on Mondays, he would put me through a sort
of sexual Spanish Inquisition and demand to know where I'd
been, what I'd done (drugs and otherwise) as well as who I'd
shagged, what their bodies were like, what positions we'd tried,
who came first, the whole nine yards.

When I'd first started working for him, I thought he was a
sad old fucker and dreaded every weekend's end because I knew
I would have the grueling grilling to endure come Monday. I
would have to quash the overwhelming desire to tell this nosy
nonce to fuck off. But I did quash it—he was my boss, after
all—and after a while I actually came to look forward to our
little confessional ritual. Over the weekend, in the midst of some
bacchanalian encounter, I would say to myself, "Julian will *love*

this," and in a way, through time, he came to be a sort of combination of big brother and therapist to me, inadvertently making me question or defend my excesses, and by recounting them, letting me enjoy them over again. I loved to see him squirm or gasp when his Holland Park sensibilities were offended. And I also loved to hear his advice or asking after some particular shag, months after the deed when they were long forgotten by me. "Oh, I liked the sound of him, Tom," he'd say, slurping his coffee. "Why don't you try for another canter round the tracks there?"

He was basically all right, Julian. A bit of a pillock, posh and therefore handicapped in his outlook, but in spite of all that I said about him, and how much I moaned about his inadequacies and the embarrassing things he asked me to do for him ("Tom, could you call them and pretend that my answer machine was broken or something and apologize and say I am excruciatingly embarrassed and try and rearrange for next week, you know, just try and make it sound like it's not my fault, there's a dear"), I actually sort of quite liked him. I suppose I must quite like him a lot, otherwise I wouldn't have stayed with him this long (seven years), and also working for him was pretty easy and I got to travel a bit sometimes, and meet people, and oh yeah, get quite a few shags. There's nothing like a photo studio, where the subject has spent a couple of hours being told they look gorgeous and sexy and amazing, to capitalize on all that outpouring of sexuality and confidence come the end of the day. You'd be amazed how far the words "You looked really great, those shots are going to be fab, we're going round the corner for a drink, do you want to join us?" can take you.

In addition to his well-heeled upbringing, Julian had had the great good fortune to be a young, posh, up-and-coming photographer around the time the British media went completely bonkers for the "young royals"—Di, Fergie et al.—in the mid- to late eighties, and his aristocratic countenance and pedigree stood him in great stead to get royal sittings that led to not only great prices for his—just above average, then—snaps, but also entry into the pantheon of classy celebrity photographers, where he has remained, bemused slightly and just clinging on, ever since.

Back to the faint

Julian's arse was not the only surprise to greet me on my re-entry into the world of the awake. As soon as he was sure I was okay, and not in need of medical attention, and after I had murmured a few calming-the-waters-type lies about not having slept well last night or eaten this morning and how after a croissant and a sweet coffee to get my sugar levels up I would be fine, Julian looked at me with a twinkle in his eye and raised his regal chin—a sure sign that he was about to make a pronouncement.

"Well, Tommy, you'd better get your sugar levels up because I have some good news, and I don't want you flaking out on me in the middle of it," he said cryptically.

"What news?" I mumbled through a mouthful of French pastry.

"I have just had a call from my agent, and on Monday we will be in New York City for two fabulous, all-expenses-paid weeks photographing the New World's finest young starlets for a spread in *Elle*. What a riot! Two weeks, one filly a day, so no hardship there, and room service at the Mercer every night. It's just what the doctor ordered, as well as the accountant, as the bookings in Old Blighty were looking a bit thin for the next wee while."

Julian laughed, and looked at me for a reaction. Frankly, I was stunned. At the moment—with all that was going on in my head, and the situation with Finn, and the fact that my blatant avoidance of Bobby and Sadie would very soon result in a big-brother-and-sisterly intervention with the inevitable outpouring of all my woes and all its patent potential destabilizing effects—all of this made the notion of two weeks of easy work in the party city of the world seem to transform my life from Ken Loach–style urban decay to *The Wizard of Oz*! I leapt from the sofa and hugged Julian as hard as my weak limbs could clench.

New York City, baby! Talk about just what the doctor ordered. Suddenly I felt the fog lifting and the color coming back into my sallow cheeks. Two weeks away from gray old London, two weeks of not having to deal, two weeks away from . . . myself. Well, not quite, but still. New York equals FUN. Anonymous fun, because even though I'd been there quite a few times with Julian on previous trips, it wasn't a place where I had roots or loads of friends and therefore calls to make and people to see and answers to "So how are you really doing, Tommy?" and annoying, hard stuff like that. I could go out and wander and look around and party and get laid and restore my batteries. When I came back I'd be my old self again, the self without a care in the world who'd never be caught crying in the disabled loo or telling Charlie my cock was his or even worried about upsetting Finn.

The last time I'd gone to New York was right after I'd broken up with India (the one who broke my heart and turned into someone else, remember?) and it had done me a world of good. I made no plans, but every night was an adventure, and I just went with it. I met people and had great talks and danced and drank and got stoned and shagged.

My favorite part of that trip was the Sunday night before we came home. We'd been shooting some bitchy old American iconoclastic novelist who in the seventies wrote books that now seem almost soft porn but at the time were groundbreaking—or so she said. Anyway, she hated being photographed. Or so she said. She actually liked all the attention and the fuss, but she was a terrible model. She did a really good impersonation of someone who was dead and had been wheeled into the studio, plastered in orange foundation and then propped up in front of the lens. The only sign that she was not in fact a goner was the copious amount of sweat emitting from her forehead and upper lip.

Modeling is not as easy as it looks, you know. Feigning naturalism for the camera is an art form, as far as I'm concerned. And all those girls who get famous and suddenly lose their second name don't get the big bucks for nothing. Naomi, Kate, Giselle, Heidi—they fucking rock. It certainly makes Julian's job easier when we have a good model (since he is a pathetic, socially inept twit who hasn't the first idea how to be spontaneous and natural himself, let alone coax it from a rigor-mortis-like novelist), and therefore, by association, mine. Anyway, the shoot was a nightmare, and the only saving grace was the cute Italian makeup boy who had the unfortunate task of trying to dissuade said novelist from going for her normal makeup look (i.e., a drag queen) and opting for something a little softer, a little more pleasing to the eye, and frankly a little less scary to small children who might have the misfortune to pick up the Sunday supplement this picture was intended for, leaf through to this harridan's visage and be forever disturbed. His name was Luca, and he was wearing leather trousers and a cutoff T-shirt that showed off not just his fabulous arse but also the hairiness of his stomach and the tattoo at the top of his back. We got chatting at the lunch table and flirted all through the rest of the afternoon, mainly due to a common disbelief that this woman, who, ironically, in her writing explored the passions and depths of being a woman alive in the world today (or quite near to today, at least in the last few decades) but who, in real life, could only barely pass at being either a woman or alive.

When Julian had finally lied and told her he had got the shot, she was packed off in a taxi back to the Upper East Side, and me and Luca got chatting about what we would do next. There was no doubt in either of our minds that we would be having sex later. After he'd finished packing up his gear and I'd finished up the stuff for the lab (Julian, of course, had run out the door the second the grande dame had gone with the pathetic cry of "God, is that the time? I'm meeting the picture editor of *Vogue* at Pastis in fifteen minutes"), he sauntered up to me, in the middle of the studio, in exactly the same spot where the grim writer had sat, glowing, only minutes before, and said, "Tommy, do you want to have an adventure?"

"Always," I replied, smiling, rubbing the dark hair on his tummy, then giving his cock a little pat through the leather.

"Eat this then," he said, popping an e into my mouth.

What a night we had! He took me to a place in SoHo called Spy Bar where you could go upstairs and look through telescopes at the people sitting down below. He introduced me to a drag king (think queen but the other way round) and the hostess of the night, a skinny, blond, typical downtown New York self-proclaimed superstar called Ice Cream Sundae. She had little raisins of nipples. I saw them when the three of us snogged and, as they say in America, fooled around a bit, in one of the dark banquettes that bordered the bar. Then we were off in a blur of taxis and clubs and more kissing and martinis and my hand rubbing on Luca's hairy tummy, getting lower each time but never wanting to spoil what I knew was to come by exposing the treasure below. At one point we got into a car belonging to the friend of someone's friend, a boy who told us he was about to move to Budapest to make porn films because he happened to have a ten-inch dick. I asked him to show me but he wouldn't, so of course, I bet it wasn't really ten inches. Everyone I've ever met who had one would show it to anyone. Wouldn't you? Anyway, this supposedly well-endowed boy drove his car the wrong way down Eighth Avenue (in retrospect, if his dick was as big as he was stupid, it was probably fifteen inches), nearly killing us and forcing him to swerve violently to avoid the oncoming traffic. It was scary, sure, but the adrenaline rush combined with the e made me really enjoy it. I know that's sort of sick, but hey, if we'd been killed at least I would've died happy. The night ended with me and Luca getting out of a cab in the Meatpacking District, near his apartment. It was about six in the morning and the road was blocked with all the trucks coming to stock up or deliver meat to the city. It was pouring with rain, and we were in that coming-down stage where everything is sort of in slow motion and your senses are nearly back to normal, and there we were, soaked, ears full of the noise of men shouting and trucks pulling out, and big rails of dead cows' carcasses flashing in front of our paths every few steps. It was amazing. When we got back to his apartment we had a bath together (my suggestion) and then we took turns fucking each other till we were exhausted and flopped down into each other's arms and waited for the day. We were too wired to sleep, too wired to come, but knew we'd just had a great, only-in-New-York sort of night together. And you know what, I didn't think of India once. Not for a second.

I had completely LIVED! And that was what I was going to do on this trip. I was going to live! Fuck all these thoughts of what am I going to do, I'm nearly thirty and where is it all leading? Fuck all of that! Tommy knows where it's leading—to New York fucking City!!

Yeah, baby!!

india

When I got home that night I was really pissed off to find Sadie and Bobby not there. And no note or nothing.

I suppose the fact that I had so studiously avoided contact with the pair of them for the last few days meant it was fair enough that they didn't keep me informed of their every movement. But nonetheless I felt a little pang in the bottom of my tummy, which I quickly diagnosed as missing them combined with a big surge of guilt due to my incognito period.

I wanted to tell them about the trip to New York, and maybe about the faint, and maybe apologize for being such a wanker.

Being in the flat on my own was weird. I had craved it since the weekend but now I wanted it to be like it normally was—music blaring, the three of us shouting to each other above it, and Sadie banging about in the kitchen, throwing leftovers from the fridge into a pot and creating some dish that we would then name as we ate it together, like "Sadiemush," a stalwart of Sadie cuisine which was basically a stir-fry of old Chinese and Indian take-aways cooked in the oven with some lentils, and "Saddopasta," so called because eating it meant we had joined the ranks of very sad people. It was a real scraping-the-barrel-nothing-left-in-the-cupboards-type meal which consisted of penne, or any pasta of a circular bent, with a sauce made of fried garlic mixed with tomato paste and honey. It was really, really delicious and belied its humble origins. Sadie just invented it out of her head. Try it, you'll be amazed. Then there was "Sadage Stew," made of the inevitable packet of sausages that was always lurking in some corner of our fridge (Bobby had a penchant for sausages from both the swine and male species). It also involved tins of tomatoes and basically things that were lying around un-used, but, again, was really, really tasty. Those were my happiest times: Bobby and Sadie and I around the kitchen table drinking wine and wolfing down something Sadie had thrown together quickly, laughing and being reminded of why we loved each other so much. Our flatmates-only dinners were more formal affairs, planned and prepared in advance and with the cooking chores divided week by week, and with some time set aside for a sensible chat about flat etiquette, the neighbors, who had been shirking on their emptying-the-bins duties, that sort of thing. But these im-promptu, we-all-happen-to-be-in-at-the-same-time-and-hungry sort of meals were the best. Unexpected things are usually more fun because of their surprise value, rather than their actual con-tent, aren't they? Like bumping into an old college friend in a bar and having an evening or reminiscing and remembering in-cidents you'd never have revisited if you hadn't had that chance encounter. It was great to know that not planning anything wouldn't necessarily rule out a great time being just around the corner.

But tonight? No plans had been made and there was no prospect of Tinkerbell waving her magic wand to fill the kitchen with the smells of comforting things like cigarette smoke and food and Bobby and Sadie.

I went through to the living room. Sadie had obviously been cleaning again—the newspapers and magazines were arranged in a fan shape, titles carefully available to the eye. After each bout of tidying, for a few hours the place felt like a doctor's waiting room, but then it would inexorably be mussed up and become again us.

The only light came from the lampposts out on the street. Long shadows fell across the floorboards as I perched on the edge of the sofa. It was red and big but tonight didn't feel as comfy as it felt when there were three of us on it. In fact tonight the sofa felt like it should be in the window of Habitat. We called Sadie the Princess Plumper. She couldn't bear to leave the flat with the cushions on the sofa all mashed up, and ran the gauntlet of our taunts every time we left together by dashing round the living room plumping them up so they would sit there, puffed up like collagen lips, ready and welcoming for the next bout of bums to drop into their fullness. Where were they? Just then the phone rang. I sat in the dark and listened to the answer machine click on. "Hello, this is Tommy, and Sadie, and Bobby."

I remembered the night we'd all crouched down on the floor beside the fireplace, giggling, to get near the microphone on the crappy little machine. We were down there for ages, and I remember having sore limbs the next day—it was the nearest thing to a gymlike activity I had undergone in many years. But it took us ages to get a message that we were all happy with and in which we didn't sound totally weird. In fact, although I know this is not one of those tradesman's-secrets sort of books where weird little hotel managers in spectacles tell you how to clean an ashtray efficiently, but still, this is worth the digression: never, never, dear reader, record your answer-machine message whilst squatting on all fours over the mike. Apart from the indignity, you will alarm your callers no end because the weird, strangulated timbre this position gives to your vox humana bears a striking resemblance to those tapes you hear on the news when kidnappers peel back a bit of the surgical tape with which they have muted their victims and force them to say a few words to assure their families that they are indeed alive.

"We're sorry we're not here, but we're either out somewhere fabulous or else we're in and can't be bothered to talk to you. When you leave your message remember that we might be here listening to it, so the more entertaining you can be the better chance you have of us picking up. Thanks for calling. Bye!"

I smiled. You rarely get to hear your own answer-machine message. With some you don't hear anything at all until the caller starts to speak. Ours was an antiquated, cheap old thing with none of that sophistication.

"Tommy, it's India, are you there? Um, you know I'm not very good at being entertaining . . ."

My stomach shot into my throat, I gasped and my whole body convulsed. I hadn't heard from her since last year, on Guy Fawkes Night actually, when I'd gone round to her new swanky apartment, paid for no doubt by the new swanky boyfriend she had so quickly acquired after she and I hit the rocks. There was even the possibility of an overlap that still made my stomach turn when I thought of it, despite her claims that yes, they'd met, they'd gone out for dinner, but it wasn't until we had completely called it the proverbial day that anything actually *happened*. And what a delightful visual that had been. Something *happening*. What, of course, had *happened* was that Karl the German, that slimy, perfectly ironed—even when wearing jeans, for fuck's sake—creep she had taken up with had inserted his slimy, German and no doubt also perfectly ironed and certainly circumcised (for clearly he wouldn't be able to stand the potential creasing presented by a foreskin) dick into the pussy of the beautiful, beautiful, but deluded, insecure mess that had been India. Who had been mine. As she had told me many times. "I'm yours." "My pussy is yours." Sounds familiar? The "my cock is yours" incident suddenly didn't seem so bad. The mere utterance of such stupid remarks was surely accompanied by an unspoken codicil that ensured they were of a purely temporary nature?

"It's just what you say, Tommy, when you're in the midst of something," she'd spluttered during that last blazing postmortem slanging match. I replied that when I was in the midst of the supermarket, in the midst of shopping, I managed to suppress the urge to tell the checkout girl that she owned my dick. And I told India she should just shut up and look pretty because that would be less painful for me and probably easier for her, as shutting up and looking pretty had been her lifelong modus operandi anyway. Then she had slapped me. Really hard. She was a nonaggressive, vegetarian, going-on-marches sort of girl trapped inside the body of Venus, so this sudden bout of violence was doubly stinging. Just then, as if on cue, the Guy Fawkes Night fireworks display in the park in front of her desirable residence began, and the sky behind her lit up with a million red sparkles and seconds later that deafening, always surprising, noise. Her eyes were completely blazing, and her cheeks were as red as the sky. She looked like a devil, an angry she-devil spewed out of the pits of hell for a brief moment to avenge all the wrongs inflicted on her sex. "Don't ever talk to me like that, Tommy. Ever," she said, quivering. "I will not be patronized by you. I loved you. I told you I was yours, and for a while I was. Then we drifted apart, and now I'm not yours anymore. And I know Karl being in my life is hard for you, but you have to get over it. Just get over it, please." And so there it was. The last words she had spoken to me. "Get over it."

Back to the answering machine . . .

"Tommy, *are* you there?" My heart was beating so fast. I guess you realized that I'm not over India. But what did she want? And why, oh bloody why, weren't Bobby and Sadie here to help me? I suppose it was karma. Maybe over the last few days they'd wanted to talk to *me* about stuff or needed *my* help. Fair enough, but all the same, I hate karma sometimes. And what swaying of the karmic pendulum had brought India, the beautiful India, who I had yearned for, gurned for, and masturbated for so often in the past year and a half, to be on the end of the line, tonight, just when I was coming *out* of a downer?

In a split second I had leapt across the room, scattering Sadie's manicured magazines to the four corners, and was grappling about on the floor for the receiver. "Hi, yes, I'm here." I tried to sound polite but guarded, and took the phone away from my mouth to hide the deep breaths I was taking due to my exertions.

"How are you?" She sounded tentative, wary of how I was

going to be with her. For my part, I didn't know how I was going to be. I just knew I was glad she had phoned.

"I'm okay. How are you?"

"Oh, you know . . . I've been better," she said.

And what the fuck does that mean, I thought, but I decided to ignore it.

"Good, good," I said, then realized that was completely the wrong response. "Erm, I mean . . . ah . . . why?"

There was a little silence. "Oh, I don't know, I just wanted to hear your voice." India had a bad habit of lapsing into bad movie dialogue. When we were splitting up she had actually said, "I don't know anything anymore." I mean, really.

I decided to get straight to the point. "Have you split up with him?"

Another silence. Then, a quiet "Yes."

So that was it, was it? Kreepy Karl had grown tired of this year's model (ha-ha, because that was what she was, a model) and had roared off in his perfectly ironed Porsche in search of pastures new. And now, little India, who all her life has defined herself by the man she is with (and she was rarely without one, believe me, the streets of London town are awash with her former lovers: for a nice girl she has put it about), was feeling lost and lonely and decided to seek solace in me, the man she said she had truly found love with for the very first time, the man who she so quickly abandoned when things got complicated, the man who, probably because he wasn't a high flyer or very important in the grand scheme of things, led her to define herself as also not very important and, oh my goodness me, we can't have that, can we? I knew she still loved me, I knew we couldn't be together. But above all I knew that it would be no good for me to see her again in the state I was in.

"So, do you want to meet up?" I asked.

"Yeah, that would be nice. What about sometime next week?"

Fuck me. Don't go out of your way, you old slapper. Calling me up after a year and a half, when the last interaction we had was a physical attack, to tell me your Hitler Youth boyfriend has now fled the nest and you need to hear my voice, but can't find a window till next week?! Fuck her! Maybe her other nights were filled with other old boyfriends who'd been slotted in after similar SOS calls.

"Um, I can't next week. I'm going to New York," I retorted, so glad I had a legitimate and—even better—glamorous reason to say no.

"Oh, well, what about before you go? I'm free any night." Ah. So delete that bit about her evenings being jam-packed with the moistening of former shags' shoulders. "I just didn't want to sound, you know . . ." She fumbled for the word.

"Desperate?" I interjected.

"I suppose so. I know I've got a cheek. Look, I'd really like to see you before you go. How about Sunday night?"

"Okay, Sunday's good," I said, a bit too quickly, dammit. Also, Sunday wasn't good. That was the day of our flatmates-only dinner, and we only ever missed it after prior flatmate consultation. It had better be something pretty important to miss the Sunday dinner, and I'd already missed last week, feigning illness after the excesses of the Dame's coke and as a means to hide from the world and then start the next few days of self-destruction culminating in the fainting episode. And as if missing the dinner wasn't bad enough, there was no way Bobby and Sadie would consider me going round to the lion's den that was India's flat, with its doorman and underground garage and its terrace overlooking the canal, as important or wise. They hated

India—well, they didn't actually hate her, just the way she had treated me. It was a natural, protective kind of hate. In the beginning they actually used to quite like her. Sadie, after her initial suspicion—any girl that beautiful being no more than a member of the "shag only, don't bring round for dinner" department—really took to her; they even used to see each other when I was away on trips. But that all changed when things started to go wrong, and I became a mess of tears and missing and everything I had believed was sure and good turned out not to be. Sadie said she was just so disappointed that India had proven her initial instincts to be right. India was too young, too unformed, too looking-over-her-shoulder-for-something-more-sparkly to be toying with someone like me. (Sadie's words, not mine, but she was *right*.) Oh, and Sunday night was also my turn to cook.

A little bit of explaining

You know how I've said I know who I am, and I know, if I'm being really honest, it's impossible to be with someone forever and how I'm a man and ergo, you know . . . Well, the bitter lesson that brought me to this creed was India.

I was in love with India. Really in love. She was so beautiful, a kind of beauty that made you stop in your tracks and just stare, and for the first time in my life, I thought that I had someone I could actually imagine being with forever. Never mind imagine, I *wanted* to be with forever. This is how it happens, I'd thought. You go through years of shagging and meeting Mister and Miss Wrong, you get jaded, you begin to see the world as a place where happy, lasting existence is only possible alone, and then POW! I met India. And it was great, for a while, for a long while. Almost too great. It was like I'd smiled too much for too long and eventually I had to stop smiling, otherwise I'd really injure myself forever.

And the anger and pain I suffered when it ended was as much due to the knowledge that I had been right all along as it was to the loss and the missing of her. It's not possible. For me, anyway, it seems. Even when you find the person you thought only appeared in soap operas, that person who makes you tingle and who you'd never dream of straying from, and who you'd happily *marry* if only you hadn't been such a ditz and forgotten to ask her. That was the thing about girls that probably made the monogamy and commitment thing easier—you could marry them and contractually pin them down to a life of security and bliss. With boys, in the absence of such a, let's face it, pretty fucked-up ritual—why should a bit of paper make you any more likely to stay with someone?—there was no metaphorical structure to ensure such a nonnegotiable pact.

Maybe if marriage was legal for them, gay men would be less promiscuous? There's an interesting theory to put to those big-oted old farts who decry both same-sex marriages and the sexual habits of gay men! Let them get married and there would be no more swimming around in the cesspits of their own making!

Anyway, it's all irrelevant. I'll never be married, to either a girl or a boy. But I could've married India. It feels so weird to say it now, but it's true. She taught me a bitter lesson, but I think I'm a happier Tommy because of it. To thine own self be true. Isn't it funny? India as a country was the jewel in the British crown, a land of beauty and plenty and, for the lucky Brits who went in and pillaged it, a paradise on earth. India the girl is much the same—exotic, serene, alluring and passive. India the country, of course, turned into a mess of civil confusion and bloodshed. See the parallel?

Fuck! I was going round to India's for dinner on Sunday night. Was this a good idea? I thought back to all the times over the last year and a half when I'd been perfectly happily out on the town and suddenly caught sight of her across a crowded bar and, bang, the ground just opened up in front of me, my stomach felt like it was going through a wringer and I just had to go home. It was awful. Once I'd spotted her getting into a taxi on my way to work from the top deck of the number 19 bus. Well, I just got off the bus and got another one in the opposite direction, called in sick and spent the day in bed. It wasn't so much the pain of seeing her—although there was some, but seeing more of her would dissipate that—it was more the *shock* of seeing her. I needed to be prepared. My loins had to be girded. And between now and Sunday I could do just that: prepare and gird. So that's all right then.

And it's about time. It's been too long that we've felt we *had* to stay away from each other. I want to be one of those people who include among their friends all their old lovers, at least the ones whose names I can remember (or ever knew). Also because it will be nice to look at her again, and smell her, and hear her tell her stories about her bizarre combination of friends—anorexics and activists.

And also, it couldn't do any harm, could it? We'd have a dinner, we'd reminisce, we might even do a bit of that "why did we ever split up" sort of thing, and it would all be just fine.

And she was the one who called me. She was the one who, Karl-less, called Mr. Pre-Karl for comfort. I am the one who, India-less, went away and thought about life and came out the other end weathered but wiser.

Oh yeah, baby, it was all going to be just fine.

10

a fairy tale about beauty

A long time ago, in a land not so very far away, there was a town where everyone was really, really beautiful. The men had handsome faces—strong cheekbones, fine noses, full and luscious lips, sparkling eyes and heads of hair so shiny and healthy that the birds of the town sometimes checked that their feathers were smooth in the reflections of these Adonises' manes. The women were no less impressive. Every morning when they awoke they pulled open the scarves they wore whilst sleeping and let their flowing tresses tumble down onto their elegant shoulders and beyond, down into the crease between their ripe breasts. There would be a flicker of their eyelashes as they left sleep behind them, then a long, slim hand would pass across a wide and smooth forehead, and sometimes, turning at the sound of their man's still sleepy stirring, they would part their peach-red lips, so ripe and full the birds were sometimes desirous of pecking them for their seed, and they would smile a smile at their man that could melt the ice floes with its warmth.

As dazzling as their smiles were their bodies: firm, of course, perfectly toned—muscular men, but never excessively so, just a natural, manly strength that came from using their bodies at work in the fields or running round the athletic tracks that could be found on the perimeter of every square. The women's bodies defined the word *pert*. Their long limbs were never too defined by intensive or repetitive tasks, but always lithe and flexible and languorous, and their hips and breasts were curved and smooth like peaches.

But the sex these beautiful creatures had with each other was not an explosion of passion, as one might expect from two specimens of such an extraordinary species enjoying the fruits of another so full and ripe and firm and mesmerizing as themselves. Oh no, this was an area where the townsfolk suffered.

For when you are so, so beautiful, and all around you is equally enchanting, there is nothing to compare yourself or anyone else with, and so naturally you come to think of yourself and your peers as normal, average, even slightly dull, and so the prospect of physical union with one as equally as dull as oneself is as exciting as reading those pages in newspapers devoted entirely to marriages, births and deaths—you know it is boring but you also know you will inevitably be a part of it in some capacity one day.

The lives of the people in this town were calm and peaceful and therefore long, but also a little bit dull. Actually, screamingly dull.

One day, the river, which, many miles above, flowed through the mountains and forests and then down into the pond in the beautiful people's town, burst its banks. One of the shepherdesses who lived up in the mountains was standing at the edge of the river bending down to swill out her mouth (as was her morning ritual) when she was swept off her feet and away downstream by the force of the angry water. Before she knew it she found herself coming up for air in a large, clear pond with a crowd of gorgeous-looking people peering down at her.

The shepherdess's name was Daphne, and although she had nothing physically wrong with her per se, she had not been at the front of the queue when God was handing out good looks. There was a slight twist in her nose, her ears were rather too large for the size of her head, her teeth were crooked or lost and her eyes rarely alighted on an object at the same time.

"Who are you?" said a young woman so exquisite to Daphne that she literally could not answer.

"Where did you come from?" asked a man with arms so brown and firm, and golden locks of hair flashing across his unfeasibly blue eyes.

"I was just about to gargle, and . . ."

Daphne couldn't finish her sentence, for the entire group that had assembled to watch her gasped. "What a beautiful voice," said one.

"I have never heard or seen anything so enchanting," exclaimed another.

"Who, me?" said Daphne, looking over her shoulder, sure that someone else had emerged from the pond behind her, but no, there was no one; they were speaking of her.

The townsfolk carried Daphne back to one of their houses, where they bathed her and laid her down under a quilt of duck feathers where Daphne fell into a deep sleep. She discovered, as many had before her, the peacefulness of sleep that is acquired when one is adored.

The next morning an exquisite young couple brought a tray of fruit and herb teas to her bedside.

The young couple had never seen anyone so enchanting, so remarkable, so sensual but mostly so desirable as Daphne. Just being near to her sent them into a frenzy of sexual and emotional confusion that is rarely glimpsed outside the pages of the most erotic literature, or the shadows of a stage door. They were literally mad for her.

The beautiful boy trembled as he held a grape above Daphne's rough mouth, and the girl felt her heart race as she glimpsed a broken vein on the end of Daphne's nose. As usually happens in situations like these, within seconds they were all together on the bed, one mass of desire and disbelief. Rarely in any sexual encounter can all the participants have thought the exact same thing: "I cannot believe how lucky I am for this to be happening to me."

Life was pretty good for Daphne for the next few weeks. Once word leaked out that this goddess would deign to engage in entanglements with the dull old inhabitants of the real world, everyone that Daphne met was eager—nay, determined—to sample her, to us, homely charms, but to them, mystical sensual prowess.

She was a little homesick, of course, and sometimes would long to be back on her little wooden porch and able to tell the rough girls from the other side of the hill just what she had been up to. How that would shut them up. But of course, they would never believe her. Daphne could hardly believe it herself.

Soon though, Daphne began to realize she was caught in a trap, because she could never leave this newfound land. If she did, she would no longer be the new Daphne, the confident, firm and toned Daphne, the Daphne that for the first time in her entire life actually liked herself.

And after all the citizens had tasted the fruits of the exotic creature in their midst, they did not, as Daphne had feared, lose their desire for more. On the contrary, their appetites were increased.

Daphne was adored and loved and feted and serviced every night of her life till she died (in the act of being penetrated by a young boy so soft and smooth he could never possibly have known the winds that roared across the hills to the north). She was still a young woman, but she died unhappy, sucked dry and disbelieving of all the evidence around her that she was indeed worthy of this attention, and too scared or lazy to move away or change her circumstances.

11

as if things weren't complicated enough

As soon as the doorbell rang I remembered. On Monday evening, as I was walking listlessly up the stairs of Highbury and Islington tube station on my way home from work, I'd turned on my mobile phone to see if I had any messages. I'd had it switched off all day, as I couldn't handle the thought of talking to anyone, and the few exchanges I had had with Julian were enough to remind me why I shouldn't switch it on. Apart from the obligatory reenactment of my weekend's sex life—the early-morning blow job with Charlie on Saturday and the coke-fingering escapade (minus of course the teary bit), I got away lightly because we weren't shooting anyone, and after he popped in to check on the state of things (my cock action, it seemed, primarily), he swept off to have lunch with some Hooray Henry friends of his at San Lorenzo (1 P.M., table for four, perhaps a fifth joining for coffee) and I was left to have a mooching-about afternoon trying to make sense of the disaster area that was Julian's receipts drawer.

The first message was from my mum, reminding me it was my gran's birthday in a week's time. She was great, my mum, not only because she served as a sort of family birthday alarm clock, but also for completely accepting the fuck-up of a son that was me ("Helen Rogers says her eldest, Brian, has a great new job in San Francisco, something to do with finance on the Internet. Doesn't that sound boring, Tommy? At least you're doing something *important* with your life"—I don't think my mum's sense of perspective has ever been the same since she heard the news of Laura Ashley's death. It affected her so much more than my dad's demise. I remember her sobbing "I felt as though I *knew* her" over and over, kneading a Paisley pattern wrap). The second message was from Charlie:

"Hi Tommy, it's Charlie here."

". . . and Finn too," piped up a little voice in the background.

"Finn was wondering, well, we were both wondering if we could come over and see you on Thursday night. Finn's got a birthday party just round the corner from you from six till eight so we thought we'd drop by after that. Don't bother to call back. We'll just stop by if we don't hear from you. And, eh"—his voice lowered, presumably so Finn wouldn't hear—"is it still mine?" Charlie was laughing as he put down the receiver and I could just make out Finn saying, "Is what still yours?"

I was in such a daze that day, and the few that followed, that I'd forgotten all about it. And here it was, Thursday night, I'd just hung up with India, and Charlie and Finn were ringing the front doorbell. Imagine if they'd been here when she called! If they had been, I certainly wouldn't be going round to hers on Sunday night, I can tell you that for nothing. It would have been more like "Oh hi, how are you, look, I can't talk right now, can you call back later" and of course, India, sensing I was not alone at home pining for her, would have been too proud to call back. Call it fate.

Finn was holding a red balloon on a little string and his mouth had the remnants of chocolate cake smeared over it.

"Dad, he *is* in! Tommy, look, I brought this for you. It's a balloon," he yelled, rushing to me and throwing both arms around my waist. As he did so, the balloon flew upward and out of his reach, and we watched it fly along the street and off, up above the council block, to who knew where.

"Sorry, Tommy, I just got excited to see you," he said.

"Don't worry, Finn. It was a nice thought, and at least we got to see it flying away. That was better than keeping it in my room for ages till it went all wrinkly, wasn't it?"

"Yeah," he said, mulling this over. "But I wanted you to have something of mine to keep." Oh dear, he was still on that one.

Charlie gave me a kiss on the mouth as he passed me in the hall. One of those that wasn't a snog but was more than simply a peck on the cheek gone east or west. It was a kiss of confidence. Confidence in himself, in his relationship with me, and confidence that he would taste those lips again ere too long. It was kind of scary.

He looked great. His eyes sparkled and he positively bounded up the stairs after Finn toward the kitchen.

I think a funny thing happens to people who have kids. The first few years they are just exhausted, haggard-looking wrecks, who float through life looking bitterly at their friends who are single or rich, and getting drunk incredibly quickly on the few, rare occasions they manage to find a baby-sitter and escape for a night and try to re-create the carefree existence and routine they had *before*. These evenings are spent, incidentally, slurring through tissues of lies about how fabulous their lives are now, then guilt or alcohol misuse forces them home early, to relieve the sitter and nurse the inexorable crashing hangover they will never recover from fully, as they will be up at some unearthly hour throwing plastic bottles of milk in microwaves and pureeing carrots.

But then, one day, something miraculous happens. I always watch for it, and as there are no real telltale signs, I inevitably miss it. One day, when the kids don't wake up in the middle of the night all the time and they speak and become interesting people to be with instead of things to just mop up after, the sallow countenance, the lackluster gait, the exhausted, drained and bored former friends disappear and transmogrify into these sparkly-eyed, fresh-faced beings, as though the wonder and glee their offspring feel in just being alive is by osmosis rubbing off onto them.

A confession

I envied Charlie. And not just for the fact that he had Finn, who was beautiful and perfect in his own right, and aside from the fact that he also represented something that I could not have, not easily or truthfully anyway. No, I envied Charlie for the way in which he lived his life. I think partly because of Finn's existence (as children force parents to live completely in the moment), Charlie had a way of being that I had yet to ascend to. It's hard to describe, but the nearest I can get to it is this: he didn't adhere to the creed that as soon as the next hurdle in his life had been eliminated, then (and only then) everything would be all right. For Charlie, there were no hurdles. Sure he had things happen that were difficult to him, but the way he thought about them and dealt with them was different from the way I thought or dealt with things. For example, for me, on one level, I saw the trip to New York as something where I would undoubtedly get wasted and behave badly and ignore all the needing-to-be-addressed issues until it was over, and only then when I returned to my "real" life would I be able to get on with stuff and start to attempt to make everything that was wrong right. On another level, of course, it was just my job, a trip that I'd taken before and would again. But it was always something that stood between me and my sorting myself out, something that no matter how fun it might turn out to be (and believe me, I was hoping it was going to be major fun) I saw as something that had to be *endured*.

Charlie, on the other hand, just did it. He got on with things, sorted problems out as they arose and looked forward to the rest of his life. And he wasn't superhuman, or supersmug either. He was normal, and that was the annoying thing. Charlie belonged to that lucky, lucky group of normal people who are not *waiting for their lives to start*.

I took the stairs rather more slowly than Finn or Charlie. It was only this morning I had blacked out, remember, and although this afternoon I'd eaten more than I had in the last five days combined—several of the mashed-up pastries and a chicken chow mein at lunchtime—I was still a little shaky. (Perhaps the excessive masturbation contributed too.)

Finn was already at the kitchen table rifling through a pile of magazines, a pair of scissors hovering precariously in one tiny hand.

"I didn't finish my collage, Tommy!" he sang out urgently, a look on his face as guilty as if he had let go of a fellow mountaineer's hand just after uttering the immortal words "Don't worry, you're safe with me."

Kids can be so serious sometimes.

"That's okay, Finn, we kept it for you to finish another time," I said, coughing slightly after the stair ordeal.

"I know, but it was a present for you," he replied, without looking up.

"You're giving me a lot of presents these days, Finn, aren't you?"

"Yeah," laughed Charlie, "what about your poor old dad, Finn? I don't seem to get any presents anymore, do I?"

"That's because I've got you already." Finn's voice was deadly calm. "I know you'll be here for Christmas and birthdays so I can give you your presents then. But with Tommy, it's different. You two might break up or something. So I want to give him as many presents as I can to show him that I love him just as much as I would if he lived with us, or something like that. You see?"

There was a deathly hush. Wow, two minutes in the door. This kid could really work it. Wow.

Charlie took all this in his stride, let it sink in, looked over at me with a faintly apologetic look on his face, cleared his throat and then said, "What makes you think that, Finn? I mean, why do you think Tommy isn't going to be around at Christmas?"

Finn kept his eyes on a German politician he was cutting out from the *Guardian*. There was a pause for a few seconds, the lull before the storm among the teacups. " 'Cos he's unreliable."

What was this all about? I may be many things, but unreliable is not one of them, I don't think. I shot a pissed-off and incredulous look over to Charlie and mouthed, "What?" The flash of guilt that swept across his face as his eyes met mine put me in no doubt where Finn had picked up the "unreliable" word. Finn continued: "You do it with girls sometimes, Tommy, and other times with other boys."

"Now, um, Finn." Charlie was flustered. He and I both, to be honest. Where the fuck was this going? "I don't think it's any of your business who Tommy does it with, do you?" Charlie had opted for the firm, what-do-you-think-you're-playing-at-young-man approach.

There was an uncomfortable pause. Finn's little cheeks began to redden, and although his head was down, obscuring his eyes, I could tell it wouldn't be long before the waterworks started. He had finished off the German and was starting to leaf through a homo mag called *Boyz*. There were naked-escort ads at the back that I really didn't want to have to explain to him right now, so I took the bull by the horns, walked over to the table, grabbed the mag from him, threw it on a chair, then picked him up into my arms, all in one fell swoop.

"All right, you cheeky monkey," I said to him as his head burrowed into my shoulder. "Let's finish your collage and get this all over with, shall we?"

I looked at Charlie for some sort of response, but all he could muster was a weak smile, half apologetic, half the-kid-does-have-a-point.

"If you finish it tonight I'll be able to take it away with me on my trip to America," I said.

"You're going to America?" Charlie and Finn loudly retorted together. Finn's head appeared from out of my armpit, his forehead crinkled with disdain. Charlie too was looking unhappy at the news.

"Only for a couple of weeks." I hate it when you have to play things down when you really want to jump up and down and scream about them. It's a weird thing that people do more and more, I've noticed. You'd think most normal people would be capable of putting aside how *they* might feel about whatever good news you have, and just simply be happy for you and even enjoy your very happiness. But oh no, not nowadays. Now it's a weak grin through clenched teeth and an at best desultory "Oh that's nice," which really means "You wanker, what about me?" or "Why didn't you tell me sooner?" What has caused this malaise? Is it the proliferation of self-analysis and therapy talk and the "I am my own best friend" sort of phenomenon that makes every utterance by someone else go through a "how does that affect me" filter first and so imbues any spontaneity at the news with a rather tight-lipped, preoccupied countenance?

I, on the other hand, know when to keep my mouth shut. And contrary to what you might be forgiven for thinking, dear reader, considering what you know of my young life so far, I know what is appropriate—like when you get introduced to someone's new boyfriend or girlfriend and you shake their hand and you realize they've had that hand round your cock once. I love moments like that. But I would never *say* anything.

And I pride myself in being able to forget my own feelings when I see someone in the midst of a burst of euphoria. In fact it's almost a hobby. I get carried away and become infected by it too. The number of nights I have ended up in some strange bar chatting to people I didn't know just because earlier in the evening, in some other watering hole, I'd witnessed the fun they were exuding at some news or some celebration and had gone over and joined in with them, just to feel it, their happiness and giddiness, and then of course their flirtiness and of course, later, their readiness to let go a bit more than they normally would. And I know a birthday or a forthcoming wedding or a promotion is slightly different from two weeks working in NYC, but the principle is the same. Charlie and Finn (and I know he's only eight and so he shouldn't really be judged by the same standards, but hey, he can do emotional blackmail and manipulation better than most grown-ups I know, so he can be bracketed with them for this too) didn't even for a second consider how I might feel about going to New York; it was all about *them*. And even if it does sadden (or annoy) them that they won't see me for a couple of weeks, they could at least try and suppress those feelings just a tad, even for the sake of politeness. Couldn't they? I mean, come on. God knows, were it not for the potential joy I was deriving from having my head forced down into a variety of pillows across the pond to block out my present state of mind, I'd be sad about missing them too.

Once, one of the actors at the Almeida had told me about why he would never go out with another actress again, never as long as he lived. It made me so sad for the acting profession that I've never forgotten it: "There is nothing worse in the world than getting a call from your agent about some fabulous job that you were waiting to hear about for ages, and as soon as the euphoria of the call is over the first thing that comes into your mind is 'Oh shit, how am I going to tell her? How is she going to take it?' "

Because she would be jealous, she would not be able to be happy for her man and the opportunity that had come his way because, as they were both actors and therefore always in some weird, fucked-up type of competition, she would always be reminded of her own shortcomings or failings and lack of job, and that would cloud her vision so much that she could never see the joy he was having at that moment. Isn't that awful? Never seeing the joy in other people? Not *allowing* the joy in other people?

Well, Charlie and Finn were giving me a pretty joyless time of it right now.

"Are you going to New York because you don't want to see me?" Finn said, his eyes piercing into mine, and his bottom lip a semi-quiver.

"What?" Where did this come from? "Of course not, Finn. Of course not." I knelt down and looked him in the eyes. "I have to go for my work. It's my job. Julian, who I work for, you remember Julian?"

" 'She's a lovely filly' Julian?" Through misty eyes Finn gave a pretty passable Julian impersonation.

"Yes, exactly, 'She's a lovely filly' Julian. Well, he has got a job photographing some actresses in New York, and 'cos I'm his assistant I have to go and help him. It's only for a couple of weeks."

"When did you find this out?" From behind me Charlie was entering the fray.

"Ah, this morning," I came back at him in a don't-even-start-with-that-one-matey voice. "Like about ten hours ago. I'm sorry I can't be any more specific." Charlie registered my annoyance, accepted it and nodded in apology. Finn was oblivious:

"But we had it all planned, Tommy. We were going to have a treasure trail this weekend and everything. And I was going to cook for you . . ." Finn's little voice trailed off as the tears started. He laid his head gently on my shoulder and sobbed. I could feel his whole body rack with them. He was a really, really sad little boy at that moment.

"Come on now, Finn, there's no need to be so sad; we can do all that stuff when Tommy gets back," said his dad, lifting him off me. But Finn screamed and kicked and more tears exploded from him at being removed from me, so Charlie had to withdraw and let him carry on sobbing in my arms. How about that? My arms. Finn wanted to be in my arms in his sadness, not his dad's. Even though Charlie smiled to me as he moved through to the living room, I could sense a frisson of aggression from him, something almost territorial. I felt really honored that Finn wanted to stay with me—honored by his trust, but also full of guilt that I'd dismissed his feelings when I'd first mentioned the trip away.

But a bittersweet cuddle can be a double-edged sword. His ability to be comforted by me, and my enjoyment of that, meant that I had a responsibility to Finn. He wasn't just part of a quirky anecdote—the funny things said by this kid whose dad I fuck—he was part of my life. A big part. And I was a big part of his, obviously. And please believe that I truly regretted it having taken me so long to come to terms with this, not to mention little Finn having to go to such lengths to show me.

A funny thing

Even though, that morning, I had blacked out due to complete bodily abuse brought about by a desire of my mind's needs to override my body's needs in a vain—and, yes, childish— attempt to push away the demons that were crowding ever closer round my mental periphery by ultimately making me stop thinking altogether and sending me spiraling toward Julian's arse; even though, with the recent self-revelations about my desire to somehow be a parent juxtaposed with the equally recent realizations that my chosen lifestyle forbids such desires; even though my head was full of India and the myriad of problems attached to the logistics of dogging off the flatmates-only dinner, let alone how I was going to handle being alone with her; even though I had just shocked myself with the knowledge that, parent or not, I had responsibilities and ties to a delicate, impressionable and beautiful little boy that were so much deeper and beyond anything I had previously imagined before tonight; even though all of this might make you think that the idea of being alone in my kitchen with Finn, his tears and snot seeping through my T-shirt and his arms and legs clamped tight around my torso, symbolic almost of the sorrow and the very rigid chance that I would someday let him down, even though all of this . . . I don't think I have ever felt more at peace in my whole life. Just for a few seconds, mind. And I didn't say happy. Just at peace, calm, quiet, dealing very basically with what needed to be dealt with, which was for Finn to feel secure. That *is* a funny thing, isn't it?

Another funny thing

There comes a time in your relationship with someone when you must face the most difficult challenge that two human beings can attempt together. It can come at any time, there is no rhyme nor reason for its arrival. Yet if the friendship is to be true it will come. With me and Sadie, even though we are the bestest of best friends and we would gladly chop off limbs for each other (we've already discussed it; I chose my left leg 'cos I play soccer with my right. Uh, yeah, I know, and the last time I played soccer was? And I use both hands to masturbate, sometimes at the same time, so the obvious one to go was the left leg), it still took us many, many months to pass this test together. However, the best thing was that the challenge presented itself to us and we passed it without even realizing. That is true friendship.

I am talking about being able to be silent with someone.

I know it sounds easy, but think about it. How many people do you know that could come round to your house, on their own, and you could have lulls in the conversation that weren't due only to one of you going to the loo or the fact that you were both watching television, and you'd feel it was a completely comfortable and comfort*ing* part of the evening? Not many, I should co-co.

Some people you never have it with, and that's okay. Julian, for instance. Never going to happen. Bobby? Didn't happen for ages and now it does fairly often but mostly only 'cos we're stoned, like last Saturday when he joined me in the bath. My mum? It is a physical impossibility for my mum to be silent in front of another living thing. Even in a restaurant she will read aloud the entire menu rather than have silence. It's probably a generational thing. She comes from a time where silence was what you did in bomb shelters and in church and when you had sex—all things that were, to her, by varying degrees, uncomfortable. So it's understandable that the notion is abhorrent to her nowadays. Understandable but annoying, 'cos sometimes you just want to tell people to press the pause button and shut the fuck up.

I have it with Finn, this ability to be silent, but the silence seeming as full as if we were both talking nonstop. And during the quiet time, as I sat him back at the kitchen table and picked up the cutout of the German and stuck a knife down the glued-up slit of the glue bottle and got him some juice and then just sat with him, I thought back over the months and months we had known each other and I realized we had had it from the very beginning. That's a funny thing too.

12

just as it was all going so well too

When Bobby and Sadie erupted home, all silence was
left behind. As soon as the front door crashed open
and the gurgle of their chatter and laughter came
ever louder up the stairs toward us, Charlie, who had been
unknowingly annoying Sadie by lying along as many cushions of
the sofa as he could—thereby pushing the cushion-per-person
plumping ratio sky high—jumped up and positively rushed
through to join Finn and me in the kitchen. We were both a little
startled to see him, and it was especially disorienting considering
we were focused on Bobby and Sadie appearing through the
other of the kitchen's doors. I remember thinking at the time
that it was kind of a weird thing to do, and that he probably
didn't want the newcomers to suspect that anything had been
amiss, and I supposed that I could understand that.

It seemed that Charlie felt guilty. Guilty that he had let Finn get upset in order to make a point to me—and a very convenient point at that, because his son was actually getting at areas of our relationship that I think he wanted to discuss but felt he shouldn't or couldn't.

Finn's face was a picture of glee when Bobby and Sadie rolled into the room. He jumped down from the chair and ran into Sadie's arms, leaning over to give Bobby a kiss too so he wouldn't feel left out. That was the thing about Finn, he thought about things like that. This kind of awareness, of course, is also why he is so good at manipulating situations and laying on the guilt to get what he wants—or rather to make you feel what he wants you to feel in order that, hopefully, you will then take action that will present a situation he will find desirable. My God, I have just realized—Finn should work for the UN. Watch your back, Kofi.

"Finn's here, what a lovely surprise! Uygh!" cried Sadie. The "uygh" bit was due to the force of Finn's little body propelling itself into her ample, though still not impregnable, bosom.

"How are you, my little soldier?" Sadie had a habit of channeling old ladies when she talked to Finn. Matronly terms of endearment such as "little soldier," warnings like "You'll take your eye out" and bedtime entreaties like "Off you pop upstairs to the land of nod" seemed to emit from her in a spooky poltergeist sort of way.

"I'm fine," Finn replied, looking back at me with a reassuring smile. "Tommy's helped me finish my collage."

"Oh, he loves a bit of arts and crafts, that one," said Bobby. "You should see what he can do with a sheet of sticky-back plastic."

"Is that an insect?" Finn inquired.

"No, Finn," his dad interjected, coming in from the doorway. "It's stuff they always used to have on *Blue Peter*."

"Was *Blue Peter* on TV when you were all young?" Finn looked around at us, incredulous. It reminded me of when I was a teenager and my mum had come into my bedroom and started singing along to the Rolling Stones song I was playing on my tape deck. The horrifying realization dawned on me that she knew the words because they had first released the song when *she* was young. I'd felt sick.

"Yes, of course it was, my little petal," Sadie channeled. "*Blue Peter* has been on TV since time began."

"And when we were little we always covered the things they showed us how to make in sticky-back plastic," said Charlie.

"Less of the young, big boy. I still cover things in sticky-back plastic. I make a living from it," Bobby jibed.

"Yes, my darling, you've also been known to wrap a few genitals in it too, haven't you?" Sadie was in good form. (And she was also right, by the way. Bobby had been known to take his work home, if you catch my drift.) But Bobby carried on regardless:

"I owe my whole livelihood to *Blue Peter*. Valerie Singleton is a goddess in my book."

"Who's Valerie Singleton?" inquired Finn, enjoying this banter. I was too. I had loved the quiet, but there was something reassuring about watching my best friends joking around. It was what we did, how we engaged with each other. Silly but witty chitchat about inane things. It's funny how meaningful inane things can be—comforting, easy things like family. And they were my family.

I took a deep breath, and let it out. I was doing that a lot, I'd noticed. Apropos of nothing, I'd heave a big sigh and feel my body sort of de-stress a couple of levels. This was turning into quite a week. And today was already something of an epic. I suddenly remembered the wank I'd had on the top deck of the bus. Now there was a story for Julian. God, to think that was only this morning. It seems like an eternity. That quiet time I'd had with Finn—how long can it have been? Half an hour? Forty-five minutes? It really did me good. It's funny when you get into a situation where you unexpectedly just have a think, especially at a time when you're doing everything in your power not to. Not that I sorted anything out or anything. It was sort of just mental downtime, and it felt good. Normally my mental downtime is chemically induced, so this was a novel experience for me.

"Who's Valerie Singleton?! Oh, young man, we have a lot of work ahead of us." Bobby feigned outrage as Finn giggled hysterically in Sadie's arms. "Charlie, you call yourself a homosexual?" he continued. "Your son doesn't even have a basic grasp of contemporary gay culture."

Charlie laughed and gave Bobby and Sadie a kiss. "It's good to see you two," he said, then looked over at me, sitting dumb at the table taking them all in in a kind of haze. It really had been quite a week. "Shall we go upstairs for a minute, Tom?"

"Er, okay," I said, and got up.

We went up the stairs to the sound of Bobby getting Finn up to speed on former *Blue Peter* presenters: "Valerie Singleton, John Noakes, Peter Purves. Repeat after me, everyone!"

"Valerie Singleton, John Noakes, Peter Purves!" chanted Finn and Sadie.

"Again!"

"Valerie Singleton, John Noakes, Peter Purves!"

Charlie and I had reached my bedroom door.

"And then of course Valerie moved on and became a grown-up on Radio 4, so it was Lesley Judd, John Noakes, Peter Purves! All together!"

Bobby's voice carried on. I shut the door and looked over at Charlie. "What's all this about?" I asked him.

Charlie looked out of the window across toward the railway line. It was behind the next row of houses, so we never actually saw the trains, but we could hear them from time to time, and one train especially, around four in the morning, made the whole house vibrate. This was the train that carried nuclear waste out of London, someone had told me. It went in the middle of the night so as to minimize the chance of accidents that might result in mass destruction, they'd said. I also thought that if it really did carry nuclear waste, then it was a good time to travel, as most activists and demonstrators would be in bed, dreaming sweet dreams of storming police barricades, blissfully unaware that a source of potential death, not to mention countless marches, was chugging past their bedsits and mansion blocks. I don't really think it's true, though. I mean, where would it be coming from? And where would it be going? They don't move nuclear waste every day, do they? And surely someone would have found out by now and raised merry hell? Islington was Labour through and through. It was a nuclear-free borough, for Christ's sake!

The reason I was able to run with this for so long was that Charlie wasn't saying anything. He had been the one who had wanted to come upstairs, and so now, here we were, upstairs, so it was only fair for him to take the lead, wasn't it?

But no, nothing. He was still looking out the window. I should have had an idea from the body language alone. But no.

"Well, what is it?" I started to feel a little panicked.

With his back still to me, Charlie said: "I think we should stop seeing each other, Tommy."

I wanted to speak but nothing came out.

"I just don't think it's good for Finn."

13

shabby

The title of this chapter is "Shabby" because that was the first word that came out of my mouth as I slumped down onto my bed after Charlie had dropped the bomb. Shabby is what I thought he was, and shabbily is how I thought he had behaved. Suddenly it all became clear. The quiet time, which I had taken for a loving, healing silence for us all after Finn's little outburst, had in reality been a time for Charlie to pluck up the courage to tell me. The getting up from the sofa had been, I was right, a guilt impulse, as he knew he had been and was about to be, yes, that word again: shabby, shabby, shabby.

But back to the bedroom.

"I'm sorry, Tommy."

"No, no, no. You're looking after the welfare of your son. I can understand that. There's no need to be sorry." I felt like one of those tight-lipped heroines from a 1940s black-and-white film—all stoic martyr on the train station platform as she gets the boot from her married amour, then crying and crying in the first-class carriage all the way home to Middle Englandville. But of course, I am not that person. I exploded.

"What the fuck do you mean it's not good for Finn? What isn't good? Me? Is that it, Charlie? Don't you want your son to be around people like me, you fucking hypocrite?"

This was really turning into a fucker of a day. Let's recap: oh yes, despair, fainting, jubilation, old wounds reopened, infant misery, newfound calm and now, to cap it all, being chucked! What next? An earthquake? Caledonian Road washed away by mudslides? Fuck me I need a drink. But that looks unlikely for quite some time, 'cos I am stuck in this fucking bedroom "talking" with Charlie, who has turned now from the window to face me and his face is red and he is obviously riled by my last little outburst, but Jesus Christ, *I'm* the one who's just been shat on! *I'm* the one who's chucked! And nobody ever chucks me. Ever. Well, *maybe* the odd person over the years didn't return my calls, but nothing like this.

And now suddenly Charlie is shouting at me. From nowhere, it seems, he is shouting like I've never been shouted at before. He is screaming at me. There are tears in his eyes and all the veins in his neck and his forehead are bulging out like a horse, and he is sort of advancing toward me—though now not like a horse, more like a furious and on the brink of committing a violent act human male—and I suddenly feel about eight years old and really, really scared. Yes, I feel like Finn. I feel like the grown-ups are turning on me and it must be all my fault.

"Shut the fuck up, would you, Tommy? Just for once in your life, shut the fuck up and listen. Listen to me. Do you think this is easy for me? Do you think this is what I want? Do you think I want to have to tell Finn that yes, he's right, he's been right all along and Tommy won't be a part of our lives anymore? For fuck's sake, Tommy, don't you see? Finn adores you and I can't bear to see how upset he'll be if we stopped seeing each other. Shit, he's upset enough already about you going away for two weeks. Don't you get it? He loves you, Tommy. And I can't bear it. Oh fuck, I can't bear it because *I* love you. I fucking love you, Tom. I actually *want* your cock to be mine, or at least partly mine. And don't you fucking dare get all lippy on me about it, because believe you me, I've tried to not feel like this. Oh fucking hell! And the real reason I don't think it's good for Finn is because I'm letting him get upset about stuff just so I can see how you're going to respond because I want to know the answers too! I want to know how you feel about me, Tommy. And I feel so fucking terrible that I'm using Finn in this way because you and me, we've developed this stupid, fucking laddish way of dealing with each other, which means we never properly communicate. And I can't bear it! I can't bear to not know. I can't bear to treat Finn like this. But most of all . . ."

Charlie is out of control now. He is shaking, and if I wasn't scared I would be worried for him as he looks like he might have a fit or something. In fact maybe part of why I'm scared is that I'm so worried about him. And now he's having trouble getting the words out 'cos big blubby tears are running down his face, and he is having trouble swallowing, he's gulping just like Finn does when he cries.

". . . most of all I can't bear to think that you won't be around, because I need to know that you're going to be in my life, Tommy. And I don't want to own you or anything like that, so really, please, don't worry. I just want to know that you're going to be around, because I don't want to fuck myself and Finn up any more than we are already. That's all. And I'm not a hypocrite, see?"

And now I'm standing up and he's coming to me, and he's heaving, I can feel his whole body shuddering and quaking. I hold him and pull him down onto the bed with me. I hold him close to me for a long time until he stops the shaking and then he lifts his head to me and we look into each other's eyes and then we are kissing, and now violence of a different kind fills the room. We are all over each other. It's out of control, a need in both of us that is out of control. Shirts are pulled up, belts are unbuckled. We are scraping at each other like two animals. And before I know what is happening—almost within seconds of us first kissing, it seems, but it must be longer—but before I can comprehend or rationalize or process a single response to what we are doing that is not a purely visceral one, Charlie is on top of me and he's fucking me. And as he's fucking me he is pulling my head round so he can kiss me and I am taking him. I am really taking him. I am giving in to him, completely and utterly and wholeheartedly, really properly for the first time ever since I've known him. I give in to Charlie, the man who has just chucked me. And I love it. I feel like my body was made for this.

Fuck me

And that, of course, is exactly what is happening. Maybe sometimes you don't need to say things. Maybe sometimes you just need to be shouted at and fucked.

So, here we are then. What a fucking day indeed. I can now add being screamed at and having consensual unsafe sex to today's list of life experiences. You couldn't make this up, you know.

After Charlie came we both lay there on the bed panting, him still inside me. I turned my head around to look at him.

"Fuck me," I said, trying not to laugh.

"Ha-bloody-ha," said Charlie.

There was silence for a moment, no sound except for our breathing. I felt him begin to pull out of me.

"Not yet," I said. I heard myself say it, and my voice sounded panicked, as if I wouldn't know what the world would be like when he wasn't in me anymore. Like one of those birds that doesn't know where to fly to when it's let out of its cage. This was an unusual feeling.

"I really needed that, didn't I?"

"Yes, Tommy, you really did." He smiled. I did too. We were both still shaking from the shock of it all, the shouting and the fucking, and now the blood was pumping through my ears and even though I knew the room was quiet and it was all over I just couldn't seem to come down, to stop my heart from beating so fast. A bead of sweat dripped into my eye from Charlie's forehead. We were sharing a lot of bodily fluids. He cupped his hand round my face and looked at me like he'd never seen me before.

"What?" I said. "What are you looking at?"

"I'm not sure. Is this the new you?"

I smiled. "No, I'm still the same. Just . . . well, you understand, don't you? I mean, you know what that was all about?"

"What? That you're a twat but I've fucked some sense into you?"

We laughed. A little titter at first but then more and more loud and almost a bit hysterical.

We kept laughing as we got dressed and prepared to face the music. We had a lot of explaining to do.

I touched Charlie's arm as he was about to open the bedroom door. He looked back at me, his face still a bit sweaty but calm now.

"You okay?" I asked.

"Yeah, Tommy, I'm fine. Let's get downstairs in case they think we've killed each other."

I looked toward the enseamed bed, as Hamlet would have called it. It really was enseamed too. Wow. Everything was so epic today.

"I love you, Charlie. And I love Finn too. And I'm in both your lives. I'm not going to let you down." Maybe the fact that I didn't look him in the eye was a bit of a giveaway that I wasn't completely confident about what I'd just said—at least the last bit.

"Thanks, Tom. I know how painful that was for you." And before I could slap him he was off down the stairs to the kitchen.

I hovered at the bedroom door and listened. I thought I'd let him do the immediate explaining. Finn was first to pipe up. "So did you have a row or did you do it?" he said, his little treble voice completely earnest. Again his future at the UN seemed so clear.

"What makes you think we did either?" I heard Charlie reply, rather lamely I thought. There was laughter from Sadie and Bobby, then Finn piped up again: "Oh come on, Dad, we weren't born yesterday. We were just taking bets about whether you had a very big fight or a very noisy you-know-what."

"Well, you know, Finn, the two things are sometimes connected."

"So you did both! Sadie was right!"

"Hooray for me," Sadie whooped. "What do I get as my prize?"

"By the sound of things I'd say Tommy's won all the prizes that are going to be handed out tonight, darling," said Bobby.

I started down the stairs, laughing and feeling lucky to have such funny people in my life.

"No, Sadie can have the collage I made as her prize," said Finn.

"But I thought you were making that especially for Tommy?" I heard his dad say, interested at this turn of events. I came into the kitchen and Finn turned his head toward me.

"Well, I was, but I can make one for Tommy anytime."

14

just as it was all going so well too, two

Bobby, Sadie and I gathered on the stairs to sing "So Long, Farewell" from *The Sound of Music* as Charlie and Finn stood by the front door, giggling and clapping. Each of us did our solo bit and then skipped up the stairs again, where we regrouped for the final, out of vision, heavenly angels–type good-byes.

We were laughing and clinging to the banister as we heard the door bang and we stayed all clung together and listened as Finn's laughter receded down the street toward the tube station. When we could hear him no more, Sadie hugged me and Bobby tight, tight into herself. "My boys," she said quietly.

We gave each other a kiss and then made our way back into the kitchen.

"I need a drink," I said, opening the fridge and scouring through the debris for a beer.

"I bet you do, my darling," said Sadie, sitting down at the table to look at her collage. "It sounded like you worked pretty hard for it too."

"Yeah, what was all that about?" Bobby was eager for details.

"It was the weirdest thing. He took me upstairs to chuck me, right? And then he went ballistic at me, and then all of a sudden we were fucking," I explained, though hearing it out loud didn't quite capture the magnitude of what had taken place.

"He wanted to chuck you?" Sadie was aghast. The collage was pushed aside. "Why? Have you two been having a bad time?"

"Is that why you've been such a Greta Garbo all week, Tommy boy? You know you can always tell us everything," said Bobby, all concerned and big brotherish.

"No, no, everything seemed fine with Charlie, and eh, about this week, I'm really sorry, I was just a bit down and, you know, I couldn't really handle dealing with anyone, even you two, my darlings."

"But wait a second, what about Charlie, why did he suddenly want to chuck you?" Sadie was a woman with a mission. "Let's just go back to that."

"Well, he actually didn't. I think it was all more about him needing to know that things were a bit more solid between us than I had been willing to let on. Yeah, that's it. You know, because of Finn and everything."

I was tired. It had been such a long day. I could only find a three-quarters-full bottle of Australian Riesling stuffed in the fridge-door shelf between the tomato ketchup and an industrial-size jar of gherkins clearly past its sell-by date. I wonder who bought that? It had been there as long as I could remember, but to my knowledge no one had ever imbibed of it. So who had consumed a quarter of it? I suspected it was Sadie. She had strange eating habits when she was premenstrual. Popping downstairs in her PJs in the middle of the night to gulp down a gherkin or two was so her. I was so tired and punch-drunk from the day that I was now free-associating about gherkins, and Bobby and Sadie were still grilling me.

"I hope you were responsible, Tommy. You do have to think about Finn, you know." Bobby, uncharacteristically, was coming over all Middle England on me.

"What do you mean by that?" I wasn't in a mood to have any more aspersions cast upon my character. I'd had them from Finn, I'd had them from Charlie, fuck me, I was getting them from myself, I certainly didn't need Bobby to add his tuppence-worth, thank you very much.

"Well, erm, uh, you know." He and Sadie exchanged a guilty look. "We're just concerned that . . ."

"We?" I interjected. Evidently a little chitchatting had been going on behind my back. I poured myself a glass of the Riesling and banged the bottle down too hard on the table, making me seem more angry than I actually was. Or maybe I really was that angry but my senses had been so battered by everyone that day that I just couldn't judge.

"Yes," Bobby said a bit haltingly. "Sadie and I have been thinking for some time now . . ."

"Oh have you?"

"Tommy," Sadie stepped in, trying to soothe me. "It's nothing bad. We just had a chat about you and Charlie and, well, it's difficult enough seeing someone, and, well, when you get involved with their child, then suddenly it's not as easy as it might be to extricate yourself, eh, oneself . . ."

"You mean, myself." I was acting like the brattish teenager who had been caught smoking pot and Bobby and Sadie were my aging liberal parents.

"Okay, yourself," she carried on. "We thought you might have been wanting to get out of the situation with Charlie but felt you couldn't because you'd upset Finn. And we were just worried about you, darling."

"And we were worried about Finn too," Bobby added. "About how he might react to it all, should anything negative have gone down. That's all."

There was a pause. I gulped down some wine. It was disgusting and vinegary. I didn't care.

Look at the day I have had.

"I see," I said, head down. "Well, you're right. I was feeling all those things."

"I know you were, darling." Sadie reached across the table and held my hand, like they do in those films when someone says "I'm Wayne and I'm an alcoholic" for the first time. The way we were going I would be getting a round of applause soon.

"It's just . . ." Suddenly I felt like I could cry. "It's just . . . things have been a bit weird lately and yes, I have been having a lot of strange feelings about Charlie and Finn and just about—oh, everything, I suppose; hitting thirty, what I'm doing with my life, you know, those old turkeys."

Sadie and Bobby were staring at me, slightly alarmed. I didn't usually do these sort of speeches. But you know what? Due to unforeseen circumstances, today was not the scheduled episode of Tommy's life.

No one said anything for a few seconds.

"Do you mean the stuff we talked about in the bar at the weekend?" Sadie looked at me knowingly. I'd forgotten about that. During the coke ramble—before the anal probing and everything going pear shaped in the disabled loo—I'd told her about the wanting-a-kid thing, hadn't I?

Even though that should have made me feel reassured—that I'd already gone over some of this territory with Sadie and she was supportive and all that—it actually made me panic more, like I'd done something wrong and had given away a silly clue earlier without thinking. Why was I feeling like this? And why was this huge fucking rock all of a sudden stuck in my chest?

"Yes," I gulped. "That sort of stuff. About, em, children, and so you know, it's kind of a hard thing to get clear in your mind, what with all the other things going on in my life, and so tonight has been really difficult, and even though it's ended really well, I mean, I pretty much told Charlie that he could rely on me and that I'd be around for him and Finn . . ."

"Oh, Tommy, that's wonderful." Sadie was beaming at me. She was so close to applauding, I could feel it.

"Tommy boy, you're becoming a grown-up," Bobby said, coming in for a hug. But it didn't feel right. I felt patronized, and as though there was a trick or a secret somewhere in all of this, and I'd failed, and Bobby and Sadie being there was suddenly not comforting at all but utterly, utterly humiliating and shameful and I couldn't take it anymore. It was all too much.

"Fuck off!" I shouted, too loud, the same sort of thing as the bottle of wine—which was now nearly empty, by the way—banging on the table. "Don't treat me like a child. This isn't like I've done well at my exams, you know. This is my life." What the fuck was I saying? And where was it going? *This is my life?*

(Again I was plunging into the realm of daytime soaps. Jesus, any minute now a very suntanned woman wearing shoulder pads and a lot of gold jewelry and huge sunglasses is going to come out of the cupboard and say, "Thomas, I know you thought I'd been burned alive in that hideous accident at our ski cabin in Aspen, but I escaped and made a new life for myself in Liechtenstein with my Puerto Rican lover, Raul. Yes, I'm your mother.")

Bobby and Sadie looked at me, frozen, desperately trying to think of the right thing to say. I could see Sadie especially was really startled. They hadn't ever seen me like this. *I'd* never seen me like this. I suppose I was having a bit of an aftershock, what with all the Charlie shouting and then the Charlie fucking, not forgetting the India stuff—which of course I knew I'd have to bring up before too long, and I was *not* looking forward to that.

"It's okay, Tommy." Bobby was trying to bring me down. He was good in these situations, I remembered from many of Sadie's monthly irrational, and apparently gherkin-fueled, days. He was good from the outside. From the inside he was an annoying cunt who I wanted to punch.

"No, it fucking isn't okay." By now I was half shouting, half sobbing. "I don't feel very good about myself these days." This was news to me. I thought I didn't feel good about everybody else. It was a surreal experience, hearing the truth come out of my own mouth, as if someone else had taken over the controls. There was me and what was going on in my mind, and then there was someone else who had taken over in a sort of psychological hijack, who was speaking on my behalf. The good thing was he was saying interesting things that I thought were pretty on the nose, so I just let him carry on.

"I'm feeling a little panicky. A lot of stuff has happened to me, and I haven't really been looking after myself, and now all this stuff with Charlie and Finn—even though it's all turned out great . . ." When I said "great" it came out far too loud and sort of high-pitched, causing Sadie to wince and Bobby to bring his index finger to his lips and whisper "Sssh." God, I was so close to punching him.

"I just feel that . . . to have you two on my back on top of everything else is too much to cope with . . ."

"Tommy, darling, please . . ."

"We're only trying to . . ."

I carried on above their protests. "You said I had to be more responsible, and that I had to think of Finn, and you're right, I do! It's true." More gulping. I paused to swig down the last of the wine. "But I really don't need to feel that you think I'm a fuck-up too." That was it, I was off. Bawling. I started to shake and I couldn't stop. My legs gave way and before I knew it I was on the floor, expunging noises that seemed to have been trapped inside me for years.

The pair of them rushed over and knelt down to me, smothering me in a kind of impromptu Teletubbies group hug, me in the center curled up like a clam, not wanting to let them in. But I did. It was all too much. This day was all too much.

After a long time of crying—the kind where you feel like you'll never catch your breath so you start to have minor panic attacks too—and a *lot* of hankies and a lot of snot, I began to calm down. Bobby made me some cheese on toast and Sadie brought down the pair of stripey pajamas I only ever wear when I'm not well, which, of course, was now. The pj's made it official somehow.

I was propped up on the sofa, Sadie having thrown caution to the wind and heaped cushion after cushion all around me to ensure maximum comfort, and there were loads of little moist blobs of paper tissue strewn about the living-room floor. They looked like tiny crumpled parachutes, some bizarre NATO airdrop of coagulated mucus. We looked at them all sitting there. They looked quite pretty actually, against the wood of the floor and the lights of the street coming in through the windows. None of us had turned any of the living-room lights on. These sorts of occasions are best kept muted, lightingwise.

I was okay now. I'd been really scared for a bit because I had lost control. As I'm sure you'll have gathered, being out of control is something I often yearn for and always treasure, but this time was different. I didn't like it. It was a kind of out-of-control that didn't have an escape hatch. There was no side door you could go through like the normal out-of-control you get from good drugs—I wasn't going to sober up or fall asleep and everything would be back to how it had always been when I woke up again. This out-of-control had no emergency exit, and I had just got back from it in the nick of time. One more step and who knows what would have happened. Thank God for Sadie and Bobby.

We sat for a while in the semi-darkness, and the semi-quiet, all three of us huggled up on the sofa, under a blanket. I felt so safe. I thought back to today, and the ridiculous roller coaster of feelings and moods I had been on. It seemed to have lasted for years. But now at last it was over. I felt a little drunk, a nice woozy drunk, and not just from the horrible Riesling. I felt woozy with all the comfort: Bobby's and Sadie's bodies next to mine willing me to feel better, and being at home, on the sofa, under a blankie, and the mellifluous tones of the traffic from the street.

Finally, Sadie broke the silence.

"Well, that was a *Truly, Madly, Deeply* moment, my petal," she said.

Bobby snorted. "That left *Truly, Madly, Deeply* at the

starting block, darling. That was *Truly, Madly, Deeply* IMAX Three-D!"

We all started to snigger and then we were off, tears of a happier kind now streaming down my face.

Truly, Madly, Deeply was a film we'd seen years ago, and there was a scene in it where the lead actress was crying during her session with her shrink, and the thing was that instead of taking a hankie from the box which was sitting right beside her on the table, she just kept letting it go and go till there were great big dribbly bits of snot hanging from her nose, and every time she breathed in they rose up a little and stayed there, shimmering, until she breathed out and they dropped down again. Even though it was truly and madly disgusting, there was something enthralling about it because you just couldn't believe that (a) snot would hang from someone's nose for so long like that without dropping off, and (b) she hadn't *noticed.* It was a really sad scene 'cos she was genuinely upset, but it was also really funny because she looked like one of those Hush Puppies dogs that emanate those strands of goo every time they sense food. Or sort of like when babies get colds and they haven't yet learned that you wipe your nose. Except this woman was in her late thirties and quite posh and also, duh, there was a huge box of hankies *centimeters* away from her. It was probably moist with the spray, it was so close, yet she never used it.

And so, of course, every time one of us had food on the side of our mouth, or any sort of unintentional bodily fluid visible to the world (booger, bit of stray coke, etc.) we'd always say "*Truly, Madly, Deeply*" and the other person would immediately examine all orifices and/or grab a napkin.

"Stop, please, I'm going to wet myself." Bobby had to get up off the sofa, he was laughing so much.

"At least, even in the midst of your despair," Sadie said, grinning madly and managing to keep a giggle down in her throat. "You had the common sense, and the class, to ask for a tissue!" She was off again, head back in a silent scream of mirth.

"Oh my God, look at them!" I cried, pointing at the dozens of scrunched-up tissues, now dried and stuck fast to the floorboards. The sight of them sent us off again, until finally, as the last chortles ebbed and we pulled the blanket back up again over our entwined bodies, Bobby said:

"So how was your day, Tom?"

"Oh God, where do I start, Bobby?"

Of course, I shouldn't have started at all. I see that now. But I honestly didn't dream that anything I would say could possibly make this momentous day get any worse. But I was tired and was caught off guard so I continued: "It's been a fucker of a day. I've not been eating."

"Why?" Sadie said, sternly. When it came to matters of food, Sadie is my mother manqué.

"Because I've been depressed, I've been in a real funk, and you know when I get like that I can't see anyone and I can't eat."

"Don't you wank a lot too?" Bobby would remember that bit.

"Maniacally," I replied. "I even did it on the bus this morning."

"Oh, Tommy, be careful," Sadie said. "You could get arrested."

"There was no one there. I checked. But I think that's why I fainted."

"You fainted?" they chorused, suddenly more alarmed.

"Jesus, Tom, did you still have your cock out when you fainted?" Trust Bobby to go there.

"No," I said, getting a bit exasperated, partly because I

couldn't get on with what I wanted to tell them, and partly because the more I did, the more I understood their interruptions. It really *had* been a weird fucking day.

"I fainted later, when I got to work."

"Thank God for that," Sadie chimed in. "I mean at least you didn't embarrass yourself in public."

"But why did you faint?" asked Bobby.

"Oh, you know, 'cos I hadn't eaten for a few days and I've been doing too many drugs and my body just couldn't take it anymore. But I'm okay now. I've eaten tons today and I feel much better, really."

"Yes, and you look it too. Not." Sadie was giving me harsh love.

"And why were you depressed?" Bobby continued.

"Oh, God, that's a big one. Probably also because of drugs. I need a little vacation from the white powder, I think. And then the whole Charlie and Finn thing, which you two so accurately predicted, you clever clogs . . ."

"And wanting to have a baby?" Sadie looked deep into my eyes when I turned, panicky, to her.

"What's that?" Bobby was bemused. This was the first he'd heard of it.

"Yeah, that too I suppose," I said quietly.

"I didn't know anything about this, Tomser." Bobby was faintly hurt.

"Well, it's not the easiest thing to bring up, Bobby, and anyway, it's only recently that I've come to realize it. I know it's weird, and I know it'll never happen, but I think it's maybe something to do with having Finn around so much, it just made me think, 'I'd like to do that with my life,' but, you know, as if! I can't even look after myself."

"You don't look after yourself when you want to punish yourself," Sadie said sharply. "It's all right to feel these things, Tommy. Other people do."

"I can't say I ever have," said Bobby. "Uncle Bobby will do me fine."

Sadie and I looked at each other for a long moment.

"So you fainted . . ." Bobby was impatient for more.

"Yeah, just for a minute, and then when I came to, Julian told me some fabulous news."

"What?" said Bobby.

"I'm going with him to New York for two weeks on Monday!"

This is where things started to go wrong. Instead of the "hooray, that's great, what a fabulous thing to happen on this awful day" type reaction I had expected from my best buddies, there was a definite tensing beneath that homely little blanket and a definite chill became apparent in the air.

"New York?" Sadie must not have heard me properly.

"Yeah, isn't it great?" I still didn't get it.

Sadie and Bobby looked at each other in a kind of conspiratorial way, obviously trying to hide the horror they both felt about the idea of me, Tommy, little bonkers, just-been-on-the-brink-of-a-nervous-breakdown, just-been-screaming, just-been-fucked, just-been-calmed-down Tommy being let loose on the nutter magnet that is Gotham City.

"What is it? I thought you'd be happy for me," I said.

"We are, Tom, we are," Bobby lied. "It's just we're worried about you. We got a bit of a scare tonight. And what would have happened if tonight had happened when you were on your own in New York?"

He had a point, of course, but I chose to ignore it.

"You need to take it easy for a bit," said Sadie.

"I will," I replied, getting a bit pissed off now. I was sure they'd have seen what a great thing this was for me. "I'll take it easy in New York."

"No, you won't. You go mad in New York, Tommy. Remember the last time you were there, that time after you and India broke up . . ."

"Oh, that's the other thing that happened today," I said, glad of being able to change the subject. "She called."

There was another collective clenching of the buttocks beneath the blanket. As I've mentioned, India was not a popular destination in our household.

The fact that Bobby and Sadie had just got me tucked up in my jimmyjams and stopped me crying made it more than understandable that the last person on earth they wanted to hear about on this night of all nights was India—the cause of quite a few similar (though not this monumental) Tommy-in-a-state evenings not all that long ago. So it was understandable, yes. Yes, it definitely was, but at the same time, I think that because the specter of possibly more anguished nights mopping up after me had suddenly reared its ugly, ugly head Bobby and Sadie were quite naturally (and I'm being blunt here) really bored at the prospect. But if I talk to her or—God forbid! Ha-ha!—see her, then that was my decision and I would face the consequences, and if, because I'm a fuck-up of a person and bi-codependent, they were going to be called in to kick-start the recovery process afterward, then that is an issue they should take up with me, and not transfer it onto her. Don't you think?

However, I wasn't going to have that chat now. In fact, I would have preferred to have no chat at all about the aforementioned artist formerly known as girlfriend. But it was not to be.

"What did she want?" Sadie said suspiciously, her languid, cuddly disposition now gone, replaced with bony elbows in my side and a shrill undercurrent in her voice.

"And she definitely called you? You didn't call her?" butted in Bobby, ever wary of my foibles.

"Of course she called me. What, you think that on top of everything else that's happened in the last few days I'm going to call her?!"

There was a knowing silence.

"Anyway, she just wanted to have a chat, you know, it's been a while now, and she feels that maybe it's time we saw each other, and, well . . . I agreed."

In an instant the blanket was thrown off and the two of them were up on their feet.

"No, Tommy, you know that's not a good idea, especially at the moment." Sadie was in full schoolmistress mode, and Bobby was similarly stern. It was both scary and horny at the same time.

"You did make us promise to tell you this, Tommy. Last time you saw her and you came back in a state, you sat us down and made us promise to tell you not to see her again. And Sadie's right, you're far too vulnerable to see her just now anyway. Look at you!"

"Well, actually, she's the one who's in a state," I said, rallying. "She's just split up with that German wanker and she's all needy, so I'm the one in control of the situation, don't you worry about me."

Coming from a man in stripy pajamas, with bleary eyes and about a hundred moistened paper tissues strewn around him, this must not have been very convincing.

"Well, we do worry." Sadie had now reached Nurse Ratched

proportions. "She's upset and lonely, and yet again, she's going to turn to you for comfort, and you, because you're soft and you can't say no to her . . ."

". . . and because you're a fucking idiot," Bobby interjected, a trifle harshly, I thought.

"And a fucking idiot, yes." Sadie picked up the baton. "You'll go there and you'll—you'll give in to her, and oh, God knows what you'll do . . ."

"You'll fuck her, Tommy." Bobby was not afraid of laying it on the line.

"That's right," said Sadie as the baton passed back. "You'll fuck her, and you'll get all emotionally involved and then you'll be in a state again and all angry with yourself and we'll be right back to where we started from."

"Don't see her, Tom," pleaded Bobby.

"Please, you told us not to let you. We worry, we love you . . ." Sadie got a bit teary. She tilted her head to one side and furrowed her brows.

"Don't fuck her."

Tommy stands his (shaky) ground

I, more than most people, know that we don't always do things that are right for us. (In fact, I am practically the poster boy for not always doing things that are right for me.) And right now, even though I heard and understood and remembered and agreed with all that Bobby and Sadie were saying, I honestly believed that seeing India would actually be really good for me. Not because she was suddenly single and needy and therefore I had the upper hand and could get some sort of retroactive schadenfreude or anything, but because I needed to prove to myself that I really am over her, and I needed to show that to her. And it was about time we put the whole thing to bed (as it were) and just got on with our lives.

I cleared my throat and went for it: "Look, you two, I'm really grateful, and I know that everything you're saying is absolutely right, but you just have to trust me on this one: I'm going to see her and I will be all right. It's important for me to be able to see her and it be okay. Bobby, you're always talking about breaking the cycle—well, that's exactly what I'm doing. I'm breaking the cycle of me and her seeing each other and fucking each other up. But I have to see her in order to do that, don't you see?"

"How about starting a new cycle of being an adult?" Ouch.

"I am being adult, Bobser," I said, trying to keep any hint of whining out of my voice. "And surely the fact that I am thinking of seeing her in the state I'm in at the moment is an indication . . . um, perhaps perversely, of how adult and strong I really am. Don't you think?"

"Whatever." Bobby rolled his eyes and left the room.

Oh God, I knew things were really bad when Bobby got this pissed off.

"You've already arranged to see her, haven't you?" Sadie said, hurt. "No wonder you were all churned up tonight. See, it's started already. Well, you're on your own with this one, Tom. We've done our best. Don't expect any sympathy from me or Bobby. She's still got so much power over you, don't you see? You ask us to try and help you, and then you slap us in the face when we do."

I didn't say anything. I knew she was right. But why didn't she understand? What a fucking day.

"When are you seeing her?"

"Eh, that's the other thing, Sadie, I wasn't thinking and I said I'd see her on Sunday night . . ."

Well, that really did it. The camel's back was well and truly broken. "You're such a fool, Tommy. You need to think with what's inside your head, not what's inside your pants. She knows we all have dinner on Sunday. That wasn't an accident."

I tried to interrupt and say no, it was me, I suggested Sunday, I'd been flustered, it wasn't fair to lump it all on India. But it was to no avail.

Sadie got up and walked through to the kitchen. "I suppose you'll just have to make up your own mind who's more important to you, won't you? Bobby and me, or India. Good night, Tommy," and she was gone too.

I sat there in the dark, my chest rising and falling too fast. I tried my hardest to take deep breaths. Just take deep breaths, Tommy.

WHAT

A

FUCKING

DAY

I tried to close my eyes and let sleep come but it was no use. When you let in fear, there's no chance of sleep till your body gives out. And that is who I realized had moved in with me recently—fear. The panic attacks, the weeping, the fainting, even the wanking—all were for my mistress Fear.

Everywhere I go now it's with me, becoming stronger every day: that feeling that something bad is going to happen. I don't know what it is, I just know it's close.

I was so exhausted. My whole body felt heavy. And now the weight of Sadie's anger pulled me down far, far into the deepest and coldest recesses of the sofa. There was no way I was going to be able to get up the stairs. I was done. I pulled my feet up and lay down on my side, eyes open, and stared out at the fluorescent sky.

15

a fairy tale about fear

Once upon a time there lived a little boy called Fred. Fred was eight. He lived with his mum and dad in a little house in a little cul-de-sac in a town made up entirely of little houses in little culs-de-sac, all exactly alike.

The planners of this town had tried, it seemed, to make everyone feel equal, and therefore the townspeople had a choice to feel either equally good or equally bad. Sadly, most of them chose to feel bad. It was actually easier that way, because for one thing you would be in the majority, you'd never have to explain yourself, and there would never be any disappointments, as no matter how bad things got, you'd have always expected worse.

Fred could see why the equally bad option might seem appealing—in theory it had its pluses. But in practice it made you gray, and gradually you stopped being the person you once were and you even began to look like everyone else. Maybe this was

162

the ultimate goal of the town planners. If it was, they had done a marvelous job.

Day after day, week after week, Fred watched his mum get grayer and grayer and the sparkle in her eyes get dimmer and dimmer until one day when he was walking home from school he saw her just ahead of him at the entrance to their cul-de-sac and he ran up and took her hand. The woman turned, surprised, and Fred realized it was not his mother at all but their neighbor two doors down. She just looked so like his mum. And that was when Fred knew that the whole thing was a conspiracy.

Why did people start to look like each other? Why did everyone live in houses that were identical, with bedrooms in the same color and pictures on the same places on every wall (sometimes when playing at his friends' houses he'd forget where he was)? Could it possibly be that if they lived and ate and worked and relaxed alike, it wouldn't be too much of a leap to make them think alike? Even at eight years old, Fred was astounded by the awfulness of this prospect, but he also was sure that it was true.

One day Fred noticed a man getting really angry because one of his neighbors had a pot of flowers outside his front door that was a different color to the flowers in the identical pots outside the front doors of every other house in the cul-de-sac, and therefore, of course, the entire town. The majority of the flowers were yellow and these just happened to be pink. (Incidentally, Fred preferred the pink ones, but he knew best to keep that to himself.)

"That's a disgrace," said the man, his gray face for once colored with the incandescence of his rage. "What do they think they're doing, having pink flowers like that?"

A lady from across the street leaned out of her upstairs bedroom window and shrieked, "I agree! It's flowers now, but what will be next?"

Within a week the family who lived in the house with the pink flowers had moved elsewhere, and the flowers were replaced with yellow ones. Fred asked his dad why they had gone, but his dad only hushed him up and said it was better for everyone now, and told Fred to go and play on the front lawn like all the other little eight-year-old boys.

As he went through the motions of throwing his ball back and forth across the little lawn that backed onto the little lawn of next door's house where their little eight-year-old boy was joylessly throwing his ball, Fred couldn't help wondering why. Why did people get angry at little things like flowers' colors? Could it possibly be because they themselves harbored secret desires to be equally different? To paint their walls with huge polka dots, or to replace their lawns with gravel and cacti? Fred thought it was.

And then he began to understand that people in the town were afraid to be different because anyone who was different was feared, and they were feared for daring—albeit accidentally in some cases, which was even more alarming—to express themselves as the individuals they were. And as we know from the pink flowers, individuality was not prized in this town.

That's it! thought Fred. Now it all makes sense. He felt so happy with himself. But his happiness was short-lived. He had the sudden horrible realization that the very fact that he had been able to work it all out meant that he was different from everyone else too.

And what was even worse, during the time he had been thinking all this, he had forgotten about playing with his ball. He had stopped in the middle of the lawn and was staring into space, his mind on higher things than throwing the silly ball, which had now, to Fred's horror, rolled off the grass and into the middle of the road, where it lay motionless and ownerless and very, very different from all the other little boys' balls.

"You there!" yelled a little boy from across the cul-de-sac. "Why aren't you playing with your ball?"

"Yes," cried another, looking at Fred nervously. "And why are you staring into space? What's wrong with you?"

Before Fred could answer, more and more little boys started shouting at him, and before long their parents and brothers and sisters had come out of the houses and were screaming at Fred for not playing with his ball, and for thinking and being different. But although alarmed by their anger and the sudden cacophony of their voices, Fred couldn't help but smile. He suddenly felt so happy, because he knew he had been right. He also knew, in that instant, that his life would not be an easy one—he was different, he looked different, he thought differently.

His thinking, and his ball in the middle of the road, made the other little boys fear him. And his smile made them angry. But Fred couldn't stop himself. His smile got bigger and bigger, because he realized that, unlike all of them, he had nothing to fear.

16

tomorrow is another day

Bizarrely, that night I slept better than I had done in weeks. Even on our sofa, which enjoyed some notoriety amongst our friends for being the least comfortable sofa to sleep on in all of London. A lot of regularly plumped cushions maketh not a good night's sleep, you see. You need a firm base. Now isn't that the truth. And we didn't have one.

And even more bizarrely, considering how I'd felt the previous evening, when I woke up, I didn't feel too bad.

Something had happened.

And as I sat up and looked across into the windows of the old-age pensioners' flats in the council block over the street, and saw them sitting at their windows looking back at me, I tried really hard to think what it was.

What had happened?

Were Sadie and Bobby still pissed off with me?

Probably. I don't see why that situation will have changed that dramatically. Maybe they'll have regretted how hard they were on me, maybe they'll even apologize, but they certainly won't be sending me off to India's on Sunday night with a clean handkerchief and a fiver to buy sweets. So it's not that.

Was I still going to go to see India?

Yes. No change there. Though in the yellow glow of morning, the whole thing seemed much less ominous than it had done in the cold light of last night. So it wasn't really that.

Did I regret the outcome of all the stuff with Charlie?

Absolutely not. It actually felt like a weight off my shoulders, believe it or not. His outburst had cleared the air, big-time, and forced me to think and say the things I've been worrying about for ages without even having to think or say very much. I just talked with my body, ha-ha. But I felt good about what had been said, or understood, I really did. It had sort of resolved things for me in the best way possible without having to do the really scary, difficult thing of bringing them all up myself. And what had really changed? I was going to keep seeing Charlie and Finn in the way we see each other now. Except we both could stop getting agitated that one of us (me) was going to end it soon and so cause major angst for us both, and more important, Finn. So, apart from the obvious calming fringe benefits, nothing really too big there. See? Accepting responsibility isn't such a big deal. Plus I got a great shag out of it.

Did I still feel that I wanted to have a child of my own?

Hmmm. Yes, that hasn't gone away. But today it doesn't feel as weird, somehow. It isn't making me feel bad or hopeless like it has been doing. I think because I actually voiced it to Sadie and Bobby and they didn't turn round and tell me I was a delusional fool. But come to think of it, they didn't actually mention it at all very much. Maybe this was due to the fact that quite quickly after it slipped out I turned into a spotty adolescent banging wine bottles, telling them it was my life we were talking about and bursting into tears. And of course the India thing sort of served as a smoke screen on this front. So that's pretty much in the status quo department too.

What the fuck is it then?

Well, I didn't wake up feeling like shit today. That is definitely something new. This, I'm sure, has a lot to do with the copious amounts of food I had last night. It was only cheese on toast actually, now I come to think about it, but that is definitely copious compared to my intake of nutrients over the last few days. I also didn't drink very much, had no drugs, and—oh, I know! I had a great big cry. That always helps.

So is that it? That's what happened? I bawled my eyes out and everything in the garden looks rosier? Why oh why does my life keep reminding me of bad TV movies?

My musings were interrupted by Bobby clomping down the stairs on his way out to work. I quickly lay back down and closed my eyes, fearful of how he might be with me after last night, and not wanting this surprising and confusingly okayish feeling I had to evaporate too quickly.

I heard him stop at the kitchen door and tiptoe through to

the living room. Then I heard him tut when he saw me curled up on the sofa.

"Tommy boy," he whispered. "What are you doing down here?"

I opened my eyes and looked up at him.

"You're a great big baby," he said, sort of smiling.

"What do you mean?" said I, rubbing my eyes, feigning waking-up-ness.

"Staying down here all night on purpose to make sure you'll have the worst night's sleep. Would you like a horsehair shirt too? Perhaps I could interest sir in some nipple clamps?"

"Now you're talking," I said, clambering up and giving him a big cuddle. "I love you, Bobser, and I know you think I'm an arsehole, and I am, I admit it, but it'll be okay. And I slept really well actually and feel much better. Thanks for the cheese on toast."

"You're welcome. You had me really worried last night, you know." He looked at me, all serious. "Look after yourself better."

"I will, I am," I said. "I'm going to get a big breakfast and take loads of vitamins."

"I didn't mean that." He looked at me knowingly. I smiled back at him, a smile that said I understand, but hey, let's not dwell. You know the kind.

"I'll see you tonight," I said. "Fancy going to Popstarz?" This was a sort of queer club that played sort of alternativey music filled with people pretty much like . . . me.

"Maybe you should have a night in, eh, Tommy boy?" And he was off. Ooh, that "night in" crack sort of hurt a bit.

I did go out a lot, I suppose. But hey, what was wrong with that? I was young, free and single, sort of. And fast approaching . . . thirty.

Shit! Of course! That was it. Why didn't I think of it before?

Of course I'm going to be bonkers. My thirtieth birthday is only a month or two away. No wonder all this is happening to me. No wonder I'm on a bender. Everyone goes a bit nutty at this stage of their lives. What was that thing Sadie had told me about? The sort of astrological thing that happens to you? Your Saturn returning, I think it was. Yeah, now I remember. Sadie got really into all that stuff for a while a few years back, and she told me about how Saturn returns into everyone's charts around about age thirty, making you reassess everything and go through a time of . . . what was it?

Oh yes. Turmoil.

Hello?! My Saturn was well and truly back in the building. I leapt off the sofa, eager to jump in beside Sadie and quiz her all about it. Suddenly it all made sense—the baby thing, the commitment thing, the needing-to-sort-things-out-with-India thing: it wasn't because I was a fucked-up loser, it was because I was nearly thirty and my Saturn had returned.

I was halfway up the stairs when I remembered that Sadie wasn't speaking to me. Shit. Well, she wasn't technically not speaking to me, there hadn't been an edict. But she had certainly given me the impression in our last interchange that she thought I was a pathetic wanker, and the last thing she would want to wake up to was me bouncing onto her bed and telling her I felt much better and could she fill me in on a little-known astrological phenomenon she had casually mentioned to me several years ago.

I went for a pee to mull it over.

A few thoughts on peeing

Peeing for men is such a dilemma because we have options. For girls there's no mucking about, it's just hike up your skirt or pull down your trousers and sit. But for boys, there's not only the decision to be made about sitting or standing, but the inherent prejudices and assumptions made about your choice that you have to battle with. You see, the done thing is to stand. Men stand up, they pull out their manhoods and they piss. That's the way it goes. That's how it's been done for generation after generation since time immemorial, and that's what it means to be a guy. But, we also have the slightly sissy—in most men's eyes, anyway— option of sitting down, taking the weight off our legs and avoiding all the potential drama of rogue sprays of pee getting on the carpet, our trousers or anyone or thing who might have the misfortune to be standing nearby. Peeing, like shaving, is hard. There's a lot to it. And first thing in the morning, your brain is not ready to deal with the *physics* that's involved in measuring distance, force of flow, direction and all that stuff. At home, I always sit. I can't bear the worry that I'm going to hit something unintended. I can so commiserate with those jet fighter pilots who accidentally drop bombs on schools or convents or Red Cross depots. (Uh, I'm kidding.) Sitting down makes peeing a more restful, worryless and so more enjoyable experience. But in public, I usually stand. This is for two reasons. First, men's toilets tend to be really stinky and you want to be in them for as little time as possible (unless of course you're off your tits and you're going into a stall to get a blow job or something), and second there is the shame factor. It's not macho to admit you sit down to pee when you're a man. The very fact that I am talking about it now will probably send tremors across the male species' world. You watch. Also of course the stalls of men's toilets are usually even more stinky and horrid than the urinals, so you only want to go into them when you absolutely have to, and sitting down for a pee is not generally enough of a necessity.

But there is a subculture of men who do sit down, in public and private. And we are growing bigger day by day, and we will not go away. It's not easy to find us, for the weight of the fear of being spurned by the upright majority is great, but occasionally, when defenses are down and the conversation turns toward toilet matters or masculinity, the question can be mooted, and more and more men are coming out from the shadows and into the sunshine, shouting (moderately), "YES! I SIT DOWN WHEN I PEE!"

Sadie was at the door.

"Tommy, can I come in? I need to talk to you."

Ooh, that sounded a bit scary. I stood up, shook carefully, flushed and opened the door.

"You're still angry with me, aren't you?" I said, very meekly, hoping it would shame her and bring her out of it. It usually worked.

"What? Oh, no. I said what I had to say last night, and if you want to go off and have dinner with your ex and have a miserable time instead of staying in and having a lovely, laughter-filled dinner with me and Bobby, then that's up to you. You're a great big twat of course, but I bless you with my love and release you from our prior engagement." Sometimes I think Sadie should be the one writing a book. But not a rambly, confessional sort of one like this. I mean one of those books about Life and How to Deal with Things, full of little sayings like the one she just uttered that you could cut out and stick on your fridge and every time you go to get the milk you see it and mentally absorb. She'd make a fortune.

"No, there's something much worse than last night, my petal," she said, sitting on the edge of the bath and looking genuinely worried. "This just came in the post." She held up a letter. "It's from the landlord. We have to move out of the flat."

"What?" I couldn't believe it. Thank God I'd felt better this morning. This news last night and I would've really fallen apart.

"He wants to sell it, and he says it'll be easier and he'll get a better price if there aren't sitting tenants," Sadie said glumly. "I really love this flat."

"Can he do that?" I was indignant. "I mean, does he have the right?"

"Our three-year lease expired in the summer, and we've been on a month-to-month thing since. I should've pressed him to sign a new one, but it just never occurred to me that he would want to sell it. You know how nice he is."

"Not that nice." The grumpy adolescent of last evening was making a return visit.

"Anyway, he's perfectly within his rights, and . . . let's see . . ." She began to read from the letter. ". . . he understands the inconvenience this will cause us all so he is giving us three months' notice to find somewhere else. Oh, and he thanks us for being model tenants." Sadie threw the letter down on the floor with a flourish and looked up at me, beaming. "Tommy, we're models!"

We laughed for a bit, but it rang a little hollow.

God, talk about time of turmoil. Was there any part of my

life that wasn't in a state of flux? Well, yes, and I was looking at her. Sadie.

We decided the best thing to do was to have a bath together and let the news sink in, then have a really fabulous breakfast, and then make a PLAN.

In the bath with Sadie

We always had baths in times of crises, me and Sadie. Together, I mean.

We talked about the previous night's row and the events of the last while and Sadie said she was sorry that she'd been so remiss as a friend for not pulling me into the bath sooner.

It felt good to be warm, and wet, and to have my head between Sadie's breasts and to be watching the little sprays of water that she made by stroking her hand back and forth across the bristly hairs on my head.

"You're in a real state, darling, aren't you?" she said softly.

"Yeah," I said, resigned, and not needing to lie. It felt good to be able to just admit it.

"I feel so much better today, though. I think because so much happened last night and so much was said. And as soon as you say big scary things out loud in front of the people you love, they don't seem so big and scary anymore, do they?" I said, again trying to find an explanation for my new, sunnier disposition and hoping it wasn't unfounded.

"No, they don't, darling. The longer that you leave it before you talk about them, though, the scarier they will become, and that's a lesson I hope you've learned, little Tomser."

"Yeah."

We lay in silence for a minute. I closed my eyes and when I

opened them I realized I was staring at her left boob. It's funny how you don't notice things like that, and then when you sort of stand back from yourself, or in this case close your eyes and then open them again, you see how weird and sort of pervy this situation could look to someone who didn't understand us. But that's the thing about any relationship, isn't it? Nobody can really understand it from the outside.

"You've got great tits, Sadie," I murmured drowsily.

"Thank you, my darling."

"Even though I don't know how things are going to be, or how I'm going to sort things out like the baby thing, the fact that I've recognized that it's a weird time for me is a really good sign, isn't it, Sade?" I asked, suddenly a bit anxious again.

"Of course it is, my love. It's the first step."

Phew, thank God for that. When Sadie said stuff like that, especially in the bath, I knew it was the truth.

Just then I remembered the Saturn-returning thing, and I sat up on my knees to quiz her about it all. She couldn't tell me very much more than I'd remembered already, but apparently in everyone's life, around the age of thirty and then again maybe in your late thirties or early forties, you reach a point where you look at your life and reassess and make adjustments and it's okay because it happens to everyone and it's even in your astrological charts so you couldn't stop it happening even if you wanted to. Apparently. I think it's kind of obvious anyway. Turning thirty is a huge step. It's like saying, Okay, I am an adult now, really, for real. Even if I act immaturely or buy Britney Spears dolls for *myself*, I am a thirty-year-old adult and I have accepted who I am and I am happy with that and so you should be too. And last night was important because it was something of a crash course in me accepting who I am. And I guess that's why I feel better this morning. Some of the circumstances haven't changed, but my attitude toward them has.

"You know what, Sades?" I said to her as she was toweling herself and I was having one last, soaky linger.

"What?"

"I'm okay."

"Yes, you are, Tommy."

I sat up, a bit teary. "And you're okay too."

"Oh, thank you, my darling, I know I am." She bent down to give me a hug. As her breasts enfolded my face I managed to mumble: "And I might not be the most together person in the world and maybe I do party a bit too much and maybe I do want some things that maybe I can't have, but that's okay too. I'm okay."

"Of course you are, Tomser. I want things that I maybe can't have too." I had a flashback to our coke jabber in the bar, and her little face when she'd said she wanted a baby.

Sadie held me for a long time, until I felt I was going to suffocate and had to pull away from her and come back up for air. I could see my face in the mirror above the sink. It was a bit purple.

"You may be okay," she said, bringing us both back to planet earth, "but you're also homeless."

Shit. I'd forgotten about that.

Over breakfast in Café Ole on Upper Street (sausage, eggs, beans and chips twice) we decided the best thing to do was to not panic and to talk it all through that night with Bobby, then start putting the feelers out and going to estate agents on Saturday. We were both a little worried because we knew we had such a good deal where we were, and prices had gone up dramatically in Islington since we'd moved in. Our landlord lived in Brighton, and hadn't quite grasped how the area had become all groovy now and expensive, and so the last time he had raised the rent it wasn't nearly as much as he could've or should've. Maybe he was just a nice man and didn't want to.

And we loved this flat. Although we'd lived together in various places of varying degrees of squalor since we'd left college, this flat was the first place that really felt like our home. We'd had a bit more money 'cos we were working in proper jobs when we'd moved in, so we were able to do things to it that we actually liked instead of covering up the cracks due to financial necessity. It was our first home, really, as adults. Proper home I mean. We'd ripped the carpets off the floors and hired one of those industrial sanders to polish the wood (I had an asthma attack because of all the dust—ah, memories, memories), we'd put up wooden shelves, not just those crappy ones with the metal bits that you screw into the walls so you can adjust the shelves to any height, oh no; we decided before we put them up where all our stuff was going to sit on them and built them accordingly. I remember we thought we were so posh.

And the garden. None of us had ever had a garden before. In the summer we used to hardly be in the house. We'd eat out there every night, convene for cups of coffee in the morning, and of course there was the newfound hobby of gardening. After a few false starts we had a beautiful garden. Creepers all around, with big pots on top of the walls to shield the prying eyes of the kids in the playground next door, and big bushes of rosemary and lavender that wafted their scent across at you when you sat in the low deck chair. We'd even put mirrors all along one side of the fence to make it look bigger than it actually was. This was Bobby's idea, so we always suspected it was also so he could stay outside and still pout at himself when he had withdrawal symptoms. On the very night the mirrors had been installed, when it was late and dark and we'd just got home from a party, India and I had crept down to the garden and lit some candles and quietly, ever so quietly, fucked each other up against the fence, she pushing against it as I came from behind her. When I managed to tear my eyes away from her beautiful white back, I could see in the mirror's reflection my fingers teasing her nipples. That was a great night, and Bobby was so happy we'd christened his mirrors.

Oh God, India again. More and more recently I keep thinking of her and me having sex. What's that about? Anyway, all that was in the past—India *and* the garden, as it turned out now—and as we got up and walked into the traffic-filled morning we resolved we'd find a new place and make it just as homey and as safe as our present one. We even shook hands on it. I just hoped we didn't have to move as far north as Scotland to be able to afford to. It would be a bit of a commute.

17

a night in

For once on a Friday night, Charlie and I didn't go out and get completely wasted. I'd been a bit nervous about seeing him after all the hoo-ha of the other night, but it turned out I needn't have worried. He was the same old Charlie. I admired him even more for what had happened too. He had brought things to a head, sorted them out, and here we were moving on to the next stage of our, em, relationship. There, I said it!

I also admired him for the other qualities he had displayed on Thursday night, but more of that later.

It's funny when someone has broken down in front of you, someone who's never done it before I mean. One of two things can happen. You can either look into their very core and feel forever closer to them for having let you see it, or you can take a peek and realize that they are an absolute freak who you must never be alone with again in case they try to pull off a similar stunt. With Charlie, it was the former, thankfully. He had showed me a side of himself that I honestly never expected to see, but having seen it I wasn't scared or didn't feel it was something I shouldn't have been privy to. It felt right. It was like the test of a friendship when you are silent together for the first time. He had opened up and I had seen inside, and it felt like a logical progression instead of a step over any imaginary line.

However, the suggestion that we shouldn't go out to a club was a little more alarming, frankly. We always went to a club on a Friday night. It was the end of the week. It was the night he came round with Finn and we mucked about and had a laugh and then I gave Finn a bath and put him to bed, then when Sadie came home from the theater she'd baby-sit and Charlie and I would go out to a club. That was what happened. Sometimes it was Bobby who baby-sat if Sadie had a hot date, but the evening always culminated in me and Charlie dancing and sweating and snogging and laughing. In a club!

Not going felt like my mum saying, "Okay, darling, this year for Christmas dinner we're going to be having beef chow mein." It just wasn't right.

And it wasn't that I was absolutely desperate to go clubbing— not like some nights when I just *need* to get to one, and dance and think of nothing except who is cute and who has drugs. No, it just felt weird, but hey, as I reminded myself, everything has been a little weird of late, so just ride it, baby.

Finn, now that he had a gentleman's agreement that I would be around for it, had told me that he'd already decided what he was going to buy me for Christmas. But he couldn't contain himself and five minutes later told me what it was (an N'Sync calendar. "Justin has his top off in September. He's got tiny nip-nips"). Then he butted in to our discussion and asked, "Do you have to be a member to get into this club?"

"No, Finn, it's not that kind of club," I'd said, wary of where this was going.

"But is there a room where you smoke cigars?"

"No, Finn," said Charlie. "You're thinking of a gentlemen's club."

"The kind they had in that Oscar Wildey film?" he asked.

"Yes," Charlie replied, patiently. "But the kind of club me and Tommy go to is for dancing. They don't do cigars."

"And there aren't many gentlemen," I added.

Finn seemed satisfied. I wanted to ask why an eight-year-old was watching films about Oscar Wilde, but when you take into account his family situation, I suppose it makes sense.

So we just stayed in! I called Sadie and told her she could go out and paint the town puce and she did. Bobby was going to a dirty bar in Kings Cross where they had a dark room, so I knew we wouldn't see him till the early hours, so Charlie and I had the place to ourselves. We ordered in Chinese food (not beef chow mein, before you ask) and we just sat and ate and had a bottle of wine and chatted, and it was actually really nice.

Once I'd managed to resolve my feelings about not being out clubbing on a Friday night, the main topic of concern for me was the whole flat business. Bobby had freaked out about it. He was certain we'd have to move to somewhere much further out to be able to get the same size of place for what we could afford.

"We're going to be living in Siberia," he'd cried. "We'll end up in a suburban wasteland miles from a tube, and lifetimes away from a decent gay bar." Bobby liked to be near the Soho scene, bless him. Sadie and I told him not to worry and Sadie added one of her Oprah-like pronouncements about how if we really believe that we can find something in Islington that's within our budget, then it really will happen. But queeny fits about going to live in Siberia were not very helpful.

I'd agreed with Sadie, but now I was starting to feel a little more pessimistic. When I'd gone to meet Charlie and Finn off the tube, I'd glanced in the window of an estate agent. Fuck me! The cheapest three-bedroom flat was nearly double what we paid now. And three months isn't a long time to find somewhere when you can't just move into the first place you like.

"You could always come and stay with Finn and me for a bit if you're stuck," Charlie had said. My face must have betrayed me, because he quickly added, "Don't worry, only if you're stuck. I'm not asking you to move in. You can drop your shoulders now, Tommy."

The thing was, he was practically in the same boat as us. He needed to find somewhere bigger. The two of them lived in a one-bedroom place, Charlie sleeping on a pull-down bed in the living room whilst Finn had the bedroom. It was getting pretty cramped. Every time I stayed over there I invariably got some toy or action figure wedged between my buttocks before the night was through.

"Thanks, Charlie," I said. "And I will if I'm really stuck. But what about Bobby and Sadie? I don't want to start staying with friends, because I know what'll happen. Months will go by and we'll get more and more desperate and before you know it the three of us have found rooms in different flats and we won't be living together anymore. And I love living with those two. No, we have to stick together. So if we're really, really stuck, you'll have all three of us!"

"Oh great," snorted Charlie.

We were quiet for a while. It felt nice, this staying in for the night with your sort of boyfriend. And the wine and the chow mein.

"Charlie," I said after a bit.

"What is it?" He put his hand behind my head and pulled me round to face him. I liked it when he did stuff like that. It's nice to feel someone's strength sometimes. I think that's one of the things I like about boys, the feeling that you aren't necessarily the strongest one.

"I just wanted to say I feel really good about the other night, about you having said all that stuff. And I want to say again that I understand the responsibility I have to Finn."

"And me," he interjected.

"And you, yeah. That's all."

Of course, it wasn't all really. I hadn't told Charlie any of the stuff that happened after he'd gone, and I certainly wasn't going to tell him about India. Why bother? It would only upset him. And I think at the moment it's best if I deal with one thing at a time. Everything in the Charlie garden is rosy, so why risk an Indian drought? And besides, I was really horny. Thinking back to the other night had got me all going, and the fact that the house was empty and we could have a replay on the sofa was really starting a party in my Calvins.

He pulled me toward him. Wow, I was enjoying this new, firm Charlie. I thought he was going to kiss me, but his mouth moved past mine and I felt his breath against my ear. "Do you need some more sense fucked into you, Tom?"

I took a little sharp intake of breath. What I wanted to do was say nothing and just pull down my jeans and my pants, lean over the edge of the sofa and just let him fuck the arse off me. I really did. But I waited a second or two—for dramatic effect—and then said, "You know what? I think maybe I do."

18

just as it was all going so well too, three

I was late, of course. My lateness was something that had always pissed her off. She thought I did it on purpose, and now I realized I had. I left the flat late, so ran down to Highbury Corner in the naive hope that I might get a cab, and was suddenly transported back (though not sadly in a fast black) to so many previous nights when I'd been on the same corner in the same situation. I was always late for her. Maybe it was because me being late meant that I wouldn't have to go through the experience of watching her arrive in a restaurant or a bar and seeing every other man in the room's head turn toward her. That wasn't a nice feeling for a boy. Maybe at first, I suppose, in the early days. When their eyes came round to find little old me sitting waiting for her, I'd wanted to shout back at them, "Yeah! I know! I can't believe it either!" But after a while that sort of smug feeling turned into an ugly, angry rage at their stares and an unease about just how much India enjoyed the attention. Oh, everybody enjoys attention, I know that, believe me, and I didn't want to deprive her of any of the fun of being looked at. I just got to really hate it, so it was better if I came late, even though, in my absence, she said the attention from the other bar patrons was not so welcome as it had been when she had me as her destination. So she would start to come later than me, and then I would double-bluff her and come later still, till finally we would always meet at one of our flats and then leave to go out together. Funny, eh? The games people play. And now I was at it again. Subconsciously maybe, and not because we were meeting in a public place, but nevertheless here I was at eight-thirty, not in a taxi, when I'd told her I'd be on time for eight o'clock. Old habits die hard, I suppose.

Sadie and Bobby were as much to blame for my lateness as me, though. When I came downstairs they were both waiting for me, a delicious dinner in front of them, their wineglasses raised, heads thrown back, laughing. They were just pretending of course. They'd been listening for me to come out of my bedroom and had started one of those laughs that only extras in films do—a sort of laugh that just starts in the middle, there's no buildup, and when it ends it's as though the person's off switch has been pressed. They were doing it on purpose as one last jibe for me not staying in with them for the flatmates-only dinner. And even though I knew it came from a place that was a little pissy, it still made me laugh, and I came into the kitchen with them and had a chat.

"Oh, Tommy, we didn't see you there," said Sadie. "Bobby and I were just having a hilarious time reminiscing about one of our previous fun-packed dinners, weren't we, Bobser?"

"That's right, Sadie. We always have a laugh of a Sunday evening, don't we? And tonight isn't going to be any different."

They then burst into another of those silly laughs and stopped as abruptly again.

"Okay, okay, I get it," I said. "I'm sure you'll have a much better time tonight than I will."

"Oh, I'm sure India will have made you a delicious dinner," said Sadie, starting to bitch.

"Yes, are you fond of lettuce?" Bobby waded in.

"Shut up, you know I'm going to go and nothing you say is going to stop me. Besides, I thought you understood that this was important for me."

"We know it is, my little petal. But you must allow us a little fun," said Sadie, gulping down some chardonnay.

"Did you pack a condom?" Bobby just wouldn't let it lie.

"No, I did not, 'cos I won't be needing one." I sat down at the table and poured myself a glass. "I'm not going to fuck her, remember."

All weekend that had been the little joke we'd had. Bobby or Sadie would sit down next to me on the sofa or pass me on the stairs and murmur "Don't fuck her" under their breaths. It was funny the first four thousand times but now it was getting a little old, to be honest.

"Hmm," said Bobby.

"Hmm-mmm," echoed Sadie.

"I am not going to fuck India," I repeated.

I did though. And that's only the half of it.

We were a funny couple, India and me. Everyone said so. She was tall and willowy, certainly taller and willowier than me. She was smart and chic and you may have gleaned that I was way at the back of the queue when chic was being handed out. She got free stuff from being a model, but even when she wasn't dressed up she still managed to look like she'd been styled. Even when she wore my clothes she looked great. A pair of sweats, an old T-shirt and a scuffed-up pair of slippers that on me looked exactly as they sound, on her became things of beauty. Her beauty was a kind that transcended the outward trappings of designer togs or makeup. First thing in the morning she was beautiful. When she came out of the shower she was beautiful. It was almost spooky.

It was just that we didn't look like we should be together. I was shorter and grungier and always looking like I'd just stepped out of bed, while she looked like she'd just stepped out of a magazine. And often she had. But it worked, somehow. We made each other laugh. She had a mind that was at odds with the popular conception of the mind of someone who looked like her. And that contradiction made her even more beautiful, if that's possible. In a way we were alike in that we looked at the world differently from most people. We didn't judge, we hated injustice and prejudice and small-mindedness, and we were just crazy about each other. One time, in the early days, I'd told Sadie that for the first time in my life I didn't feel like going out anymore, 'cos India and I were completely happy just staying at home looking at each other. And the sex was amazing, that was also a great connection. We were both really into each other's bodies, almost to the point of obsession, and completely uninhibited physically.

And she didn't take any shit, from me or anyone else. Once, a guy in a bar who'd been eyeing her up came up to her and, within my earshot, said, "Don't you mind your boyfriend being shorter than you?" It was on the tip of my tongue to say back,

"Don't you mind that asking questions like that makes people think you're retarded?" but before I could, and luckily too, for he was a scary big bruiser, India retorted, "It's all the same when you're lying down." India was cool.

One of the saddest things about us breaking up, apart from the heartbreak, the missing, and the despair of knowing that nothing, but nothing, is forever, was the fact that the kind of man you'd have expected India to go out with—someone rich, smooth, tall, well groomed, with a big car and an apartment like something out of one of those coffee commercials (where even people with perfectly normal jobs and incomes seem to live in airy lofts with amazing views)—was exactly the type of person she did in fact go on to go out with, the aforementioned Karl, he of the ironed slacks and the Porsche.

It's kind of annoying when people revert to type, isn't it? Or if not type, everyone else in the world's idea of their type. Annoying and sad, too. For Karl wasn't her type, really. Karl was solid and reliable and secure and tall and dull, but he'd always be early and she'd never have to write him checks to pay off his Visa bills, and he'd never dream of asking her to do a threesome and he certainly would never fuck boys on weekends when she was out of town. So I guess he had his pluses.

But now Karl was gone. And weirdly, I was driving up in a taxi to Karl's apartment, the gated, twenty-four-hour-securitied, coffee-commercial apartment high above the city that India was still living in. All of a sudden, the proximity to her, and her still being ensconced in the Nazi's lair, sent alarm bells ringing in my head: Why was she still in his flat? Why hadn't she moved back to her place? Maybe they hadn't really broken up. Maybe it was just a trial separation thing and my visit was a sort of audition to see how she felt about the outside world, and if I failed it she'd run straight back and hide in Karl's muscly arms. (They were *bulging,* actually. I bet if he was ever in a holdup and the robbers shouted, "Put your hands up," he wouldn't be able to raise them above elbow level and so would be mown down, a revenge killing for all us skinny blokes.) With this happy visual in my head I pressed her buzzer, and without a word, she let me into the inner sanctum that was Karl's coffee-commercial courtyard.

There were two elevators, and one was already there, but I decided to wait for the other one because the last time I'd been here, on that fateful Guy Fawkes Night when she'd slapped me, I'd kicked the wall of the other elevator as I was leaving, and I wanted to see if the big dent I'd made was still there. Plus it would make me a bit later.

I was really disappointed to see that the dent had gone. I suppose it was a year and a half ago, but the elevator was smooth, metal and . . . ironed.

She was waiting at the front door for me. I stopped in my tracks when I saw her and just took her in. She was having an au naturel day. Her hair was all curly, its natural way, not ironed straight like she had it most of the time, and she was wearing *pajamas.* Aye, aye.

"Come on, dopey, don't stand there gawping! I've hardly anything on," she said.

"I can see that," I replied, continuing down the corridor to join her. "Are you expecting an old lover or something?"

She didn't say anything. She just smiled and pulled me into her in a big hug. Fuck, she *was* tall. My nose was resting on her shoulder, and the first thing that hit me was the smell. Her smell. Everyone has their own smell, and hers was imprinted on my brain forever. It wasn't just the perfume she wore or anything like that, it was her. Months after we'd broken up I'd found an old shirt of hers jammed down the back of my chest of drawers and I could still smell her on it. I've still got it. I've also got two pairs of her knickers, but we don't have time to go into those right now. Smells are so important. It's the first thing I do when I'm with someone new, give them a good sniff.

"It's so good to see you, Tommy. I've missed you." She pulled me out of the hug and looked down at me, her hands on my shoulders. It felt a bit like when I was little and I'd visit an auntie I hadn't seen for years. India's next line should have been "Now let me have a good look at you." Instead, it was me that spoke.

"I've missed your smell."

We went into the flat and she asked me if I wanted a beer. I didn't really, but I wanted to see her have one. That was another great thing I'd missed: the sight of a gorgeous big model swigging back a Corona from the bottle. Of course, this time it was a Beck's. Another reminder of Karl that spoiled somewhat my dewy reminiscence. I had a sudden panic that the whole evening would have a German theme: bratwurst, apple strudel, beer, with Strauss (Richard, not Johann) playing throughout, culminating in a nightcap of schnapps and a Kurt Weill singalong.

She took a long slug of the beer, wiped her pajama-clad forearm across her mouth and smacked her lips. "That's good," she said, and burped.

"Ja," I replied, still in my whimsy. *"Das* ist *gut."*

A shadow crossed her face. "Okay, very funny. I think we should just talk for a bit and get the whole Karl thing out of the way, because I didn't ask you round here for an evening of snidey comments." She held my gaze.

"Okay, see ya." I started toward the door.

"Tommy, don't spoil it. I know this is weird, but it's weird for both of us. Let's try and be grown-ups. Remember that?"

Bitch.

"Well, when did you start drinking Beck's?" I asked, petu-lantly.

"Oh, for God's sakes! Get over it!"

There she goes again with the get-over-it thing. Bells were rung and buttons were pressed. Suddenly it was a year and a half ago and the room was filled with fireworks. "That was your parting comment when we saw each other last time," I said calmly. "I have got over it, believe me. The very fact that I'm here is proof that I've got over it." I paused, she said nothing, so I decided to carry on.

"You used to drink Corona, and now you drink Beck's. I just didn't know your taste for Germans extended to beer, that's all." This wasn't going too well already.

"Fuck you." India swore! Oh my God, India swears now. I can't wait to tell Sadie.

"You know you probably will have by the end of tonight," I said, and left it there, hanging to see what she would do. I can't believe I said that! I had no intention of getting all smutty with her, at least not so early on. When I'd left the kitchen Bobby and Sadie had given me one last chorus of "Don't fuck her," I dutifully repeated that I wouldn't, and I'd really meant it. It just slipped out.

She looked away from me, her mouth open in that kind of "I don't believe you said that" way, and then she blushed. And that was when I knew it was going to happen. She blushed and then she looked back and she smiled and said, "Sit down, you dog."

We both relaxed after that. It had come out of a roaring flashback of hurt and it could well have ended the evening before it had begun, but it had the effect of relaxing us both, and if recrimination and the acceptance of sexual tension is what we needed to relax, so be it. Don't knock it till you've tried it.

I sat on the sofa, splayed out and comfy. She sat on an armchair across the wooden coffee table (hewn from the Black Forest, no doubt). The flat was actually quite nice, all dark wood and books and patterned armchairs with cushions you could sink into. There was a telescope by one of the windows, which I thought was an interesting little insight into Karl's psyche.

"So you've split up?" I started. What was I now, her therapist?

"Yup," she said, taking another slurp of the Beck's. "He wasn't the man for me."

I raised my eyebrows.

"You know how that can be." She smiled.

"Oh yes. I know." She looked sad. Her eyes were lowered and she bit her lip.

"Do you want to tell me what happened?"

She looked up and a tear slid slowly down her cheek. "Shit happened," she said.

I got up and went over and knelt on the floor in front of her. I rested a hand on her thigh, not a very comforting gesture I know, but I didn't know quite what to do. It was all a bit confusing. I wanted to stroke her face and brush away the tear that had now come to rest on the side of her lip. I wanted to pull her into my arms and rock her gently until she felt better. But should I? Could I even? What would that be saying: "There, there, don't worry that you split up with your boyfriend, I'm here, the last one you split up with, to help you pick up the pieces"? I don't think so.

I wanted her to come to me. I wanted her to be the one to reach out for comfort. And it wasn't a power thing, I just had my dignity to think about, you know what I mean?

She put her hand on mine, sniffed and said, "I'm starving, are you?"

Dinner was a mixed bag. She'd never been very gifted in the cooking department, a symptom no doubt of a pathological fear of eating in her formative, early modeling days. Now she'd grown older and had become a woman, so it wasn't as imperative for her to be twiglike to get modeling work. Gone were the days when she'd blanch at the offer of a french fry. Also she'd discovered the step machine and other equally, to me, mind-numbing activities at the gym, so she could afford to eat the odd meal that wasn't celery. Incidentally, did you know that celery is the one thing you can eat that actually makes you *lose* weight? Yes. You burn up more calories with all that chewing than it contains, apparently. India once told me that.

There was celery in this dish. It was supposed to be a stir-fry, but it seemed heavier on the stir than the fry. Oil was still the enemy, I presume. There was brown rice too, natch, that you had to swallow by the globule rather than the grain.

The good bit of the dinner was that we talked. Although a little vague about the cause of their demise ("We both wanted different things," "It's for the best for both of us" and other assorted *Hello!*-magazine-style sentiments), she did tell me that the reason she was still here at Nazi HQ was that she'd rented out her own flat earlier in the year, and the lease wouldn't be up for another month or so. I told her about my flat-lease issues, and she said I could move in with her for a while. If I was stuck. That sounded familiar.

"I don't think that would be a very good idea, do you?" I'd said.

"Well, it would be better than you being out on the streets," she'd replied.

"And what do you think Karl would think if he came back to get his mail one night and found me curled up on his sofa, sipping his Beck's?" I asked, curious.

"I wouldn't care if Karl came back and saw you on the sofa curled up with me, Tommy. I don't care what Karl thinks. He's been very kind and let me stay on here for a while, but it also suits him very nicely because he's traveling with work for the next eight weeks so he'd have needed a house-sitter anyway. Stop talking about Karl, would you?"

Karl, I'd forgotten, was the head of a model agency and yes, you've guessed it, India was one of his "girls," as those in the model business so delicately call their clients. For the next two months he was jetting off round his various worldwide branches as well as doing a bit of "scouting" for new talent. I'd heard this phrase before and it had always puzzled me. How exactly, I wonder, do modeling agents "scout" for new talent? You hear stories about teenage girls in malls, out shopping with their mums one minute and the next thing they know they're sashaying down the runway in a Valentino wedding dress, being heralded as the Next Big Thing at the couture shows. But I fancy that most scouters' methods (including Karl's) involve hanging around bars eyeing up totty, then luring them back to their hotel rooms to "check out their potential" with the promise of a fat contract and/or an expense-accounted minibar. Call me jaded.

"So what have you been up to?" Ah, this is the bit where she tries to find out if I've got anyone new.

Oh, you know, doing a lot of drugs out of girls' bums, fainting at work, wanking on buses, crying, making collages with manipulative infants, getting shouted at, buggered, being told to the point of annoyance not to fuck you.

"Nothing much," I said. "Same old thing. Propping up Julian, having a laugh with Bobby and Sadie."

"How are they?" Her face lit up at the mention of their names.

"Great, great. They send their love," I lied.

"Send them mine, will you?"

"Yeah." Not.

"So . . ." she began. Here we go. I could see it coming a mile off. She was so transparent. ". . . is there anyone special in your life?"

What a fucking stupid thing to say. What she meant was: Are you free? Do you have a significant other? Is there someone in your life that has taken my place? I wanted to say back that I had lots of special people in my life, her included, but I was just being bolshie and I was onto my third beer and my belly was practically empty and I didn't want to be doing chitchat. I wanted to be in bed with India. I wanted to do the shortcut-to-intimacy thing. I wanted to be inside her, and then do the talking.

I thought before I spoke. The pause, I knew, would be painful for her, but that wasn't why I left it. I wasn't sure if I wanted to tell her. I didn't know if she deserved to hear it. And also, to be honest, I wasn't sure of the answer. But out one came.

"There are two people, actually."

She choked a bit on her beer. "What are you like, Tommy? Who are they?"

"Well, one's called Charlie."

"Man or woman?"

"Man. He's thirty-nine, gorgeous, all Mediterranean skin

and lovely long arms, and he's a laugh and very together and he gets me."

"That's lovely," she lied.

But I wasn't finished. "And he's got a great cock."

Interestingly, she stiffened at this remark, and she shook her head slightly. I couldn't tell if it was condescending or affectionate or a little bit of both. "And the other one?"

"Finn. Charlie's son." There, I'd said it.

"He's got a son?" She looked a little shaken by this news. "That's great. I mean, you're great with kids. You love kids, don't you? How old is he?"

"He's eight. He's great. Who do we appreciate?" I was being such a brat.

"I'm really pleased for you, Tommy." She looked at me, a smile fixed on her face, and I was sure I saw her eyes begin to mist over. But before I could be certain, she said: "Oh, there's pudding, I forgot."

She got up really quickly and headed off into the shadows. I got up too. I didn't know why. I just did. I didn't know what was happening really, but I was fired up and she'd walked away so fast and I followed her toward the light that was coming from the fridge door she had just opened, and I said, "Why did you and Karl really split up, I mean, really? None of this 'we drifted apart' stuff. Just tell me!" My voice was raised; it surprised her. Me too. The light from the fridge hit her eyes and I saw she was tearing up again. She looked so fucking beautiful. Never mind why did she and Karl split up, why did *we* split up?

She looked at me, defiant. "He wouldn't give me a baby."

We didn't have the pudding

It's funny how things happen. It's funny how wrong you can know something is, but you still jump in and do it. It's funny how even when you're in the middle of the thing you know is a really bad idea, you can still find new reserves of stupidity to make the bad thing even worse. And it doesn't feel like stupidity, that's the other funny thing, it feels like the most natural thing in the world.

I told you already that I had fucked India. But I lied. I *made love* to India. And I know that one of the first things I told you about myself was my absolute abhorrence of that phrase, but there you go, that's what I did. There were extenuating circumstances, after all. If Charlie found out I'd uttered that phrase he wouldn't be best pleased. Mind you, if Charlie found out I'd done the deed, not just uttered the phrase, he wouldn't be pleased at all.

And I made love to her without a condom. And I stayed inside her when I came. She wanted me to. I wanted to too.

In that moment India and I had been prepared to take the risk.

It's too hard to explain it. You had to be there really.

But I defy you to say that you haven't had times in your life that you've looked back on and thought, "I can't believe I did that. What the fuck was I thinking of?" Well, hello, this was one of those times for me. Well, hell, one of many times, but it doesn't get any easier to say no or to be wise, okay?

Like India said, shit happens.

a fairy tale about risk

Once upon a time only a few decades ago, in a land quite far away, there lived a young man named Alex. At the time this story begins, Alex is sixteen and starting to experiment with sex. Alex likes sex. He was a rare boy in that he had no shame about it. For Alex, sex was a beautiful thing. When he was younger and had his first orgasm, he felt like he had discovered what his body was for. And the first time he was not alone when he had sex, the other person—a girl who he knew from school—felt it was beautiful too. And luckily for Alex, she had no shame about sex either and they both passed an evening that was the best anyone could hope for when losing their virginity. For it was passionate, it was easy, there was no shame attached and above all it gave them both pleasure.

This first time gave Alex confidence, and over the next few years he continued to enjoy sex, unbridled and unashamed.

Occasionally the subject of protection came up. Early on, in Alex's sexual journey, a girl asked him if he had a condom. He hadn't, and so the evening ended pleasurably enough, but a little sooner than Alex had anticipated. Soon after, Alex overcame his embarrassment and went into a shop and bought condoms, and in the privacy of his bedroom, he read the instructions that came in the box and tried one on. The next time he was asked for one, Alex was happy to oblige, and happy that his trial at home made him look a more seasoned user than he actually was.

Soon after, Alex heard of a new disease. It came from a land across the sea and it was sexually transmitted. For a while no one really took any notice. The land across the sea was far, far away, and its inhabitants, to most of Alex's acquaintances' minds, were slightly histrionic. But soon the disease could not be ignored. People were dying. Alex saw images of them on TV. And soon Alex could sense fear all around him.

Before too long, everyone was wearing condoms. It was taken for granted that no young man or woman would go out of an evening without them. When Alex heard stories of his friends having "forgotten" to wear one, or using an excuse involving the phrase "in the heat of the moment," he became angry and chastised them.

Even though he was "safe," which was the word that came to be used for a sensible condom user, Alex still feared. There were stories about how penetrative sex might not be the only source of infection. Gum shields and condoms during oral sex were discussed among his friends, but Alex had felt this excessive, and after discussing it further with a medical man, he decided the risk involved was minimal, and therefore worth taking. So he ate cock and he ate pussy unprotected. But he also began to have nagging fears about the times, years ago, before the disease had been invented, when he had had unprotected sex. Stories abounded that the virus might have been around for years and only recently detected. Maybe, although he had always been "safe" since it had become known to him, he was one of the unlucky ones.

So Alex had a test. He talked with the doctor before the test, about his sexual activity and history, and although the doctor, a handsome young man with a shaved head and an earring, told him he felt he had nothing to worry about, Alex still had many sleepless nights until his test results were back from the laboratory and the doctor told him they were negative.

Being responsible, and not one to challenge the odds, Alex had tests regularly, just to be on the safe side, and he got so used to condoms that he no longer felt embarrassed buying them or having them around his apartment.

Then, one night, in the heat and intermittent darkness of a club, Alex caught sight of a beautiful boy who had come out of the darkness because he had caught sight of Alex. Very quickly it was decided that the two boys would spend the night together. Alex knew, by instinct, that the boy thought like him when it came to matters of sex. He could tell there was no shame in the boy's eyes, and he looked forward to what the night would bring.

But the night brought Alex a surprise. The beautiful boy, who had a beautiful cock, and who wanted to penetrate and pleasure Alex, said he didn't like wearing condoms, they were uncomfortable, they diminished his pleasure. Alex laughed, because he'd heard this story before, and he told the beautiful boy that if he wanted to penetrate him, he would have to wear a condom or not at all. The beautiful boy tried to win Alex round by teasing him with his beautiful cock, but for Alex there was no question, and the beautiful boy grudgingly put a condom on.

The beautiful boy and Alex fell in love. It was love so quick and strong and passionate that Alex found himself overcome by it, and eventually, out of control. And so when the day came that the beautiful boy didn't wear a condom when he penetrated Alex, nothing was said.

Nothing was said because, in the instant that he could have said something but didn't, Alex reasoned that he wanted to know what the beautiful boy felt like without a condom, so much so that he was willing to take the consequences of this action, whether the beautiful boy was being truthful about his former safeness or not. It was a huge decision, but made in an instant, as, for the beautiful boy, Alex was prepared to take the risk.

When they had finished, Alex felt it was worth it. The closeness and intimacy and the thrill of the risk had so pleasured him. He never again asked the beautiful boy to wear a condom, nor did the beautiful boy ask it of him.

Sadly, within a few months, the beautiful boy and Alex's love was over. It had been too quick and strong and passionate, and the beautiful boy disappeared as quickly as he had appeared from the shadows of the club.

And Alex was left feeling as foolish as the friends he had chastised years before, but understanding now how easy it could be to take so many risks for so long.

Alex went to his doctor, who told him he was a fool. Alex waited for the test results to come back from the laboratory to find out whether his foolishness, and his risk, had a price.

The test came back negative, and although relieved, Alex was also so very sad. For now he no longer could tell if the risk had been worth it.

20

the morning after and the night before

Charlie and Finn came round early to wish me bon voyage. I was still asleep and Bobby let them in. Finn bounced onto my bed with a card he'd made and a bag of boiled sweets which he said I should suck on the plane so my ears wouldn't pop. I still had India's smell on me, and I felt worried that now Charlie would sense it as he kissed me good-bye, but he didn't. I'd got away with it. In my own weird, deceptive way I felt I'd achieved what I needed to achieve without letting my friends down and without fucking myself up.

As it turned out I was so wrong. But at least I'd got a good shag out of it.

Afterward, when we were getting dressed and India had rung me a taxi, there were words of remorse and disbelief that it had happened, but there was also a mutual understanding of why, and that somehow, that frenzy, that foolhardy whirlwind of passion had given us a kind of closure that we both needed. We kissed at the door. I didn't want to sleep over and she didn't ask me to. We'd done the intimacy thing. In the light of the fridge, on the kitchen floor, we became closer, literally, than we'd ever been before, and in so doing had freed ourselves from each other forever. I think.

There was, inevitably, the no-condom thing to consider. She said not to worry, she was past the fertile time of her cycle, and I said not to worry, I've been tested recently and anyway I'm always safe. But still . . .

I was home fairly early, for me anyway, and Bobby and Sadie looked up proudly at me from the sofa and gave me a round of applause because they, of course, believed the reason I was home at a reasonable time and not creeping in shamefaced at seven in the morning was a reason for rejoicing and proof that I had not done the very thing I had indeed done.

It was easy to lie. Because if you left out the fucking-without-a-condom bit, everything that had happened with India had been what I'd hoped: we saw each other, we talked, we had some form of closure, and future meetings would no longer be full of dread. It was perfect, it seemed.

But I smelled of her. I was scared when Bobby and Sadie hugged me that they could smell it too. But they couldn't. I was safe.

21

virgin and whore

Someone, somewhere, had made a big mistake and was no doubt going to be severely reprimanded. For I, little Tommy, who, when traveling with Julian, was used to saying adieu to him at passport control and not seeing him again till our huge trunks of camera equipment came shuddering down onto the carousel at the baggage claim, discovered at the check-in that this trip was different. For someone, somewhere—whom I bless and curse by equal measures, for now that I have tasted the hitherto forbidden fruit of first-class travel I will never be happy in coach again—had sent not the usual combination of first-class ticket for Julian, economy for me, but first class for both.

I nearly cried. Well, actually, after Julian had elbowed me to stop contradicting the check-in girl and accept that it was indeed true, I nearly cried.

And so it came to pass that Tommy, just weeks short of his thirtieth birthday, entered his first first-class lounge. Wow. I couldn't believe my luck.

I look at Heathrow Airport in a totally new light now. It is no longer that melting pot of race and creed, united only in the common goal of banging into as many other people as possible with their luggage carts and bags of duty-free. Oh no, now it is Tutankhamen's tomb, because I know that in the midst of this airless darkness there is a golden place of tranquil beauty. It's called the Virgin Upper Class Lounge.

Talk about how the other half lives. Julian, who being upper class himself didn't seem to see the irony, called it simply "the lounge." He knew the drill, and took me around like the headmaster of Eton patiently explaining to a scholarship boy on his first day all the workings of this newfound world of privilege.

They have a *salon*. In the lounge. You can get your hair cut, you can have a massage or a facial. It's unreal. By the time our flight was called I wanted to stay in the lounge forever. I wanted to live in it. There is a man who'll polish your shoes, and dammit if I wasn't wearing sneakers that day. There is a little Astroturfed area where you can hone your *putting* skills. There are a couple of those arcade games where I watched businessmen line up to put their feet in little slots, grab on to little poles and with the aid of the virtual-reality screen in front of them pretend to *ski*. It's insane, really. They also have delicious food, I mean really delicious, and as much of it as you can eat in the time before your flight, and booze, and it's all, get this, *free*. I feel like my mum, because I start to steal little things like toothbrushes and razors that are casually lying about in the loo, to take home for Sadie and Bobby as souvenirs. Oh, and the staff are really cute, all dressed in sexy red outfits, some of them with those little pillbox hats worn (as it is always reported in the tabloids of the Queen when wearing any form of headgear) at a jaunty angle.

I couldn't believe my luck. Now I understood why Julian always seemed a little perkier than me after a transatlantic flight. Not for him the hanging around fluorescent-lit waiting areas, with only the purchase of some cut-price vodka or a Big Mac to ease the Orwellian gloom. And not for him the blood-clot-inducing confinement and plastic-trayed, plastic-wrapped, plastic-content meals of the economy cabin. I've since read that there's actually a medical condition called "economy-class syndrome" that attributes thrombosis of the legs or something equally menacing to long hours immobile and squashed at thirty-seven thousand feet. They keep that quiet, don't they? I think I actually read about it in a magazine in the Upper Class Lounge.

The purpose of all this luxury is of course to ensure our captains of industry arrive on foreign shores as refreshed and pampered and self-confident as possible, so when nasty little foreigners try to con them out of our kingdom's riches they will eat them up, spit them out and send them home whence they came. For me, it was just a time to relax and review what had happened the night before. And it didn't seem half as bad as it would have in economy, I'll wager.

The lounge and the flight (which was almost laughable in its opulence—a menu like a restaurant so you could eat whenever you liked, endless champagne, little goody bags to take home, a video library with all those films you'd meant to see but had never got round to and, oh yes, my favorite: "Would you like your manicure now, sir?") made it feel like I was on my holidays, so it was something of a shock to be lugging camera cases into a van at JFK whilst Julian sat on his (fat—remember?) arse, mobile phone wedged to his ear.

Suddenly the natural order returned and I felt like the little boy in *The Prince and the Pauper* watching how the other half lived again, spoiled forever because I'd stepped over the social divide.

Tommy takes Manhattan

When we'd dumped the stuff off at the studio we were going to use for the shoot, we checked into the Mercer in SoHo, Julian's New York hotel of choice, and the source of happy memories for me. It's their baths, you see. America, as a nation, has never fully embraced the bath. They normally have these truncated things, where you can't lie down properly, as though submerging all of your body would be in some way hazardous. Indeed, during my extensive research on this topic, I've gleaned that there is something of a sanitation issue for Americans when it comes to the bath. The land of the free is a shower-obsessed country, where—and bear with me if this seems puerile, but this is actually the reasoning—the water runs off the body and immediately down the drain. It is common for numerous showers to be taken each day. A bath, of course, means that the body is immersed in nonmoving (and to take this logic to its ultimate and grisly conclusion) *stagnant* water, full of the dirt and grime the body has just discarded. So it's no wonder that lounging in the bath for hours is seen, by our American cousins, as a decadent and debauched European custom, fueling further the huddled masses' fears that we are all smelly, garlic-loving, cheesy-foreskinned layabouts. But the baths in the Mercer are, thank God, huge. Not just huge by American standards, but huge for Europe too. You can easily fit three people in there. I know, I've tried. You can have two people fully stretched out and not touching! They're amazing, and a brave, symbolic stand against the majority hygiene lobby.

What with the time difference and the snooze I'd had on the plane, I was raring to go, and the night was young. I'd showered (when in Rome . . .) and remembered the other reason why the shower is the cleansing method of choice this side of the pond. They're so strong. I nearly got blown out onto the bathroom floor by the water pressure. That's another area where the New World can beat the Old hands down—plumbing. So after my skin had lost its redness and my heartbeat was stabilized, I was refreshed and dressed and ready for adventure.

We had an early start the next day. The subject—the first in our series of shoots of hot, up-and-coming actresses (or hottish actresses with hotter publicists, depending how you chose to look at it)—had a name I'd never heard of, but her power was such that we were all going in to shoot her three hours earlier than originally planned because she wanted to have lunch with her mother. Bring her mother along, I'd said, but being just a lowly assistant, invisible at a photo shoot to all but freakishly down-to-earth celebrities, I had little say in matters such as these. So it would be an early night. Just a few drinks, and a scout of what was on offer for the rest of my trip—and that might include people as well as places. It was something of a mission for me to have as much fun on this stateside jaunt as was humanly possible.

Maybe it was the result of the recent personal turbulence, or the imminent big three-oh, I wasn't sure and I didn't care, but I knew that somehow these two weeks were a sort of last hurrah, a New York farewell to my twenties and the heralding of a new stage in my life when I got back to London: a new home (hopefully), a new type of commitment to Charlie and Finn, a new ease with India and soon a new decade where the prospect of having a child might not seem as alien. I don't know why this last topic should have suddenly seemed more tangible. Maybe it was being in America, where I'd heard of several people, single men and gay couples, who had adopted children and weren't regarded as degenerate fantasists. I also had two weeks away from having to think about it again, and that always makes things rosier in my book.

Walking out onto the streets of New York is always like walking onto a film set. No matter how many times I come here I always get that feeling. Maybe because most Europeans' knowledge of New York has come from films, but the whole place has a surreal quality to it that I can't take seriously for the first few hours I'm there. Maybe when you live there you become inured to the steam belching up from the manholes in the street, the omnipresent sirens, the pretzel vendors, the yellow cabs and the battles that can ensue on any corner to claim them, the *attitude*. But to the ingenuous visitor like myself it all seems like a movie still come to life, and we, finally, are part of the fairy tale we'd always imagined New York to be. I've also found that the best way to view the city is to look up, always look up. There are treasures to behold that you could easily miss. There are whole worlds up there, architectural follies, fading ancient billboards, lives to be glimpsed through apartment windows—for in a vertical city stuffed onto a tiny island, the inhabitants have come to accept, and expect, they will be observed from time to time. Everyone in New York knows they are watched. So next time you're there, look up, you'll be amazed.

I looked up all the way across town in the cab I took to the East Village, to a little bar I'd frequented on previous trips and where the bar staff might know me, and hopefully fill me in on what was new and who was news. That's another thing about this place—people talk to you. It's never long before you're in a conversation—or even in a friendship—when you set out on your own for the night. For this is a land of immigrants, and New York is a city where everyone has come to fulfill their dreams— sometimes the dream is simply to *be* there—so its inhabitants place great importance on reaching out to others, maybe to find out where you're from and what your dream is, or maybe to ask if you'll be a part of theirs.

The bar was tiny, and when totally packed would only hold about forty people. At this early hour there were only about a dozen or so East Village types hanging out, smoking and knocking back beers. I love the East Village. I feel more at home here than I do on the West Side. It's more scruffy and the people have a sense of style that I can relate to—sexy in a dirty sort of way and not so concerned with labels or body shape. However, here, the majority body shape was mine—skinny—so I felt at home and I blended in. Apart from when I spoke, of course. That was a giveaway. Ordering a drink at the bar in a British accent would turn a few heads, and initiate new conversations. Sometimes it worked incredibly well. Once, a smart Upper West Side type of girl, who had a sort of new millennium Doris Day look (it was working, believe me) and who seemed a fish out of water in whatever dingy joint I'd found myself, turned round and said, "Oh, you're British! And cute! I just love cute British boys! Do you want to come with me to the ladies' room and *snog,* cute British boy?" Americans loved using the snog word. So I said yes, and we did. Her name was Dorothy. I told her I'd always been her friend, but she didn't get it. Considering I was tumescent in her presence when I said it, I suppose it was understandable.

The guy behind the bar remembered me. It was nice to be able to walk in somewhere three thousand miles away from home and have the barman know you. Mind you, I'd bought some pills off him before and I may even have done mild frottage with him in the small hours of a night long past. I can't say for certain, it was that kind of bar.

"Hey, what's up?" he said. I never knew quite what to say to that greeting. "Nothing" would be an easy way out, but it seemed kind of rude, putting a stop to the conversation before it had begun.

"I'm good," I said, remembering the lingo, and continuing with the obligatory "How are you?" I think his name was Brad, or Chad, or something equally monosyllabic and quintessentially American.

"Haven't seen you for a while," he continued.

"No, it's been a long while, I just came in from London today."

"And so you're out for a night on the town?" He smiled.

"That's right." I smiled back. He was cute. Goatee, shaved head, an eyebrow ring and a Boy Scout shirt with the sleeves ripped off revealing a dragon tattoo down his right upper arm. Kind of rough, kind of nasty, kind of just what the doctor ordered.

"What are you doing later?" he said. This was so easy it was almost laughable.

"What are *you* doing later?" I asked, flirting back more seriously.

"Ah, you, I think." He laughed. "Can I get you a beer?"

His shift ended at midnight. Until then I waited, drinking and chatting, to him initially and to others as the bar got fuller and he got busier. I couldn't believe I'd got off to such a good start. As beer followed beer, and new faces appeared in front of me, London and the mess I'd left behind me seemed light-years away. It was only this morning—that was the weird thing about traveling, you could pack so much into a day if you really tried—when Charlie and Finn had awakened me, and only last night that I'd lied to Bobby and Sadie about India, but all of that now drifted far away into the back of my mind, which was, of course, exactly what I'd hoped for.

Is that bad? The desire to blot out those in your life who mean most to you? But if travel broadens the mind, it must surely by necessity diffuse your attention. And that's all I was doing, really. The beers and the chats and the flirting and Brad (for that was his name) were all just diffusing my attention momentarily, and the pill I was inevitably going to take would certainly broaden my mind.

My life was continuing on another continent, except I wasn't in it. But it would still be there when I got back. This was a brief time when I could reinvent myself. Tonight I was just a boy in a bar with no ties, no former girlfriend, no sort of boyfriend with a son, no nagging thoughts about fatherhood, no fears that my twenties were ending and I wasn't the person I wanted to be. Tonight at least I was the person I wanted to be—just a drunk boy in a bar who was going to get laid.

22

tomorrow is the same day, actually

I didn't have time to make use of the big fat bed that was waiting for me at the Mercer. Not to sleep in anyway. I sat on it occasionally, and leaned and knelt on it, but I never properly lay down in it and closed my eyes.

I lay in the bath though. With Brad and a boy called Peter we'd found as we were leaving one of the many bars we'd trolled around after Brad had knocked off work. He was talking to the doorman, trying to get in by saying he was on the DJ's list, and his English accent caught our attention and we just ordered him there and then to get into a cab with us, and he did.

Peter was a student (bless!) doing a film course here for a few months, and was missing home so was only too happy to have a new friend from Blighty to reminisce with and, because of his penury, a posh hotel room to lounge in and a minibar to raid. He was twenty-two, and although he had the uniform of the arty student underclass his hair was too neat and his nose was too fine and it came as no surprise when he talked about his past and phrases like "weekend place in the country" and "sent down" revealed him as a posh boy, a little damaged product of a liberal education (Beadales) and absentee parents. He was blond and pale. He and I looked positively blue lying next to Brad's swarthiness.

We had a great time. We'd taken e, but instead of going to a club and just dancing all night (for it was a Monday, even in New York), we'd just gone back to my hotel room and chatted and enjoyed the drug together, occasionally doing a spot of dancing to one of the CDs I'd brought with me, or kissing or bathing, but it had that beautiful, innocent feel to it that ecstasy can bring where it's not about desire or sex but sensation. I do this occasionally and then always forget how good it is until the next time comes along. We were sharing a common experience that let us be intimate and open together, and completely uninhibited about ourselves and our feelings. We told each other things we'd have taken ages of knowing someone to tell if we hadn't been high, but there was no worry that this trust would be abused because the others were doing the same thing. We hugged and said how lucky we were to be with each other, and how tonight had brought us all together for this magical time.

That's the great thing about e, it's such a leveler. You feel fantastic and alive and exhilarated, yet completely safe. Me and Brad and Peter would always have a special bond now. We'd been naked, both physically and emotionally, we'd laughed and just lain quiet in each other's arms. It was great. It was also a really strong e—another New World boon, like the plumbing.

It was about five in the morning when I began to think that there wasn't any point in me going to bed. I had to meet Julian downstairs in two hours' time and anyway I wasn't sleepy at all. I was a bit woozy, especially after all the baths I'd taken, but I knew there would be no point in lying down and closing my eyes because the combination of the time-zone difference and the drug and the worry that I'd be missing something would have me up again in no time. And if I did nod off, I'd no doubt wake up more groggy and disoriented than I would do staying up. There was also the worry that I had to go to work and deal with Julian chattering away (he was a morning person—a sad indictment of anyone's soul, I always thought) and to appear as though I hadn't been up all night doing class A drugs. I wasn't that worried, though. That's another great thing about e, little things like getting up or being tired later are suddenly put into a new perspective when measured up against the way you're feeling at the time and the insights you have into *what really matters*.

Peter had crashed out, so at least someone was going to get the use of the bed. Brad and I knelt down to look at him. He had a little smirk on his face, as if his slumbering body couldn't help but manifest the night he'd had. He looked about twelve years old. I had a sudden panic that if I left him here when I went to work and the maid came in, she'd think I was a pedophile, but it went away. I felt very protective toward him, this total stranger, a little boy lost in the big bad city. Thank God we'd kidnapped him when we did. Who knows where he might've ended up if we hadn't?

Now the baby's asleep . . .

Brad and I were left alone as the world started to trickle back to normal, whatever that was. The day was coming and the drug was ebbing, so our innocence was too. We managed to catch it at just the right time, where we had the horniness back and yet still that incredible hypersensitivity from the pills, so having his mouth round my cock or his cock in my mouth was truly, and in all aspects, the best of both worlds.

Brad, sadly, was a fully fledged member of the hygiene obsessives' club. I swear that practically on the point of coming he was reaching out to turn the shower on. And after being in and out of that fabulous bath maybe four or five times in the course of the night, please note that we *showered* after sex. I wasn't going to, but he looked at me as though I was insane so I buckled and joined him. I don't see what's wrong with it though. I like having semen on me. I like the feel of it when you rub it across your tummy, and I like how it stretches and dries and you're reminded all day of how it got there.

Wakey, wakey, rise and shine

Because of his jet lag, Julian had already been up for a few hours when I met him in the hotel lobby, and he was super-perky.

"Morning, Tom! And what a beautiful morning it is. Have you been out yet? I woke up at the crack and took a little stroll down to Ground Zero. It really is an incredible sight, the television doesn't do it justice. Fell into a chat with a policeman—oops, sorry, cop—who told me there are fires still burning underground. Might take years to put them out. Absolutely amazing."

As Julian prattled on, I marveled how not even something like the World Trade Center disaster could curb his enthusiasm. Not that he was unaffected by tragedy, far from it, it was just that his background, his "bloody hard work but great fun" attitude, his inherent gusto, made him incapable of just taking in an experience and letting it settle. It was his smoke screen, I knew.

I'm sure what he really meant was "Fuck me, I went to Ground Zero and I was really moved and awed by the enormity of what happened and the chaos that still reigns there," but he couldn't say that. He was so full of zest. I was once asked to describe him, and after a long while of choosing my words carefully I said, "He's hysterically buoyant."

He was a little bit too hysterically buoyant this morning, and I, as you know, was feeling a little drained, so I made up an excuse about having forgotten something from my room and went back upstairs. Brad was getting dressed and ready to go. He had to wait tables at a diner in the East Village. He was an actor, after all.

"Brad, do you have any of that coke left?" I asked. We'd had a little bump last night before we took the E's, and I just knew it was the only way I was going to get through the morning if Julian kept up the way he was going. If you can't beat them, join them, I say.

When we arrived at the studio, there was the usual hanging around and chatting, but I made the most of the coke and got unpacked and set up incredibly fast. There was a drama because some clothes hadn't got there yet, and Ms. Starlet, who even though I'd never heard of her was actually in the number one box-office film in America for the past two weekends, was about to arrive and she would not be best pleased, her publicist told a quaking stylist, if she didn't have a Gucci option. Of course the fact that we were shooting her practically in the middle of the night might have had something to do with the garment tardiness. I bet the PR people at Gucci who were "sending stuff over" (another of my favorite fashion-talk phrases) wouldn't even be up yet, let alone in their offices ordering couriers. A compromise was reached, after the publicist had perused the racks, that they would both try to push her toward the Nicole Farhi or the Miu Miu, and if she felt there wasn't enough color, the Cynthia Rowley. This way, she might not even notice the Gucci wasn't there at all, and we would all be spared her wrath and live to fight another day. Phew!

Even with my cocktail of no sleep, post-e floatiness, coke burst and coffee high, I couldn't help thinking that it was ridiculous for three grown women—publicist, stylist and fashion editor from the magazine—to be stressing out about something so stupid at barely eight o'clock in the morning, especially when Ms. Number One at the Box Office had about a hundred other options on the racks to choose from. But I kept my mouth shut, and so did Julian, who, ever fearful of confrontation, suddenly for the first time in his life became interested in makeup and busied himself discussing the "vision" for this morning's subject with the makeup boy. This amused me greatly because normally Julian's "vision" consisted of blasting a key light into their eyes to give them a sparkle, then sending them home so he could get back to the hotel for a cocktail.

That was the best thing about working for Julian: photography wasn't his passion, nor was his range terribly great, so once he'd got the nicely lit, blemish-free, middle-of-the-road image that the clients required, he was done. I've spoken to other photographers' assistants who tell horror stories about their bosses' perfectionism and hours of overtime they sometimes work to get the shot. No, it suited me fine that Julian was average. Sometimes, when I could see that a model was capable of more, or with just a little tweaking the look of something could be more interesting, I'd get a bit frustrated, but not for long. Julian's pictures were Julian's pictures, and if I needed to vent my artistic frustration, I could always pick up one of my cameras at home and have a muck-about. I rarely did these days, though. Over the years working with Julian I'd taken my own pictures less and less. Either I just got lazier or his ordinariness just wore me down. Maybe a combination of the two. Occasionally I'd get one out and take a few snaps of Sadie. She was a great model because she was completely unselfconscious. My favorite photo ever is her on the loo, face in her hands, elbows on her knees, knickers and jeans at her ankles, just staring into space, with the bathroom door wide open. I've also got a few nice ones of Finn. The camera loves him, and he knows it. I've even persuaded a few of the past occupants of my bed to pose, and some of those have been okay. It's nice to photograph someone naked when you know their body. I've usually been naked when I've shot them too, so that makes for a good feeling of ease in a picture. I'd burnt most of the ones I took of India. When I looked back on them, I didn't see my girlfriend, I saw a model, and the professionalism and tricks she'd acquired over the years for the camera. There were a couple when she'd let me in, and I'd kept those.

Surprise!

Ms. Number One at the Box Office turned out to be a real sweetie. It's amazing how sometimes the machine that surrounds actors, and other people's expectations of how they should behave, can completely distort your impression of them until you meet them. She couldn't have given a fuck that she didn't have a Gucci option. She came in wearing a sleeveless white top with NEEDY emblazoned across the front (which gave me my first inkling that she was going to be anything but), a pair of drawstring pants that probably cost a fortune but looked sub-Gap, and flip-flops. She introduced herself to everyone, including me, and apologized for having asked for the time to be changed but explained that her mum (actually, her mom) was visiting from Alabama and had never been to New York before, so she wanted to be at home to greet Mom when she arrived from the airport. I could tell her publicist was practically willing her to be difficult about something, but she wasn't. She was just a nice girl, pretty in a sort of pouty but homely way, and respectful and kind and without any bullshit. Now, maybe it was the remnants of the e floating through my veins that fed this opinion, but I don't think so. She knew what to do in front of a camera (not as logical as you might think for a film actor—a lot of them get really self-conscious when they have to stay still) and so Julian was happy, and by 12:35 she was out of the door and we were twiddling our thumbs, trying to find things to do to make it seem like we'd done a full day's work.

It can be that easy. It should always be that easy. There was a bit of a discussion with the fashion editor and the stylist about tomorrow's subject—a girl I recognized from one of those teen horror films that seem to be made with ever more alarming alacrity these days. I wonder why our culture is so obsessed with seeing its beautiful youth terrified and hacked up?—and before too long I was in a cab with Julian heading back to the hotel, looking forward to a few hours' revivifying nap. But it was not to be.

23
Tommy's nightmare

I wake up in the flat in Islington and there is nothing there. No Sadie, no Bobby, no furniture even. They have moved to a new place but they have forgotten to tell me. I am wandering round the bare rooms looking for a note or a sign that might tell me where they have gone to, where we are living now.

And then I am running down Upper Street in Islington, right in the middle of the road, screaming for them, and get this, I am *naked*. And my feet are all cut from running on the road and my body is bruised from falling down all the time, but I will not stop, I cannot stop. I have to find them. When I get all the way down to the bottom of Upper Street, to the Angel tube, I hear a voice I recognize shouting, "You're going the wrong way, Tommy." I look around, but I cannot see where it is coming from.

"You're going the wrong way." It is India.

"Where are they?" I beg her. But she is gone.

I run back up Upper Street and up the Holloway Road, screaming and screaming and looking for a movers' van or some clue to try and find them. I stop suddenly, for I can hear a child's voice. It is Finn. I can hear him crying. I am frantic by now. Eventually I look down a side street and there he is, sitting sobbing on the side of the pavement. "What's wrong, Finn?" I ask.

He looks up at me, his eyes red and his face crinkly with grief. "What is it?" I repeat.

"Daddy told me you made a baby with India," he sobs. "How could you do that, Tommy? I wanted you to be my second dad."

I kneel down to him and try to hold him, but he pulls away. "Don't worry, Finn," I say. "It'll be all right. I'll look after you."

"How can you look after me?" he screams. "You're just a child too."

And then suddenly I see them, Charlie and Bobby and Sadie. They are carrying boxes from Charlie's car into a house. It must be our new place, but why is Charlie there? Is he moving in too? I am shouting at them and waving, and finally they see me, but instead of looking happy that I have finally found them, they hurry toward the door of the house, away from me. I run faster and think I will be able to catch them because they are carrying big boxes so are slower. I am at the bottom of the steps to this strange house and Charlie is just edging in the door, the last of the three to do so. "Charlie, wait!" I cry, but he turns round, looks at me with hate in his eyes and slams the door in my face . . .

. . . **and then I woke up.**

24

running from the volcano

That night it just started. I felt it coming and I knew it was too strong to resist so I just let it in and hoped that I would be able to hang on and survive it for long enough until it went away.

I spiraled. From the moment I woke up from that fucking dream I just spiraled.

It felt like a volcano had erupted. Everything was shaking and I was running and screaming and trying to get as far away as possible from it, from what was behind me.

Tommy's depression rules . . .

don't work here. It's gone beyond that now.

Tommy's depression rules.

Exactly. If I admitted it to myself, that I was drowning, that I was really going under, it would win, I *would* drown. So I blocked it out. I had no choice. The first step was that if I started to believe the dream had never happened, then eventually it wouldn't have. That would be the first step.

I had been able to do it before. If something had happened that I didn't ever want to think about again it was easy. I made a decision that it had not in fact occurred, and the more times I thought it, the sooner it would be erased from my memory forever. It's just an act of will.

But not this time.

Maybe because it had started with a dream, nothing tangible, no palpable events to bury, I couldn't make it go away. It floated all around me, blowing in fast like a fog when I least expected it, leaving me stranded and lost and ever more desperate to turn to a drink or a pill or a bump or a body to preoccupy me and bring me succor, however brief, before the skies would cloud again, and I would feel its mist moisten my face and I knew I was done for till the next drink or pill or bump or body.

I stumbled through work, sleeping at lunchtimes behind a screen at the back of the studio while the others chatted and ate and wondered aloud where I'd gone. After a few days, Julian pulled me to one side and asked me what was wrong, and said that I should "buck up" because questions were starting to be asked and how I must remember that I am a representative of him when I'm at work and the very least I could do was to stay awake and eat with everyone else. So I did a bump of coke in the bathroom just before lunch, then chatted merrily, entertaining the magazine people with funny stories and gossip, or asked polite questions of whatever actress was in that day and got her and her publicist coffee and behaved, all the while pushing a few leaves of lettuce round my plate, feigning praise for the chicken or the pasta salad I hadn't tried, because eating was the last thing I could or wanted to do. And Julian was satisfied because, being socially inept, he relied on me to supply the wit and the sparkle at shoots that made him, by association, seem more ebullient and "now," and relieving him of those scary duties meant he overlooked my sluggishness in the mornings or my sudden bursts of energy after a visit to the loo, or the shadows under my eyes that were becoming darker and my eagerness to be out of the studio as soon as the day's rolls of film had been sent to the labs and the lights were switched off. He even began to call my room to invite me for drinks or the occasional dinner, perhaps because he was lonely and needed an escort but more likely to keep an eye on me and ensure I had one early night that would also include food. He was worried about me. I can see that now. But I didn't want his worry, I had too many of my own.

Being worried was no use to me.

So I ignored his calls and eventually they stopped. It was easy to avoid him. Each day I would get to work before him, several times arriving there straight from a stranger's bed or an after-hours bar and creeping into my little nest at the back of the studio and dozing till I heard the hair and makeup people setting up. I'd get up and have a shower in the studio bathroom and a few espressos to pep me up and I'd be fine. Yeah, I was just fine. Not having one of my most outgoing phases certainly,

225

but fine, just a little bit quiet, just a little bit on the back foot, just not letting on. It can be done. Apart from my lunchtime duties as court-jester-cum-waiter, always made easier after two or three bumps, I was able to coast through the day.

And most people, especially those who've only known you a number of days, don't assume you need help unless you ask for it.

TOMMY'S

DEPRESSION

RULES

TOMMY.

What Tommy did about it . . .

When I got back to the hotel each night, I'd try to sleep for a few hours, then take a shower. The bath had lost its allure somewhat, as lounging in it in my state of malnutrition and drug abuse would make me light-headed, and of course any activity that involved the possibility of reflection had to be assiduously avoided. No, the bath now became a sort of attraction in my drug-use theme park, used only to enhance a high or ease a comedown, or as a venue for sex. The shower, on the other hand, was now an important component in my daily routine of stimulation. I used it like the coke, and increasingly the crystal meth that I was snorting daily—as a means to stimulate and refresh.

Sometimes when I was really high, too high to be brought down so it was okay to have a sly think about it, I'd marvel at how quickly it had come. And how. It wasn't the nightmare really. It had been the catalyst certainly, but it hadn't told me anything new. No dream can really tell you anything new, technically speaking, because it's only made up of stuff that's already swilling around inside of you already. Unless you're a psychic, and I am not. No, the dream a subconscious slap in the face to remind me of the lies I'd told and might yet tell, and the pain I'd caused others as well as the pain I'd caused for myself. It was a guilt dream, everyone in it turning away and shutting me out because that was how I felt they should treat me. But it had been successful in making the guilt of dreams breed the guilt of day. My guilt was turning into shame but even more quickly into fear, and on the few occasions when I was sober enough to feel it, the fear had increased and begun to be accompanied by a rising panic that sent me rushing back to my world of drink and pills and bumps and bodies. The circle completed and the downward spiral increased.

I'd never understood before how, in those films that earnestly replicate the confessional tones of AA and NA meetings, people would say they used drugs to numb themselves and to block out the pain they felt when sober. For me, drugs have always been, even in my wildest excesses, truly recreational. I did them to have fun. Of course I did them to block out my real world and enter a better one—they don't call it "high" for nothing—but it wasn't because my real world was so terrible that I needed to deny its existence. I just liked how the other one felt. Now it was different. I needed more and more each day to keep the real world at bay, to dodge for a few hours my fear, my mistress Fear, who was well and truly back in the building after her recent, brief respite. And I did have fun, when I was on e or coked up and just talking shit to anyone who would listen, or fucking. I did a lot of fucking. That was good. I liked it, because all I thought about was the now, and the feeling the fucking was giving me. And even if you're suicidal, fucking is fun. Why else would we do it? It's the one thing that will take *anything* off our minds. So yes, I had fun. But the fun got briefer and harder to acquire, and the gloom more difficult to dodge unless there were drugs constantly available to shorten the gaps. I quickly became a fixture on the downtown lowlife scene. I got to recognize the same need in others quickly, like a starving fox that can sense who is the weakest of the flock. So I was drawn instinctively to those who would want to stay up and get messy and get dirty and then do some more when the first time was finished.

At the weekend I stayed in bed for two days and sweated and watched TV and had hallucinatory dreams that scared me to start with but excited me too much to not make them happen again. I'd discovered ketamine, a drug originally intended for tranquilizing horses, but now being used more often to alter the brains of our young and impressionable. On Friday I bought two vials to try it out and they were empty by Monday morning. A couple of times I blacked out because I'd snorted too much and my body had shut down (quite safely, don't worry, you can't die from it), and I'd just waited and enjoyed the K hole because when I was in it, it felt nice. Just a sort of nothingy nice where my mind would be still functioning but sort of frozen, and that was why it was nice. And eventually when I came round I'd have a swig from the carafes of orange juice I'd ordered on Friday night from room service (four of them, they were the only things on the menu that didn't turn my stomach), then my sugar levels would start to pick up and I'd do a bump of coke and I'd feel back to normal and able to have another bump of K. I heard some people in the States call ketamine "Special K," and since in Britain, Special K is a sort of goody-two-shoes breakfast cereal, it wasn't too big of a leap in my mind to give it a good association, almost healthy. It made you slow down, after all. Slowing down is good for you, isn't it?

In the shower on Monday morning I'd remembered the phone ringing, and someone being in my room.

A boy I'd met in a club on Thursday night had come round and he was pretty messed up, but then we got really wasted and really dirty and used a lot of drugs while doing a lot of sex.

Now is not the time to titillate you with it.

Let me just tell you that the parts I can remember were full of abandon. I had abandoned any form of responsibility for my body.

And the rest, like the time he came round, the day he came

round, how long he stayed and how he left, is all missing from my memory.

I stood in the shower, wondering if I dared remember more. But suddenly I'd had it. I'd fucking had it. Sometimes, enough is enough.

I was fed up with feeling like this. I was fed up with trying to find out how low I would go, how long I would endure it.

Tommy's depression rules?

I got straight out of the shower and found the little plastic bag of e's I'd bought and took one.

25

the optimum day

had it all worked out. A really good system. This was how
it worked best:

1. Have shower and bump of coke, depending on how recent
the last bump was. If fairly recent, have shower only, then . . .

2. Take an e, washed down with orange juice. Orange juice
is important because it speeds, and can revive, the e's reaction
and is good for you.

3. Go to work and amaze people with my zest and joie de
vivre at such an hour, especially when compared to last week's
early-morning demeanor, causing others to think "Aww, he's
just shy and takes a while to warm up to new people" and
Julian to say he was happy to see I was back to normal and had
taken the weekend to rest up.

4. Drink a lot of water. When it is remarked upon say I am doing a cleanse. Which I am, in a way.

5. Choose music for the CD player, thus single-handedly changing the atmosphere in the studio to where everyone is following my lead and having a little dance and chatting and enjoying themselves.

6. Segue into lunchtime, continuing with my court-jester bit, only this week the interest is not feigned. I am totally nutted on e, after all, so even the dullest homilies of a twenty-three-year-old starlet are fascinating. Drink a lot of orange juice. See 2, above.

7. Do another e during lunch. Detection of the ensuing overlap period, which can cause varying degrees of delusion, is masked by the sluggish after-lunch feeling that always permeates a shoot, even for those who are sober. If it gets really bad, use this time to pretend to need to make work-related phone calls and, because mobile phone reception is better outside, leave the building and walk the streets for fifteen minutes.

8. Try to ensure that mind doesn't wander and be back within reasonable time so as not to alert suspicion.

9. Carry on and enjoy the rest of day, leaving smiling and happy.

10. Get back to hotel and bathe. Enjoy the last of the e before starting the evening.

11. Do some crystal to ensure clarity of mind till morning. Quite a lot.

12. Go out. Meet/find people. Drink a little alcohol. Martini is now the drink of choice—pure spirits, without sugar-laden mixers, are better for you—and a lot of water.

13. Take coke for purely recreational and social purposes until the evening moves back to hotel room.

14. Begin to include K in drug intake, possibly e, as well as coke, culminating in . . .

15. Sex, in which poppers—otherwise known as amyl nitrite, a liquid whose fumes are snorted and which causes the heart to beat faster and the blood to race to the brain, thus enhancing similar symptoms caused by sexual excitement—are added to the above list to heighten sensitivity.

16. Drink water. Repeat combination of the above until back to . . .

17. Have shower, etc.

And it worked! Of course I was totally off my tits all the time. But the addition of the ecstasy in the daytime made the whole thing a win-win scenario. I got to feel every sensation I liked best at some part of the day. I enjoyed work. Some nights, if the sex was rough and long enough, I even slept a bit. I had become able to push my body to the point of exhaustion and so miss out the bit before sleep where I'd let *it* in.

It didn't get a chance to get in because I had made wall-to-wall protection around myself. I had beaten it.

The sleeping bit sometimes even meant that I was late for work. On the Wednesday I'd slept till eleven and was only wakened by the phone ringing and Julian on the other end of the line, secretly enjoying the return of my usual self (India wasn't the only person I was late for) and happy to slip back into his comfortable character of eye-rolling, tut-tutting older brother who would now have source material for jokes and ribbing of me throughout the day, to which I responded cheerily because, of course, I was in ecstasy.

On the Friday of the second week, the day before we were due to leave, the phone woke me up again. Between me and the phone lay a sleeping man, whose name I couldn't remember, but who had fucked me hard just hours before whilst pushing my head down into the very pillow he was now softly slumbering on. I leaned over him and picked up the phone, rehearsing my apologies to Julian.

"Tommy? It's India. I'm pregnant."

splash!

The first thing she said was that she knew that we couldn't talk properly about it now, and so should meet up when I got back to London at the weekend. She just wanted me to know. I thought that was nice of her. She was very nice on the phone, actually. She told me not to worry. I hadn't said much. She did most of the talking.

After she hung up I sat in a daze for a while. I watched whoever he was get up and start to put on his clothes. He had a great body, lean, and a scar on his shoulder from his days in the army, he'd said. I wondered how you got scars on your shoulder from being in the army these days. They didn't use bayonets anymore, did they?

"Bad news?" he said, pulling on a T-shirt that had NYPD written on it. He was so butch.

"Eh, no, I don't think so," I said, trying to fathom what had just happened. I couldn't. It was too early and I'd done too many drugs. I just stared at him for a moment. "How did you get your scar again?" I asked.

He stopped and looked down at it, rubbing it fondly. "Oh, I was in an accident involving a tank." Of course he was.

"Were you inside the tank?" I was bemused, and I sensed somehow this scar had a less manly history than he would have liked.

"Actually, no. It was during tank training and some rookie lost control. I was standing nearby, though, and it was coming toward me, so I dived for cover and cut myself open on some glass." He had stopped dressing and was standing still, answering my queries patiently, a little uncomfortable, almost like he'd been hauled up in front of some military tribunal. Except that he was naked apart from his T-shirt and his cock bobbed about a little bit as he talked.

"Why was there glass on the ground?" I continued.

He looked sheepish. "Actually it wasn't on the ground. It was a bottle of Coke I'd been holding at the time and I forgot to let go of it when I took the dive."

"That was stupid, wasn't it?"

"Yes sir, it sure was." He smiled weakly. "Should I get dressed now or do you wanna suck my dick some more?"

I looked at him, standing there in his New York Police Department T-shirt, of which he wasn't a member, but he had simply bought the T-shirt as he knew the idea of a big man like him also being a policeman was something of a wet dream for any hot-blooded queer. And strangely, like the stupid soldier he once was, he was waiting for my orders. Whether he was to engage in activity once more, or to accept a new movement order and recommence kit replacement.

It was perfect. He wasn't really an army vet who had battled hand to hand on covert missions on some oxymoronic peace-keeping mission. He wasn't even a policeman. He'd been discharged from the army when a virus-infested mosquito had bitten him and he spent the bulk of his initial training in the medical facility. He now worked in a bank in Queens. Everything about him was a mirage, mythologized like the scar into a version of what he knew other people wanted him to be. Unless you were me and, in shock at the news that a foolish moment the Sunday before last had produced a growing fetus thousands of miles away, had just decided to quiz him to pass the time because you were incapable of processing what you'd learned.

Even his cock looked different now. Before it had been a military weapon, thick, heavy, designed to withstand the most aggressive of combat with unknown opponents. Hard-wearing, resilient, dependable, something every little boy could look up to and admire. Now it was just a lump of something not very pretty that looked more suited to banging nails into wood than going into my mouth.

"I think you'd better go, soldier," I said.

Fuck me. I am a father! The details of what this might entail shouldn't concern me now. India had even said so. And anyway, details don't really come into it when you are contemplating the marvel of having made another life. I was a father! How in the midst of all this shit can something so beautiful have happened?

I was singing in the shower, my mind racing more than ever. I'd done an extra line in honor of the baby, my baby, and now my head was full of the future. I was making a mental family photo album. The pages turned, and there was me and a beatific child in the hospital, having its first bath, at the christening, its first birthday, on a rocking horse, taking its first step, going to school, winning the sack race at sports day, learning an instrument. I was flying through images of the future. But that's exactly what they were, images, where any blemishes could be removed like in Photoshop on the computer. And I was distracted further when I noticed that India was nowhere to be seen in this album. Not anywhere. Not even in the hospital. Maybe she was taking the photos, yes, that must be it.

It was weird to suddenly be given this. A child was, after all, the answer to my prayers, wasn't it? I wanted to be a dad and now, right this very minute, I was! I had been for nearly two weeks and I didn't even know it. That was the amazing thing. But how sad that from practically the second of its inception its father had been so unable to commit to his reality that he embarked upon a self-destructive, drug-crazed binge. Yes that was sad. It was time to take an e, I thought.

I wanted to call Sadie and Bobby and Charlie and Finn. Imagine, a little half brother or half sister for Finn! Or half cousin, would it be? Whatever, a little friend for him to play with eventually, and to help look after in the playground when the other kids started to bully.

But I couldn't call them, because it was a secret. My and India's little secret. She'd told me not to tell anyone till we'd talked on Sunday, but even so it was a secret, because the baby's existence was proof that I'd lied. Oh. My child was a lie. But it came from beauty and love and that was what mattered. And it would have beauty and love. It would *be* beauty and love. The e had kicked in now and I was in a cab on the way to work. I'd felt a little dizzy when I was in the elevator, but I was fine now. I was a father!!

Work absolutely flew by. I was dancing and singing and

hugging people, and when they asked if it was because I was happy to be going home I said no, I'd got some good news but I couldn't say what. It was a secret, a beautiful secret.

At the end of the day the magazine bought us champagne. They were delighted with Julian's work, which in turn delighted Julian, for this was a big job for him and there were definitely the prospects of more in the offing now. I was so happy for him. I really was. He was such a good person. He deserved it. He deserved to be happy.

I took three e's that day.

We all drank the champagne and laughed and I cranked up the music on the CD player and persuaded the stylist and the hair and makeup people—all lovely people, by the way—to have a little dance. Even Julian joined in. He looked like he was bobbing up and down on an invisible space hopper, arms flailing to his sides with each bounce. It was sweet, and I really felt so fond of him.

Then it was time to pack up and leave, and I wanted to dance more. I'd stopped wanting to blurt my news out, I'd just placed it somewhere in my mind that I could visit it and smile. I was so happy. It was only about nine o'clock, too early for the big clubs to be open, but I couldn't wait. So I went home and showered—see, I even love showers now, look at that, who'd have thunk it?—and then I ran out to a bar up in Chelsea that had a dance floor and sometimes boys would appear on a platform above it and showers of water would start above them and they'd get all wet and do a little dance for a bit and then go and dry themselves off and then go back to serving drinks. It was such fun. And I just wanted to dance. I met great people, strangers who I'd never see again, so when they asked me why I was so happy, I was able to tell them.

"I'm a father!" I beamed.

"You're a father, and you're in Splash?" one laconic but cute boy said.

"Oh, it's called Splash? I get it, with the showers and everything? That's great. Yeah, I'm a father. Isn't it weird?"

"Yeah," he said. "I gotta go to the men's room." And I never saw him again. But I didn't care! That was what was great about it all, I didn't care! If I died tomorrow I would have *lived*. I would live on. 'Cos I was a father.

"Do you want some coke?" I asked one of the boys, there were so many and they all had started to look alike.

"Sure," he said, and we started through the throng of heaving bodies toward the toilets. "I'm a father," I shouted back to him, in a spontaneous combustion of joy and disbelief.

"Okay, Daddy," he'd said. "Whatever blows your whistle."

27

becoming a man

At about four in the morning the drugs ran out, as I knew they would. It was timed perfectly because in the morning we would be leaving for the airport and so finishing them proved that I had bought sensibly and planned well.

But even as the last vial was carefully filled with water, shaken vigorously, then drunk—waste not, want not—I still felt the urge to run screaming through the corridors of the Mercer Hotel crying, "Who's got drugs? I need drugs!" I didn't, don't worry. I could've made a call and a guy would've been round in minutes—hell, he was round here practically every night—but I didn't.

Because I know when to stop.

Okay, so you're raising your eyebrows and mentally tutting, but listen to me. Who saw this trip as exactly what it became—a drug and sex binge that would act as a sensory cushion to my worries back home? Me.

Who had completely embraced the above, especially when the worries began to surface again? Me.

And who now, on the Saturday morning at the end of the two weeks of scheduled debauchery, was in a cab on the way to the airport without a milligram of drugs on his person and no intention of buying them or imbibing them for a very long time hence? You got it.

I'm not stupid. I knew I was in trouble. But I knew I'd be in trouble before it started, so that rather diminishes the reckless irresponsible argument somewhat, doesn't it? I think of it as more a structured loss of control. And I don't care what you think. I was on my way home now to pick up the pieces. I was weaker physically, certainly, because I hadn't eaten in a while and my jeans were falling off me because I'd lost so much weight and I looked a state, my eyes were yellow and my skin was gray and I was sweating and breaking out in spots. Poorer definitely, because I'd ingested a couple of grand's worth of class A's in the last two weeks, but believe me, please, when I tell you I felt stronger and richer than I had done in years, maybe ever.

I turned right as we boarded the aircraft instead of, as on the way here, to the left. The ticket error had been detected and I was back where I belonged, in economy. It was good in a way. There were no distractions like manicures or hand massages, and no cute girls at the bar serving champagne and chocolates to get up and chat to. It was of course, and please pardon the pun, in the economy section of the plane that I crashed. My body only. It was now many hours since I had taken any drugs and my body was beginning to notice. There's a condition amongst weekend drug users known as "Suicide Tuesday," where the aftereffects of the previous Saturday night's excesses suddenly catch up with you. Well, as you can imagine, there was a little more than last Saturday catching up with me. Now the pain and the nausea and the sweat that I'd suppressed for two weeks because of a constant stream of replacement stimulants that delayed them were given full rein. I felt like total shit. I tried to sleep, but my jaw was grinding and my stomach was aching and of course I had the shakes. These, luckily, are all symptoms pretty easy to hide in the economy section of a commercial airplane, having so many striking similarities to the behavior of a normal passenger in that class of travel. I had to keep peeing, though, and the woman who was sitting next to me asked to move so I had two seats to myself—fuck, I used to think that was a luxury! I didn't know I was born—and I was able to curl up on them, my head on a pillow against the window, and let my system start to recover. It wouldn't fully for quite a while, I knew that, but I just tried to take one thing at a time. Get through the flight, Tommy, and then face the next challenge—eating a meal!

Julian, when we'd said our customary farewells before he disappeared to "the lounge" (not a patch on the one at Heathrow, he'd promised me, so that was good), had been taken aback when instead of the usual cursory, see-you-later-type remarks I'd said: "Julian, I owe you an apology."

"What?" He looked startled, sensing there could be some dalliance from the social norm ahead.

"I've been on a total bender these past two weeks and I've not been very much help to you, and I know you've covered for me, and I just want you to know that I was going through a weird time and I needed to lose myself for a bit, and so I'm sorry I haven't been a very good assistant."

"Oh, well, thanks, Tom. I have been a bit worried, you know," he blustered.

"I do, Julian, I do know that. And I'm grateful. But there was nothing you could have done, this was my own thing, and again, I'm really sorry. I'll make it up to you."

"Just get yourself back together, that'll make it up to me," he said, and coughed, realizing he had expressed a little too much emotion. I could have kissed him, it was so heartfelt. He's all right, Julian.

"I will, I promise."

home

I got home to Islington about ten. Sadie wanted me to meet her in the bar at the Almeida after the show but I'd said I was too tired.

"*You're* too tired?" she'd laughed down the phone at me. "You must have had a rare old time, Tommy boy. I'll be home about eleven and I want to know every detail. Bobby said he'll drop by too after dinner before he goes out. It's some big homo party tonight in Vauxhall, so he can't stay long. Something called 'Probe' or 'Throb' or 'Piss.' "

"Fist," I corrected her. "It's an opportunity for like-minded gentlemen to meet up and share common interests."

"Oh good, I thought he might be going to have sex or something awful like that. Maybe he'll make a few lamp-shade contacts."

I'd missed her. I'd missed Bobby too. And I couldn't wait for the morning to see Charlie and Finn, who were coming round for breakfast. But no one was going to see me tonight.

I needed to have a bath. I was stinking. Even I thought so, so it must be really bad. I was exhausted, my body ached, but I knew the hot water would make me feel better. My jaw was sore from grinding my teeth, and from the gum I'd chewed almost incessantly in New York.

When I saw myself in the bathroom mirror I was shocked. Feeling shitty is one thing, but I really looked like shit. Apart from the spots and the grayness I've mentioned, I'd no idea I looked so skinny. All the bones in my chest were poking through my skin. The bottom of my ribs jutted out where once there'd been a straight line down to my tummy. It was bad.

But believe it or not, as I looked at myself in that mirror, it hit me that for the first time in my life I was looking at a man. Not a boy anymore. A man. I am man enough to take the consequences of my actions, I thought. And man enough to know that what I have done was stupid and dangerous and crazed. I am man enough to know that I have come back to face some very difficult situations and experiences, but also man enough to say I would not have changed a single minute of the last two weeks for anything. I set myself a test and I passed it. I dared myself to go to the farthest point that I could go without a safety net, without even the mental capacity to always know how far away I had traveled, and I had come back. And the fact that I had come back from that was proof that now I was a man, who understood himself and would now plan his life accordingly. Look through the pages of any self-help book and you will see platitudes like, "Sometimes we have to go to the very lowest point we can go in order to be able to commence the climb up again." Or, "Others can advise or commiserate, but we are the only ones who can truly help ourselves." (They don't call them self-help books for nothing.) Well, from the moment those drugs ran out on that last night, I knew the only way for me was up, and I was the only one who was going to help myself. It was done, I'd had my fill.

I'd seen the other side, and fun though it was, I knew it was also temporary. India's news may have been a catalyst or a wake-up call (literally), but actually it was an internal alarm clock of my own that heralded the new me. Those two weeks had changed me. How could they not?

I'd taken risks and cheated fate, and there had been no one to tell me no, or to pull me back from the brink. I was a man, and sometimes a man needs to do that—to be primeval and animal and to go to the dark cave. But a real man also comes back and acknowledges how important the visit there has been.

Now that may sound pathetic and pointless or like an excuse to you, but I don't care. Ask yourself if you could've done it, or better, still do it, before you pass judgment. This is my tale, Tommy's Tale, and in every tale the hero has a rite of passage, doesn't he?

Well, that last passage was mine. So fuck you.

ONE YEAR LATER.

YES, REALLY.

WE'RE DOING ONE OF

THOSE TIME-JUMP THINGS!

off the holloway road

Y ou know what the weirdest thing about all of this is? (Aside from jumping ahead a year?) The weirdest thing is that right now I'm sitting in a garden. And the house whose garden I am sitting in is the house off the Holloway Road that I saw Charlie and Bobby and Sadie walking into in that dream I had in New York last year. The very same house. The one that started the spiral. I swear to God. So maybe I am a bit psychic after all.

The sun is shining and I'm taking a break from gardening. I've been making Finn a pond so we can have fish. Fish are his new passion. He can name you any species of fish you care to point at (in *Latin* too) in the London Aquarium, and he's been on at me ever since we moved in about making a pond. It's actually not too difficult. There's a bit of digging, obviously, and I had to get Bobby to help me with all the pump stuff, but it's done nearly. Just a few plants to go in (they keep the water clean and feed the fish. I'm all about ecosystems these days) and it's done. I'll surprise him with it tonight when he gets home.

Sadie is upstairs doing exercises. She's suddenly become an exercise nut. I can hear the video through the open living-room window, some screeching harridan entreating her to feel the stretch. You don't feel the burn anymore, apparently. That's all last century and Jane Fonda and likely to induce coronaries in perfectly healthy twenty-two-year-olds. Now we feel the stretch. You'd think they would go easier on women in her condition, but no. It's good for her, though; she's got to get into shape for what lies ahead.

Bobby's upstairs too, on the second floor, in his *studio*. Yes! The money he spent renting his old workspace he put into an extra room here so he can work from home. I love it. We see more of him, and I can pop in anytime and give him a hand or just have a cigarette and a chat. He's got a boyfriend. Met him the night I came back from New York, at *Fist*. Funny, eh? To meet the love of your life when he's wearing leather restraints and a cock ring, in the middle of an orgy. But they're really happy. He's called Tim and he's a teacher, so he's a great boon to have around if none of us can help Finn with his homework. He's also got a really lovely laugh and a pierced cock that Bobby says is like having the xylophone played on his fillings when he goes down on him.

Charlie is great too. He turned forty this year. I don't know what is harder to comprehend—me being thirty or having a boyfriend who's forty. Both the boyfriend and the forty have taken a bit of getting used to. Note the omission of the "sort of" prefix. He's a great man. I always knew it, but this past year he's demonstrated it so much. A couple of months ago, when we were thinking back on all that's happened, he said to me:

"You're so strong willed, Tommy."

"I know," I replied. "But so are you."

"Am I?" said he.

"Yeah," I said. "You're here, aren't you? You waited around. You're tenacious."

"It was worth my while, though, wasn't it?" He smiled.

"Yes," I said, and I knew it was true.

What happened . . .

Where do I start?

Well, India had an abortion. While I was doing cold turkey on the plane back from America, she was in a posh clinic in Harley Street having Tommy Junior "terminated," as it's so delicately and succinctly put by our friends in the New World. My mobile phone rang that night, as I was lounging in the bath with a Mario Badescu purifying mask on my face. There's never a right time for a man to hear something like that, especially when you haven't been consulted about it, but still. Naked and exhausted and wet and wearing a potion to try and ease the tide of drug-induced acne can't be far from the worst.

I saw her the next day. Our scheduled meeting to "talk" took on a different light. We both looked like shit from our individual trials, but before she could begin to explain I'd said:

"I understand. It was the right thing to do. It's the wrong time and the right thing to do. You couldn't bring up a child on your own, and you know it wouldn't have brought us together, so you did the right thing. I understand. I wish you'd let me know, but actually it's probably for the best that you didn't, because I would've only tried to stop you and that would've been wrong. For you."

"And what about for you?" she'd asked, amazed at my calm, and reason, but remember I was a man now.

"Me? Well, I would've wanted it. I would've taken it. But you'd have never just given up your child, would you?"

"No," she said quietly. "And so that's why I . . ."

"I know. Don't worry. You'll meet someone and you'll get pregnant again, and it'll be right for you to have a baby with him. With me, it's not. It never was when we were together, so it's even less right now."

"Thanks, Tommy. I never thought you'd be so . . . so understanding."

I smiled. "Yeah, well, I know what it feels like to want a baby and it not to be the right time."

I'd wept when she'd told me. The tears dribbled down through my purifying mask and into the bath water. But they weren't tears of anger. I didn't want to have a child with India. What a disastrous idea that would be for everyone concerned, and probably many who weren't. They were tears of frustration because I wanted a child, and now, even when I had actually fathered one, it still wasn't possible. I didn't blame India—why would she possibly want to have a child with me? We weren't going to get back together, and even if we did we'd both know in our hearts it would be for all the wrong reasons. So what were the alternatives? That she'd bring up the baby on her own and I'd take on the role of some sort of wacky uncle who would berate her about access rights and endanger, with my jealousy, any future relationship she might have with another man? No, she was right to have the abortion. Right, and within her rights. I couldn't be angry with her. I knew how much she wanted to.

I don't see India anymore. Even if she still lived in London I don't know that I would. We're just trouble for each other.

Anyway, she's moved to L.A. with her new boyfriend. He's the head of some film company. And oh, she's acting now.

The very next day, me and Bobby and Sadie went to look at a new flat. We all had high hopes. It was one of the few we could afford in the area we wanted. The pressure was on, and they'd been looking frantically in the weeks I'd been away. This one came with a great recommendation from the estate agent. "Needs a little bit of work, but amazing potential," she'd said cheerily, lying in that way all estate agents are bred to lie. It was a total shit hole. Think of the loo Ewan McGregor dived into in *Trainspotting* and imagine that squalor and filth throughout a three-bedroom flat and you're halfway there.

Sadie cried. Bobby just looked out of the grimy kitchen window and said, "Suburbia. I know it. I can feel it coming. Enfield, Stepney, Penge. Just shoot me now, would you?"

It was there that I lost it.

I kicked a wall. I hadn't kicked anything since the elevator of India's apartment.

"OH, FUCK IT!" I raged. "Fuck it, fuck it, fuck it!"

Sadie stopped crying. Bobby turned from the window, all thoughts of suburbia momentarily dispelled.

"Why does it all have to be so fucking difficult? Why does it have to be like this?"

"We'll find another flat, Tommy," Sadie reasoned, her hands outstretched as she moved slowly toward me, as if I were a wild animal who might bolt or scratch at any second. "Don't upset yourself. You're just all weirded out from the jet lag and the . . ."

". . . the drugs," said Bobby helpfully, also edging nearer as though I were on a ledge about to jump. "You're probably still crashing, love."

"It's not that, for fuck's sake," I screamed. They both stopped in their tracks. "India had an abortion. India had an abortion. She was carrying my child. I fucked her that night before I went away, and she got pregnant and she had an abortion. And she didn't tell me, and that's her right, and she was right to do it, but why the fuck does it all have to be so difficult?"

They were both dumbstruck by the news, but any disappointment in my betrayal of their trust in the act of fucking India was superceded instantly by their concern for the way I was dissolving in front of them. I started to shake, and noises began to emanate from deep inside that scared even me.

"Oh Tommy, you stupid fucking bastard. I'm so sorry," Sadie said quietly.

"It's okay, it's okay," I tried to respond, but I could hardly get the words out due to the dry tennis ball that appeared to be lodged in the back of my throat. "But I should never have seen her, and I should never have fucked her and I should never have lied to you two . . ."

They both began to remonstrate with me. My deceit, bless them, was the least of their worries right now. They had a potential nervy b on their hands.

"But it's for the best," I carried on, unable to stop the shaking and the heaving. "I really believe that. It's just that I feel so stupid for wanting it so much, you know? I've told you . . . I really want that, a child, and I think I'd be a good father, I know I would . . ."

Bobby was by my side now, his arm on my shoulder, trying

to stop the shakes that were overwhelming my whole body. "I know, Tom, I know. It just wasn't the right time," he said.

"But when is it going to be the right time?" I howled.

"The right time for what?" asked Sadie quietly, interested to find out where I was going with this.

"The right time for a family. The right place to be a family." I gestured at the pit of a room we were standing in, and just stood there, shaking my head back and forth, weeping. I was exhausted and crashing and undernourished, even though I had been plied with food by the pair of them from the moment they'd seen me on Sunday morning. But it was more than that. It was everything. It was what it was about.

"But we are a family, Tom. We're your family, remember? Me and Sadie." Bobby had both hands on my shoulders now. I could feel him taking the strain of my convulsing.

"And there's never a right time," said Sadie strongly. "That's only for people who read *Women's Weekly*."

"Then why can't the right time be now?" I sobbed, crumpling into Bobby's arms.

"There, there, Tommy boy, don't cry. You'll only get us all started. You're just a little tired and you've been on a bit of a bender and everything seems worse than it is. It'll be fine. Shhh. Shh."

There was silence for a few moments, apart from the creaking and heaving of my sob-wracked frame. Finally, Sadie stood up. "The right time can be now," she said, a tremble in her voice. "Tommy, would you please be the father of my child?"

So that was how it started. It's funny how when something has been voiced for the first time, its very voicing quickly enables itself to become a possibility and then a certainty, and before long so many lives have been changed by it, all for the better I might add. And it all started out of tears and frustration in that horrible flat on Highbury Green. I'd even bored myself latterly about how much I want a family. And yet I'd bashed on so much before about how my friends were my family. It seems easy now to see that the natural progression was to combine the two. To have a child with them, and make an extended family that we would all share in. Daft, eh?

Of course, it all looks much simpler on paper, and with hindsight. It wasn't as easy a decision as it feels it ought to have been now. There were many sleepless nights of talking and worrying and wondering if we were doing the most stupid, irresponsible thing in the world. Bizarrely Charlie was the one to finally push us off the cliff and send us giggling into the night, giddy with excitement that yes, we were going to actually do it, we were going to have a baby together. When I'd told him about the India episode, his response was identical to Sadie's: "Oh Tommy, you stupid fucking bastard. I'm so sorry." No anger, no blame, no judgement. And when I went on to mention what Sadie had proposed in that dingy pit of a flat that afternoon he was equally as sanguine.

A couple of weeks later, when he came round to pick me up for our weekly clubbing ritual, he walked into the kitchen and saw the three of us at the table in another tortured discussion about if and when and why and how it would all work, and he looked at us and said, "Jesus Christ, just do it! Just do it! No amount of talking is going to prepare you for what it's like. It's a huge responsibility. No one in the history of mankind has ever been prepared for it. But you want it. You both really want it, and that's all that matters, so do it. And you're not alone. You've got Bobby, and you've got me and Finn. We've been through it, we can help you. And believe me, you'll never, never regret it."

You know how I've been prone to making up fairy tales? Well, now I felt I was in one.

And there was another big thing that happened: I let Charlie in. I just looked at him differently one day and I let him in. Right in. (And hello, who wouldn't? Any man who'd overlook his boyfriend fucking his ex-girlfriend then encouraging him to have a child with his best friend has got to be a keeper, right?) He just wants me to be happy. I'd been resisting and resisting him all this time, and eventually I just stopped resisting because it seemed stupid not to. Now it's hard to remember what I was afraid of, because it all feels right, and like I've always felt this way. He doesn't want to own me, he doesn't want to change me, he just loves me and wants me to be happy and he wants to be happy with me. And I want to be happy and I love him, so what was I waiting for? It's just another part of becoming a man, I think. I was man enough to let in my man. And so Finn got his way, eventually. I am now his second dad.

He's the real king of willpower.

We found this house the day Sadie got the official news from the doctor that she was pregnant. I'm Captain Super Sperm, apparently. It only took one time. We timed it carefully though, and she lay with her legs up in the air against the kitchen wall for hours for maximum effect.

The first time we saw the house we all loved it. It really feels like a home. There's stained glass in the window of the front door, and an ancient rosebush trailing up the wall. It was in a bit of a state, but it didn't take much imagination to see that it could be amazing. There are six bedrooms. Six! Sometimes at bedtime it feels like an episode of *The Waltons*. One of them is Bobby's studio, and the others are Sadie's, Bobby's, mine, Charlie's and Finn's. Yes, they moved in too. What with the extra money Bobby puts in for his studio and Charlie and Finn's share, it costs us just a tiny bit more than the old place did. And it's just so nice to feel you're going to be somewhere forever. Even if we aren't, because nothing is forever, remember, it's a nice thing to *feel*. To be settled, and secure. I've been working hard to get it sorted out before the baby comes. Plastering the walls and painting and stuff. I'm Mr. Handyman these days too. I know my way around a power drill like the back of my hand. The garden is huge. When we moved in, the grass hadn't been cut for ages and it looked like a meadow, full of wild daisies that we quickly picked and made into chains. It was so beautiful. We had our dinner in the middle of it that night, all five of us. We were all so relieved and happy, and tired from all the moving boxes and the up and down the stairs, but none of us wanted to go to bed. We wanted that night to last forever, lying in our meadow, wearing our daisy chains, looking up at the sky, home.

Charlie and I have separate rooms just because we feel we should. It's not like we don't sleep together every night or anything, but it's good to know we have our own spaces, and I kind of like inviting him into my room, or being invited into his, for the night. It's sexy. It's adult and sensible and sexy. That's all you could hope for, is it not? Eventually, when it's older, the baby will have one of our rooms, but that'll be fine, and it's a long way off. Oh, and there's a cellar, which is a blessing when Bobby and Tim get hot and horny. No more strangers handcuffed to the bathroom radiator for us.

We didn't *do* it, you know. Me and Sadie. The deed, I mean. We talked about doing it, but we felt we'd both laugh too much and it would be weird and not the best way to introduce our baby to the world. We looked on the Internet and sent off for a sort of plastic syringe thing and I wanked into a cup (which is so much harder than it sounds), thinking beautiful thoughts and sending out healthy, loving vibes, and then ran through to Sadie's room and we put the cum into the syringe and squirted our baby up into Sadie's womb, where she remains, growing bigger by the day. Yes, it's a she. And she's going to be called Daisy, after that first night of the meadow.

I don't work for Julian anymore. We all realized that one of us was going to have to give up work to look after the baby and do all the house stuff, and I volunteered. I'd never liked my job. Photographic assistance was never my vocation and now, suddenly, I had the chance to change career and do something with and for people that I loved, so for the first time in my life I know what is meant by job satisfaction. Plus I no longer have to talk dirty for my boss every Monday morning.

I told Julian a few months ago, and he was really happy for me. And although I miss the routine of it a bit, because it's hard suddenly becoming your own boss in a job you're making up as you go along, I don't regret it at all. He calls sometimes, and one night he came to dinner, looking so fearful when he arrived, as if he were entering a sort of hippie commune that he wouldn't know the rules of. I think he thought you needed vaccinations to come this far north of the river. Maybe I'll freelance for him a bit in the future if he's really busy, and if I'm not—which doesn't seem very likely. I've been trying to get as much of the work done on the house as I can because I know that when the baby comes it's going to be pandemonium. And who knew how much cleaning there was to do in a four-story house? But I've got really into it. I've got a system, and it's working. Sometimes I laugh about how it's all ended up. I mean, I'm a housewife, for fuck's sake! But it's what I want to be doing. And how many people do you know that can say that? I just never thought this was what would make me happy. But if doing the laundry and picking up Finn from school (many raised eyebrows there, I can tell you) and grouting the bathroom tiles is the answer, for me, for now, then how lucky am I to be the man who's found what makes him happy?

And soon Daisy will be here, and I can't wait. Every time I think about the future I smile. That's something new. I used to think all that stuff about "You *can* change your life" was a crock of shit, but you can. We did—me and Sadie and Bobby and Charlie and Finn all changed our lives.

And don't worry, I've not completely turned into a Stepford wife and think that it's all going to be easy. It won't be. There are tough times ahead, I'm sure. Change is hard for everyone, even when it's change for the good. But now, instead of worrying about the future, I'll just wait for the future to come and deal with what needs to be dealt with then. Charlie did fuck some sense into me that night. I'm not waiting for my life to start anymore. This is my life, and I like it.

So, I bet you're probably wondering, Has Tommy been tamed? Has the party boy who would never be tied down, except to the bed, disappeared forever? Has ecstasy been replaced by domesticity? Is the only time he's on his knees in a toilet when he's fixing the cistern?

No, shut up. I still get to play. I still have fun. Everyone needs their fun, don't they, even homemakers. Everything in moderation, remember, including moderation. And you can take the boy out of the party but you can't take the party out of the boy. I've changed, yes, because my circumstances have, but I'm still the same Tommy.

How the fuck do you plant bulrushes in a *pond*?

acknowledgments

Thank you to my friends who have inspired or supported the writing of this novel. And sorry to those who will be horrified by it.

I would also like to thank Judith Regan, Dana Albarella and Paul Schnee at ReganBooks for their dedication, and Jonny Geller, my agent, for his patience.

An Excerpt from Alan Cumming's Memoir

Not My Father's Son

Coming October 2014

Then

"You need a haircut, boy!"

My father had only glanced at me across the kitchen table as he spoke but I had already seen in his eyes the coming storm.

I tried to speak but the fear that now engulfed me made it hard to swallow, and all that came out was a little gasping sound that hurt my throat even more. And I knew speaking would only make things worse, make him despise me more, make him pounce sooner. That was the worst bit, the waiting. I never knew exactly when it would come, and that, I know, was his favorite part.

As usual we had eaten our evening meal in near silence until my father had spoken. Until recently my older brother, Tom, would have been seated where I was now, helping to deflect the gaze of impending rage that was instead focused entirely upon me. But Tom had a job now. He left every morning in a shirt and tie, and our father hated him for it. Tom was no longer in his thrall. Tom had escaped. I hadn't been so lucky yet.

My mother tried to intervene. "I'll take him to the barber's on Saturday morning, Ali," my mum said.

"He'll be working on Saturday. He's not getting away with slouching off his work again. There's too much of that going on in this house, do you hear me?"

"Yes," I managed.

But now I knew it was a lost cause. It wasn't just a haircut, it was my physical shortcomings as a laborer, my inability to perform the tasks he gave me every weekend and many evenings, tasks I was unable to perform because I was twelve but mostly because he wanted me to fail at them so he could hit me.

You see, I understood my father. I had learned from a very young age to interpret the tone of every word he uttered, his body language, the energy he brought into a room. It has not been pleasant as an adult to realize that dealing with my father's violence was the beginning of my studies of acting.

"I can get one tomorrow at school lunchtime." My voice trailed off in that way I knew sounded too pleading, too weak, but I couldn't help it.

"Yes, do that, pet," my mum said kindly.

I could sense the optimism in her tone and I loved her for it. But I knew it was false optimism, denial. This was going to end badly, and there was no way to prevent it.

Every night getting off the school bus, walking through the gates of the estate where we lived, past the sawmill yard where my father reigned and toward our house, was like playing a lottery. Would he be home yet? What mood would he be in? As soon as I entered the house and changed out of my school uniform and began my chores—bringing wood and coal in for the fire, starting the fire, setting the table, warming the plates, putting the potatoes on to boil—I felt a bit safer. You see, by then I was on his territory, under his command, I worked for him, and that seemed to calm my father, as though my utter servitude was necessary to his well-being. I still wasn't completely safe, of course. I was never safe, but those chores were so ingrained in me and I felt I did them well enough that even if he did inspect them I would pass muster and so could breathe a little easier until we sat down to eat.

My father was the head forester of Panmure Estate, a country estate near Carnoustie, on the east coast of Scotland. The estate was vast, with fifty farms and thousands of acres of woodland covering over twenty-one square miles of land. We lived on what was known as the estate "premises," the grounds of Panmure House, though by the time we lived there the big house was long gone. In 1955, as one of many such austerity measures forced upon the landed aristocracy, its treasures were dismantled and then explosives razed it to the ground. All that remained were the stables, where on chilly Saturday mornings during hunting season I'd report, banging my wellies together to keep the feeling in my toes, to work as a beater, hitting trees with a stick in a line of other country boys, scaring the birds up into the air so that drunk rich men could shoot at them.

Attached still to the stables was the building that had been the house's chapel. Now it was used for the annual estate Christmas party and occasional dances or card game evenings for the workers. We lived in Nursery House, so called because it looked out on a tree nursery where seedlings were hatched and nurtured to replace the trees that were constantly felled and sent back to the sawmill that lay up the yard behind us. My father was in charge of the whole process, from the seeds all the way to the cut lumber and everything in between, as well as the general upkeep of the grounds.

It was all very feudal and a bit *Downton Abbey,* minus the abbey and fifty years later. I answered the door to men who referred to my father as "The Maister." There were gamekeepers and big gates and sweeping drives and follies but no lord of the manor, as during the time we lived there the place was owned by, respectively, a family shipping company, a racehorse owner's charitable trust, and then a huge insurance company.

I didn't know it at the time, but I was living through the end of an era of grand Scottish estates, since they now, like Panmure, have been mostly all dismantled and sold off. Looking back on it, it was a beautiful place to grow up in, but at the time all I wanted was to get as far away as possible.

I had seen my father's van parked by the tractor shed as I walked by. So he was home. But maybe he wasn't actually in the house, maybe he was talking to one of his men in the sawmill or in one of the storehouses or sheds. It was the time of day when they were coming back from the woods and cleaning their tools before going home. I couldn't see my dad, although I didn't want to be seen to be looking for him, in case he spotted me and he'd know that my fear was guiding my search. That would be his opening. Maybe there would be someone in the yard who'd come to see him, a farmer or even his boss, the estate factor (or manager), who would allow me to get by him without inspection.

I turned around the corner into the driveway of our house at the bottom of the sawmill yard, and I could see there was a light on in his office. My heart sank. He was sitting at his desk in the window and he looked up when he saw me. Immediately I straightened, tried to remember all the things he'd told me were wrong about me recently. I prayed my hair was combed the way he liked it, my schoolbag was hanging on my shoulder at the right angle, my shoes were shiny enough. It probably took only ten seconds before I reached the front door and was out of his sight, but in that flash a myriad anxieties about my flaws and failures had whirred across my mind.

He was on the phone, thankfully. He didn't come out of his office even until after my mum came home from work, and I always felt a little lighter having her in the house. She finished making our tea while we chatted. Then we heard the noise of him approaching through the house toward us and we were quiet. We both knew it was not a good idea to speak until we had appraised him, and tonight apparently it was not a good idea to speak at all.

My father sat in his chair at the kitchen table and immediately my mother set down his plate of food in front of him. This is how it always happened. Any deviation, let alone any complaint about the food, could start him off. Without acknowledging her or me he lifted his cutlery and began to eat. He ate like an animal, not because he was messy or noisy, but because he tore at his food, with strength and stealth and efficiency. It was terrifying to watch.

My father was silent for a while after my mum spoke, and I hoped that my going to the barber's during school lunch break the next day would appease him. All I could think of was getting to the end of this meal and upstairs to my homework, or better yet far into the woods with my dog to hide. But my mouth was so dry and there was a lump of fear stuck at the top of my chest that made it hard to swallow. I had to get some water or I was going to choke or, worse, cry. I got up from the table and moved toward the sink. I picked up a glass off the drainboard and began to fill it.

"What the hell do you think you're doing?" he said, not quite shouting yet but still too loud, as though he had been waiting to say it, eager to make the next move, and now here it was.

"Eh? Did you hear me?"

"I need to drink some water," I gasped.

"Put that glass down!" Now he was shouting.

My mother said very quietly, "Ali, leave him."

My father rose from his chair and everything went red. At the same time that he began shouting at me he grabbed me by the scruff of the neck and I was being dragged across the kitchen, through the living room, through the hallway, out through the porch and the front door and across the yard to the shed where we kept our bikes. He threw me up on top of a workbench. He was *baying* now, not just shouting. You couldn't understand what he was saying, but I knew it had to do with my hair and my water drinking and how fucking useless and insolent and pathetic I was, but it wasn't coherent. It was just pure violent rage and it was directed at me.

There was a lone bare lightbulb hanging from the shed ceiling. I remember looking up at it as he scrambled in a drawer behind me. Soon my head was propelled forward by his hand, the other hand wielding a rusty pair of clippers that he used on the sheep we had in the field in front of our house. They were blunt and dirty and they cut my skin, but my father shaved my head with them, holding me down like an animal.

I was hysterical now, as hysterical as he was, but I knew he enjoyed hearing me scream and that it would be over quicker if I was quiet and limp. But that was so hard. I was in pain and shock and I still hadn't had a drink of water and I felt I was going to pass out with trying to catch my breath. All I could do was wait for the end. Eventually it was over. He pushed my head one way then the other in order to inspect his work, then threw the clippers back in the drawer.

"You get your hair cut properly! Do you hear me?" he said, rage abating, coming down, spent.

"Yes," I tried not to whimper.

He whacked me across the back of my head and was gone. The shed door banged and I was left to climb down from the bench. I made sure to clean up the mess. I gathered in my hands the clumps of my hair that had fallen to the floor and took them to the trash can outside. I returned to the shed once more to make sure everything was back to normal and then switched off that lone lightbulb and headed back into the house. I heard the sound of my dad's van heading up the sawmill yard and I stopped for a moment, filled with shock and relief that he was gone.

In the bathroom I drank some water from the tap. Bits of hair fell into the sink as I drank and I could feel droplets of blood on my neck. Finally I stood up and stared at my reflection.

I looked like a concentration-camp inmate, and I wanted to die. Really, in that moment I wanted to die. My mum tried to tidy up the mess with scissors, to make it look less uneven, but there were patches that actually had no hair left at all, that couldn't be disguised. I would have to go to school looking like this. I cried all through the night. The next morning my eyes were so red and puffy they were almost closed, but I was glad because they detracted from my head. I told my teachers I had reached up to a high shelf and knocked over a jar of creosote (a wood preservative made from tar) and some had gotten in my eyes. When asked about my hair, I said I had tried to cut it myself.

Now

I have had more hairstyles than most men my age have had hot dinners.

It doesn't take a genius to work out that part of the reason I have so enjoyed changing the color, length, and look of my follicles over the years has something to do with reclaiming the power my father took from me in this regard (as well as many others) as a child. My hair has been blond several times, it has been short and spiky, long and floppy, sleek, shaggy, and everything in between. I've even faced the clipper demons and shaved my own head more than once.

It took a while to get to this place, though. In my late teens, there were several occasions when I was in a hair salon and would suddenly feel nauseated, and twice I actually vomited, not realizing till many years (and quite a lot of therapy) later that my body was manifesting physically what I could not yet cope with emotionally. I clearly had some deeply suppressed and deeply painful coiffure memories. But after I had left home and was free from my father's grip, I began to make my hair a symbol of my own freedom. One time at drama school, in a particularly semiotic act of self-assertion, I actually agreed to my youthful locks being dyed purple by an overzealous hairdressing student and went back to the parental home for the weekend with my head held high, and nothing, not a word, was said about it. (I did wear a purple sweater as well, in an attempt to divert all the attention, but still, it was ballsy, don't you think?)

I suppose what I am saying is . . . I am okay. I survived my father. We all did—my mother, my brother, and me—literally as well as figuratively. But as with all difficult things, it was a process. But more of that later.